PRAISE FOR

NAZARETH'S SONG

"NAZARETH'S SONG by Patricia Hickman is rich with characters living real in hard times. Jeb Nubey seeks God by trial and error, like most of us. Fresh and triumphant."

—LYN COTE, AUTHOR OF *WINTER'S SECRET*

"As deliciously Southern as black-eyed peas with corn bread! . . . a heartwarming read."

—LAWANA BLACKWELL, AUTHOR OF *THE GRESHAM CHRONICLES*

"As cozy as a patchwork quilt, Patricia Hickman's NAZARETH'S SONG carries within it the hopes and dreams of a small town . . . and if you read it with an ear cocked to listen, you just might hear the angels sing."

—ANGELA E. HUNT, AUTHOR OF *THE DEBT*

"This story beautifully illustrates the challenges and rewards of unselfishness, forgiveness, and loyalty. I couldn't put the book down."

—JANELLE SCHNEIDER, AUTHOR OF *BRITISH COLUMBIA*

"Full of insight and compassion—and an interrupted romance, a rebellious teen, shady business deals, wow!—NAZARETH'S SONG is a rich, satisfying read."

—GAYLE ROBER, AUTHOR OF *WINTER WINDS, AUTUMN DREAMS*

"Hickman, a writer with a flair for exacting and lyrical, but never cumbersome, description, delivers fresh-picked words again and again. I love the way Patty writes! You will too."

—LISA SAMSON, AUTHOR OF *THE CHURCH LADIES* AND *THE LIVING END*

more . . .

"A humorous and poignant parable of how man plans and God prevails. I thoroughly enjoyed it."
—FRANCINE RIVERS, AUTHOR OF *ATONEMENT CHILD*

"Hickman's prose rings with gritty authenticity and stark, lyrical description."
—LIZ CURTIS HIGGS, AUTHOR OF *THORN IN MY HEART*

"A new book by Patricia Hickman is always an occasion for delight. She is a gifted author with a deft touch at all the elements of fine storytelling."
—T. DAVIS BUNN, AUTHOR OF *WINNER TAKE ALL*

"Hickman kicks off her new series with this gentle, enjoyable yarn about four misfits cast adrift in Arkansas during the Great Depression . . . [She] tells her story with warmth, humor, and some lovely descriptions . . . The ending . . . is sweetly satisfying. Hickman is a talented writer, and readers will likely sympathize with her unlikely ragtag group of characters."
—PUBLISHERS WEEKLY

"I love Patty Hickman's vivid language and rich descriptions. Her characters pop off the page and, in this latest novel, steal your heart."
—LISA TAWN BERGREN, AUTHOR OF *WINDCHILL SUMMER*

"In a carefully and beautifully written story of home and family, Hickman reminds us that even when we hide, love finds a way."
—LYNN HINTON, AUTHOR OF *FRIENDSHIP CAKE*

NAZARETH'S
SONG

Also by Patricia Hickman

Fallen Angels

NAZARETH'S SONG

PATRICIA HICKMAN

WARNER
Faith

NEW YORK   BOSTON   NASHVILLE

Copyright © 2004 by Patricia Hickman
All rights reserved. No part of this book may be reproduced in any form or by any electronic or mechanical means, including information storage and retrieval systems, without permission in writing from the publisher, except by a reviewer who may quote brief passages in a review.

Scripture quotations are from the King James Version of the Holy Bible.

Cover design by Beck Stvan
Cover photo by Christopher Felver/ Corbis

The Warner Faith name and logo are registered trademarks of Warner Books.

Warner Faith

Time Warner Book Group
1271 Avenue of the Americas, New York, NY 10020
Visit our Web site at www.twbookmark.com

Printed in the United States of America

Originally published in Trade Paperback by Warner Faith
First Mass Market Paperback Printing: June 2005

10 9 8 7 6 5 4 3 2 1

To Lou Davis, a dear aunt
who loves God through loving others

I wish to thank April Goff of the Arkansas Historical Archives for her tenacity in helping me locate all those difficult-to-find facts, books, and maps of Arkansas during the Great Depression years. Also a warm thanks to Howard Hattabaugh for his extensive knowledge of history of the lumber industry in Arkansas. Much heartfelt appreciation to the tour guides of the Hot Springs National Park Visitor Center and the Fordyce Bath House for sharing their amazing history. And thanks to them as well for the historic Hot Springs maps. Thank you also to the Warner team for their commitment to the Millwood Hollow series. And again, thank you to my wonderful father- and mother-in-law, Ken and Gaye Hickman, for allowing me to pick their brains regarding Arky-isms and the customs and traditions of the ordinary folk of 1930s Arkansas.

NAZARETH'S SONG

1

Millwood Hollow cast the kind of dreamy mood that drew women into its center, the way morning trickled through the pale green mist of dawn and the trout stream meandered in an elegant train around two hundred tree trunks. The quiet veil of virgin light belonged to Millwood Hollow, just as the noise of rattling Model-As and newspaper boys shouting into the dry September air belonged to Hot Springs. The leaves hung soft and green on the thick limbs, each overlapping another, strung from the sky to the earth like happy fabric squares cut and laid out for a winter quilt.

Such a place might rekindle schoolteacher Fern Coulter's interest in him, Jeb Nubey thought, although he did not know for certain. Fern could not be figured out in an instant. Jeb knelt on one knee and practiced a speech, careful to bar any idle flattery. Fern's intellect would not buy into sentimental sweet talk, and if he so much as hinted at manipulation he would lose her altogether.

He remembered the afternoon she had dumped him. On the hottest August day that swept dust and shimmering ghosts of heat through town like a mean spirit, Fern had confessed, "Jeb, it's a crying shame, you know, the way I fell in love with an ideal and not a man. I blame myself, not you."

"I'll be making preacher soon, Fern, if that's your worry." He had realized too late he might come across a mite anxious.

"Something good will come of all this," she had said. "You'll move on, make something of yourself. I am proud of you, so don't get the wrong idea."

"Gracie says I'll be getting a certificate from this school in Texas he hooked me up with." Jeb had stopped short of saying he would have it framed. He could feel his legitimacy spilling out of him like he had sprung a leak there in plain sight of Fern. Looking back, he should have walked away right then with what little dignity remained.

"The last thing you need is someone loving you for what you're trying to become." She had worn a pair of jointed earrings that kept tapping the sides of her face like the forelegs of a praying mantis. "You deserve better." She picked up a sack of something she had bought that morning at the Woolworth's, then climbed into her rattling Chevy coupe and tooled off to start the next hour of her life without him.

Jeb had tried to tell Fern how he reached for her same ideals with the muster of a fighter pilot. But he was left watching her drive away as he fumbled for words that would not come.

Fool that you are, he had thought to himself.

Fern's blunt here's-the-deal, take-it-or-leave-it way of letting Jeb down had left him grasping for another chance, although his oldest charge, Angel, had judged him duly demeaned.

Now, in the secret chapel of daylight, he balanced on one knee until it came to him that his posture suggested matrimony. If Fern so much as laid eyes on him in such a position, she would turn and walk away before he had the chance to explain his lesser intent of starting over with courtship. So he found a place to sit on a fallen tree and spent several minutes piecing together a speech that might convince Fern to give thought to the idea of seeing him again—over coffee at Beulah's. No. Dinner. Dinner would be better, since their first go-around had taken them past the stage of coffee and a biscuit.

How well he remembered the night she had come nigh to giving herself to him. That alone had much to do with Fern's gradual pulling away from him, along with the fact she had said she loved him—before the truth came out, that is. That Jeb was not who he said he was.

Jeb slumped down, exhausted by his thoughts. His year under the tutelage of Philemon Gracie had taught him how to bring out the message inside the Scriptures, picking away at every word until the application rose from the story like a bubble below the lake's surface. Gracie had taught him porch chatter—how to yammer on about everything from the best place to buy buckshot to how to feed six children on three dollars a week. But Philemon, not a minister to dabble in matters as impractical as romance, had not mentioned how Jeb could win back the affections of the schoolteacher who hated him for pretending to be someone he wasn't. Even knowing he was working to become a legitimate preacher had not improved her trust in Jeb. The history they shared smacked of too much bitter and not enough sweet.

Returning to his orations, Jeb practiced a few well-turned phrases, got up, sat back down, then threw open his arms and said to the trees, "Fern, I'm not the same man you once knew. I've learned the difference between what is right and wrong. I want to ask you to forgive me and . . ."

His voice weakened at the sight of Angel, his fourteen-year-old charge, staring at him from across the rear of the acre behind the church. Her gaze held a pitiable anticipation, as though she expected every last ounce of his manhood to wither up and blow away. She shrugged and called over to him, "I liked you better as a liar. At least you was believable then."

❋

Jeb stopped his truck when he saw the face of the boy, aged by hard times, selling homemade items alongside the road. Everyone in Nazareth had fallen on hard times. But nobody wanted a handout, no matter what the rest of the country thought. Buying homemade wares from a neighbor lacked the sting of blatant charity. Edward Bluetooth's family was known for making and selling goods along the stretch of road right outside downtown Nazareth, as well as for being good fix-it people for the county's farmers.

Jeb was supposed to be on his way into town on an errand; Gracie had sent him to pick up a sack of nails and some wood to repair a window in the church. He hit the brake and pulled the truck to a stop next to the boy's stand.

Edward Bluetooth attended the county school often enough to fall behind and yet get a free lunch and be counted in the rolls. He'd never had the look of a boy, just

a small twelve-year-old man with a Fuller Brush salesman's spiel and yellow teeth. He sold his family's wares
on the side of the road—mostly leather things and
squares of lye soap cooked up with lavender to hide the
unpleasant stench when his momma stirred up potent
batches out in the front yard.

Jeb picked up a pair of moccasins stitched around the
toes, with leather straps and tassels that tickled the calf.
Edward had a hungry look about him that pinched Jeb's
conscience. He'd heard the Bluetooths had left the
Appalachians on foot and hiked all the way to Arkansas
to try to find a place where they could set up shop and escape the starvation of the hills. But the Depression had
put every person—Indian, Negro, and White—in the
same boat.

Before Jeb could lay down the shoes, Edward said to
him, "Those are real good moccasins."

"I'll give you fifty cents, Edward," said Jeb.

"You don't believe me. Try 'em for a month. If they
don't work fer ye, you bring 'em back. I'll give you back
your dollar."

"Too much."

"Seventy-five cents. Bottom dollar, Preacher."

Jeb handed Edward all the change from his pocket.

"You still owe me a dime, Preacher, but if you'll
not mention it to anyone, I'll let you slide. You is lucky.
The moccasins wear just as good at sixty-five cent as a
dollar."

Jeb pulled his foot out of his right shoe and tried on a
moccasin. "Feels good, Edward. You make them?"

"Nobody in the Bluetooth family has my way with
leather. Best hands in the county—fingers touched by

God, my uncle says. Wait to see how they do for you,
then you'll be runnin' back for more."

Jeb smiled at the boy's pitch and climbed into the cab
of his truck. As he drove off, he glanced back at Edward.
The boy had already pulled up shop and was walking
down the road with his entire business in a time-punctured
satchel straining with his shoemaker's knickknacks.
Leather straps dangled out the bottom. He was whistling
a song that sounded like a Christmas carol in the middle
of September.

Jeb drove on to the parsonage wearing Edward
Bluetooth's moccasins. When he pulled up, Reverend
Gracie, the minister of Church in the Dell and his mentor
and teacher, waited on the front porch. The instant Jeb
pulled into the dusty circle of roadway that led to the
house, Gracie pulled out his pocket watch to check the
time. He lifted himself out of the rocker and waited for Jeb
to come up and seat himself. Once settled, the parson
chatted about the county fair for a moment, more talkative
than usual. Then he spotted some pages sticking out from
under the jacket Jeb had laid over the top of his work.
Little if anything ever got past Gracie's eye for detail.

"Good. You brought your notes. I can't find my
glasses. You'll have to read a bit of your thesis to me.
Eyes are getting old," said Gracie.

"I don't have your flair with words," Jeb admitted.
Gracie had loaned him his old papers from the little Bible
school he had attended up north. The preacher's writing
had a quick pace about it—like a general, all hurry-up-
and-let's-get-on-with-things. Jeb's thesis felt like lead in
his hands. He had inked out and written over so many of
the words, the paper looked blotchy, as though penned by

Angel's little brother, Willie. He hesitated. "Maybe I should rewrite it."

"First-thesis jitters. I had them too. May as well get over it. Let's see it." Philemon had lucid eyes that changed from green to blue depending upon his mood. They were eyes that could see straight into Jeb with candor, probing all the way past his insecurities and straight into his fears.

Jeb laughed. He had come to know a different Gracie from the black-coated penguin who had waddled into Church in the Dell with his three astute city children. Only with Jeb around did Gracie fall into jesting.

Jeb read a line or two, cleared his throat, and then began again. He'd gone through a couple of paragraphs before he realized Gracie was staring into the dusty road beyond the parsonage. "I'm boring you. If it's lousy, just give it to me slowly."

Gracie pulled a blanket around his shoulders, allowing the corners to hang like an old lady's prayer shawl. After a pause to gauge Jeb's mood, he spoke candidly. "I'm afraid I'm not well, Jeb."

At twilight each evening, the slow final drain of summer into September sent everyone in town out onto their front porches. Even from a mile up the road, just before Marvelous Crossing Bridge, Jeb could hear the neighbor girls' carefree laughter, filled with the joys of coming of age and the mystery of boys and not the least bit dampened by the Depression.

"You been to see the doctor yet?" Jeb laid aside the thesis between them on the porch, his rocker slowing to the same steady, lulling creak of Gracie's import from Germany.

"Down around these places, it's difficult to get good care. Dr. Forrester in Hot Springs says I've gone and got myself a nasty stomach disorder."

"You thought about seeing Ethel Bluetooth? She's the best yarb woman, you know, and lots of things can be done for a stomach complaint," said Jeb, unconsciously examining his new moccasins.

"If it weren't for the children, I'd not blink an eye about staying. I can't imagine how things would turn out for them without me. Bad enough they lost their mother. I'm terrified for them."

A flock of Canada geese startled the sky all at once and dived beneath the line of trees, calling out to one another that winter would soon flush all warmth from the hollow. Jeb shifted in the rocker, wanting to steer the conversation back toward safer topics. But he noticed the beads of sweat above Gracie's upper lip and the diluted color of his cheeks and temples. He said, "Reverend Gracie, you and I both know this town took a long time to find you and get you to come and pastor Church in the Dell. You can't leave."

"Ever notice how life is one big fleeting chapter after another? You take Saint Paul. Never could settle in one place."

Jeb stopped Gracie's hand as it tapped the chair arm. "You can't be bad sick. God wouldn't allow it."

"Don't presume to second-guess God, Jeb."

Jeb drew back, respectful of his mentor.

Gracie began to lay out the plan he had mentally organized over the course of the last week. "We'll give the congregants time to grow accustomed to the idea. I've heard of another doctor in Hope who might be able to help me until I can get to Cincinnati." He caught Jeb's deflated look. "I don't mean I'm throwing in the towel just yet, so don't look at me like that."

Jeb still knew of those in Nazareth who had not forgiven his phony preacher stint when he'd used the Welby children as his family for a front. He had been on the run from the law not one year ago. The memory of his brief season of crime still weighed him down, not only in his own mind, but in the minds of the townspeople who had believed he should be lynched. Looking back on all of it—Angel's wrinkled scheme, his puerile belief that he would wind up the town preacher with a girl like Fern on his arm—still left him astonished that he had not been struck down by the Almighty. It was like him to run. He had not meant to stay long enough to get found out and arrested. But the omnipotent One had laid out a different plan.

The thought of Gracie's duties being suddenly dumped in his lap gave him a queasy feeling, like looking out over a canyon while the ground eroded under his feet.

"Your thesis opener isn't bad. I'd like for you to bring me a fresh new sermon. Tomorrow."

"What makes you think I'm ready to preach, let alone step into your shoes?"

"Man like you hates to accept defeat. You're like the young boy pedaling uphill with all his brothers watching. I know you've been trying to prove yourself to everyone in town. Including that schoolteacher."

The girls from Marvelous Crossing raced down the road, followed by the Welbys. Jeb could see Angel leading the chase with elbows crooked and bare feet pounding. Little dusty ghosts of red clay trailed behind them.

His obligation had somehow become his family, he realized. Jeb had never heard about youngens being put out
when he was growing up. These days it was the same as
being orphaned—nobody around to see to your meals
and teach you the ways of the world from a comfortable
perch. Either way, you had better find a body to latch
onto or starve. Like the Welbys, past things had put him
out too. But Nazareth had become their place to land.
Odd the way they had become a family—Jeb, Angel,
Willie, and Ida May—like someone had knitted with
threads of cotton and wool a thing of comfort. Although
the biggest, Angel, had her prickly ways.

Jeb felt Gracie slipping away from him, as though he
were being cast to sea. "Six more months with you, and
then I'll take that platform, Reverend."

"I know this is hard for you, Jeb. Give yourself some
mulling-over time."

"People here count on you, like you're the man of the
house when it comes to Church in the Dell."

Gracie spoke to himself as he checked off a mental
list. "So much to tell you. Things like how to keep your
mind on the flock and out of town politics. I'd better
write all this down. Where'd I put my glasses?"

Jeb hated to tell him they were right on the bridge of
his nose where they belonged.

Gracie picked up the thesis and passed it back to Jeb.
"Best you read me a little more. The sun is going down
and we're low on coal oil."

❖

Nazareth's bank had just closed when Jeb arrived downtown with the small offering Gracie had given him to de-

posit. Jeb had seen more squeezed from corn than was wrung out in that offering plate. He tapped on the window glass where the clerk, Finn Dudley, was pulling down the shade.

"Finn, can you take this deposit for Reverend Gracie?" Jeb said, knowing Gracie carried more weight than he.

Finn's gaze made a half-circular examination of the bank lobby behind him.

"For the church, Finn."

Finally, with a sigh as reticent as pond mist, the obliging clerk pulled out a ring of keys. Jeb smiled at him through a circle drawn in the window dust by a youth. He met Finn at the counter, where the clerk carried out the transaction while talking about the piping hot supper he had waiting for him back at the house.

"Sorry to keep you from your supper, Finn."

Finn mentioned that the wife could always throw an extra tater in the pot if he would join them. Jeb mulled over the invite, all the while knowing he had three more mouths to feed besides his own. But before he could respond the front door snapped open. Asa Hopper came into the bank like he had just bought it.

"Evening, Asa," Jeb said, even though Asa looked past him.

"Mr. Mills is gone for the day, Asa." Finn kept his eyes on the deposit, which would have been his habit anyway, so as not to lose count. But it seemed he did not want to give Asa the satisfaction of looking into his eyes.

"This Depression ain't no excuse to just haul off and kick a man when he's already fighting to scratch together two nickels, Finn!" Asa had a bearlike countenance, brown eyes liquid as kerosene. He held up a letter that had the bank's address at the top. "Ain't no one who could come up with this kind of money in two weeks. I got big deals, I tell you, that will land me in the money— but not in two weeks."

"It's none of my business, Asa." Finn kept counting the money.

Jeb knew the church offering was paltry and figured Finn had counted it three times by now. "I'll be out of here, if you two are needing to do personal business."

Finn's fingers turned white around his fountain pen. "No need to hurry off, Jeb. I can't help you, Mr. Hopper. Your business is not with me, but you already know that."

"You tell that banker, Mills, this is not my last time to come looking for him. If I want to see him, I know where he lives." Asa wadded up the letter and tossed it on the rug where people wiped their feet. Then he turned to leave and slammed the door behind him.

The big clock near the door clanged out the hour of six o'clock as though it timed Hopper's exodus.

"I should have locked up behind us," said Finn.

Jeb felt responsible for the whole scene with Asa. Finn had already wrapped up his evening clerk duties and might have motored halfway home by now if he had not wangled his way inside. "I should have waited until to-morrow. Is something wrong with Asa Hopper?"

Jeb had never known much about Asa. His wife, Telulah, was a woman as slight as a frail twig in winter, even seeming at times to snap in two if any of the other women tried to engage her in everyday talk. Some Sundays she came with their brood of five youngens, al-though usually it was with just their youngest, Beck. But Asa never visited the church. Not for Easter sunrise service or even shadowing the wife at the church picnics like other men that preferred Sunday on the creek bank.

"Asa's like every other poor old Joe in the country—needing relief but not knowing where to get it. I wish him well, but I can't help the man."

Jeb recalled that the Hoppers owned a large spread of land just outside Nazareth, a place running over with several big, strapping boys who looked like men years before they'd come of age. "Don't we all wish this Depression would let go? Been like an old mean dog, tearing up people's lives as it lopes down the road."

"Here's your receipt, Jeb. Or should I call you Reverend Nubey?" asked Finn.

It was the first time since Jeb had lied about being a preacher that he'd heard the title Reverend in front of his own name. He figured he would have to let it settle on him until he no longer felt like a fraud, like he'd been cut out of the newspaper in little Gracie silhouettes. He thanked Finn, stepped around the wadded paper on the rug, and opened the door.

Hopper yelled out the open window of the jalopy driven by his oldest boy. "I'll be back tomorrow, Dudley! You tell that to Mills!"

Jeb hesitated long enough to watch Hopper disappear around the next block. "Finn, go on and lock up behind me. It's getting late." He waited until Finn had locked the door.

When the sun set, it was as though all Jeb's energy drained with it. He was as tired as the day had been long.

2

Angel came running out of Honeysack's General Store holding a newspaper under one arm and hair ribbons in the other. As she seated herself next to Willie and Ida May, who sat in her brother's lap, Jeb said, "I asked you to get a newspaper and that's all." He took the newspaper from her. "I can't have you spending money we don't have, Biggest."

"Ida May and I can't go to school without ribbons."

"Your hair is fine. Vanity never did no one no good." Jeb cranked the truck engine.

"Fellers shouldn't get involved in a girl's business. Here, Ida May, take two, one for each braid."

"What's that supposed to mean?"

"It don't mean nothing. Let's hurry before we're late."

Jeb slowed the truck to goad her. Angel huffed in exasperation.

"Men like you don't get women—how we think and such, and what we got to have."

"I knew women in Texarkana who would disagree with you."

"Floozies don't count as real women."

"Last time I checked, women was women, big, little, purty, or bad."

"What's a floozie?" asked Ida May.

"If you knew women, you wouldn't have so much trouble keeping one. A woman needs a man to spend his last dime making sure she has what she needs."

"You got a lot to learn, Biggest, about men and women."

"Be stubborn, then. And single."

❄

The drive away from the schoolhouse was quiet. Jeb had deposited all three Welbys at the school drive so that he could be the first to see Hayes Jernigan, the lumberyard boss, about more work at the lumbermill. The way he had it figured, with what he'd made last week, he could pay off his debts at Will Honeysack's store and still have extra for daily grub.

After speaking with Hayes, Jeb waited outside the lumberyard office while Hayes figured his numbers and payroll. Finally, to while away the time, Jeb pulled his old banjo out of the pickup. His brother, Charlie, had dug it out of their mother's attic and sent it to him over a month ago. Jeb played an open note, placed his finger over the middle fret of the first string, and then chimed the note. He plucked the fretted note next, but found it low. After adjusting the bridge, he plucked the note again, chimed it, and found it right.

As he waited for the yard boss to appear, he strummed a tune about a sailor. It set the lumberyard dog to barking, so Jeb played faster, laughing at the mutt the men called Dawg for lack of a better name. Dawg squatted in front of him, his tail swaying, friendly-like, a hairy pendulum.

Jeb felt the weariness of study and work easing out of him as he played. He had stayed up too late trying to tend to the obligatory sermon, all the while sensing Gracie looking over his shoulder. Then he'd stared up from his bed for hours, troubling over how some townspeople of Nazareth still looked down on him and the Welbys. The duties of the clergy seemed to hang over him like a hammer, ready to pound out of him any hope for gaining respect if he took the job before his time. If he ever did take the pulpit again, he told himself, he would prove his sincerity for reaching for so high a mark as the station of clergy.

Then his mind had run to worry, to finding a way out of the fight for everyday survival. He did not know how he could keep the Welby children without this lumbermill job or even afford to keep up his studies and work at the same time. He had not planned well for everyday life. But what else could he do but keep trying? The youngens had no place left to go. Angel had written to her aunt in Little Rock so many times he couldn't bear to see her watching every day for a letter saying her momma had gotten well. Much less a note from a daddy who had left the children in the care of an old girlfriend and then disappeared with a wave of migrant workers.

Hayes Jernigan exited the office and shambled across the quiet lumber lot, counting a few dollar bills. Jeb's heart sank.

"Nice picking for a preacher. Dawg seems to like it anyway." Hayes laughed at the mutt's interest in Jeb's playing. "A few of the boys put in a word for you. Tuck Haw especially."

Tuck played pool down at Snooker's every evening

with the other lumbermen. Jeb had stopped in to say a polite word to him and the other lumbermen last Friday night, but they mostly kept to themselves. It surprised Jeb that Tuck had spoken up for him, what with that particular group of men not finding favor first of all with a former con man but worst of all with a man intent on the study of church doctrines and such.

"They asked me to keep you on, Jeb. But I got to do what I can to hang on to men with tenure." He handed Jeb his final pay. "If we hadn't gotten that deal to build barrels, I'd be losing lumbermen that's been eating sawdust since they was born. I hate that I don't have no more work for you. I hope you find some." He studied for a bit, as though rehashing what he had just said, and then added, "What I mean to say, Jeb, is it's a cryin' shame I got to let you go, what with those youngens you been carin' for. My wife won't hardly talk to me for it."

Jeb thanked him anyway. "I'm obliged to you, Hayes."

"You still countin' on preacherin', I guess. Some people believes they's good money in religion."

Jeb counted the coins from his pocket before adding the dollar bills. "One day, Hayes. You ought to come to church."

"My wife would agree," said Hayes.

Jeb knew that even Hayes had heard how he had skulked into town over a year ago pretending to be a preacher to feed himself. He figured Hayes's churchgoing wife had more to do with the lumberyard owner hiring him than he had admitted. Jeb had hated how first one man downtown and then another always kept bringing up the past. But Hayes had kept his opinions to himself for the most part. After several months Jeb had finally felt a friendship forming between them. But Hayes's letting him go said that business priorities had finally overridden camaraderie.

"Wish I had more work for you, Jeb."

With what Hayes might have paid him over the next two weeks, Jeb could've stretched out beans and corn bread for that long. Now he would be back at the general store by Monday, most likely, delivering seed to farmers again.

Hayes walked him out to the truck. "I ain't seen a banjo around these parts in a while. I had a cousin who could play like the devil."

"My momma once said it was of the devil. After she died, I felt bad every time I picked it up. Only reason I got it is because my brother, Charlie, sent it to me. Seems a shame to hide it in the attic."

"I'd like to hear you do another tune sometime. I like good fiddling and banjo playing. Makes me forget my troubles for a bit. Maybe it is of the devil, but I like the sound of it."

Hayes heard a dinner bell ring and glanced up toward his office. His wife, Molly, waved a brown bag of something fatty from the grassless path to the office. Hayes told her to wait inside. "You drop by and tell us how you're doing from time to time, Jeb."

Jeb left him to tend to his meal.

The road from the mill to downtown Nazareth wound for miles, with rocks spitting out from under the tires like vipers. If he had turned right at the crossroads, he would be headed toward Hope. He had driven the kids there in July to buy a watermelon. Willie had eaten it until the bottom half of his face was stained red.

The thought of sending that boy and his sisters to places unknown quickened Jeb's anxiety.

He headed straight and aimed for downtown Nazareth. He had to meet Reverend Gracie at the bank. Gracie intended to let Horace Mills, the banker, know of the upcoming transfer of the pastorate to Jeb, maybe by Christmas or even sooner. Mills and his wife had at times been the sole support of Church in the Dell, other than the families who tithed from their pantry or henhouse when cash had become such a rarity. Gracie had often sought advice from Mills about financial matters.

Jeb parked alongside the walk that ran in front of the bank and pulled out a fountain pen given to him by Freda Honeysack from the general store. She had called it a good-faith gift when he had begun his apprenticeship with Gracie. Through the glass of the bank's windows, he saw the back of Philemon Gracie's head colored like frost. He had arrived early and taken a chair to wait on Jeb. When he saw him he waved him inside.

Jeb had never known Reverend Gracie to cater to anyone, let alone Mills. But he had always shown his appreciation. Still, Jeb remembered how Horace Mills had changed toward him when he'd told him how sorry he was for the scam. Horace had not taken much stock in Jeb's conversion, paying him as much mind as he would that lumberyard dog.

"I hate to bother the banker on his busiest day," Jeb said now.

"Mr. Mills has supported Church in the Dell when no one else could. Better that we tell him about the change rather than surprise him."

Mills's office door opened and then stopped partway

as though it had a spring weighting it from inside. A muffled voice, low like a man keeping secrets, followed the drawling door.

Asa Hopper appeared. His anger drew up his elongated jaw and turned his face pink as pickled eggs. Behind him came a tall young man who looked to be the oldest Hopper boy, skinny with a face that looked stepped on. Hopper leaned back inside the office and yelled something critical and then closed the door. The boy lagged behind, mumbling monotonous echoes to his father's angry rants.

"Hopper has it in for Mills," said Jeb as they watched the two leave.

"I believe we're next." Gracie lifted his body from the wooden chair as though it took all the strength he had mustered from breakfast to do so. He sipped on a bottle of medicine like it was milk and then hid it away inside his coat.

From the office Mills called an older woman, Mona, inside and then sent her right back out. "Reverend Gracie, Mr. Mills is ready to talk with you."

Jeb issued a sigh that emptied him all the way to his feet. "It might be best for you to tell him without me present. I'll leave and come back later."

Gracie thanked Mona. Then he touched Jeb at the back of his arm and gave a gentle thrust forward, allowing Jeb to enter ahead of him. Jeb felt more illegitimate than when he had come into town posing as Gracie himself.

"Reverend Gracie, glad to see you," said Horace before eyeing Jeb.

Jeb extended his hand, to which Horace responded with a politician's squeeze. "I guess those Welby children are keeping you busy. That Angel is growing like a weed."

Horace could immediately put people at ease, even those he tended to dislike. Jeb relaxed.

The banker's office had a leather smell—not like well-worn saddle leather but like the shiny leather of a gambler's study. Jeb wondered if the door behind Horace's desk chair led to the man's genuine working desk, cluttered with stacks of papers and loan applications. This room had not one speck of dust. His desk had atop it only one gold magnifying glass and a fountain pen that Horace tucked into a desk drawer.

Jeb and Gracie sank down into the two soft leather chairs that faced the desk. Gracie had a way of swallowing up the silence in a meeting with a pensive, reflective look about him, as though he owned the quiet and was preparing to fill it with brilliant, perfectly selected words. Jeb sat forward, prepared to look equally astute, until he saw that the coat sleeve around his wrist had frayed, with threads protruding like an old woman's whiskers. He dropped his hands.

Horace sat forward, his dark worsted jacket scented by the faint suggestion of a cigar he had no doubt extinguished before the minister turned up. "Have you been to see the doctor, Reverend?"

"A few times since we last met. How is Mrs. Mills?"

"Bossy and loving it. Preparing for our daughter, Winona, to come home. She has a break coming up from her classes. Wants to take off a semester. For what reason, I couldn't tell you, but who can figure out what goes on inside a girl's head. Amy is her usual anxious self, rolling out pie dough and keeping her kitchen help busy."

Jeb shifted to one side. His right elbow sank into the leather, which deflated like a tire beneath him.

"Horace, I'll be brief. Doctors in these parts are big on honesty but low on know-how. I'm all my girls and Philip have in the world."

Mills's gaze trickled over to Jeb and then back to Gracie.

"My brother and his wife live in Cincinnati and they have the highest regard for a doctor they want me to see."

"A visit to Cincinnati would do you good," Horace said.

Gracie lifted as though the chair were swallowing him whole.

"Not leaving for good, though." Horace's brows made a gray ledge beneath the age lines that mapped a near perfect tick-tack-toe in the center of his forehead.

"Jeb is near ready for his ordination. He's studied like the wind, like I did at his age."

Jeb saw how Horace examined him for any sign of a blemish. Before the banker could raise a complaint, he sat forward. "Mr. Mills, I know my past is shady. But Reverend Gracie has taught me well. I trust his teaching. I love Nazareth, and I want to serve Church in the Dell."

"Jeb's passed every seminary course I've had mailed to him," said Gracie. "He has agreed to preach this Sunday. It will be his first time since his apprenticeship with me began."

Jeb's stomach did a flip-flop.

"And his first time since he was jailed for fraud and attempted murder," said Horace.

Jeb felt as though his entire body had gone numb, like his whole bottom half had been run over by a tractor.

Horace's smile spread like the opening of a dam. "Ha-ha! Just joshing you, Jeb. Or is it Reverend Jeb?"

Gracie, if he were elated, hid it soberly. "I can't stay in Nazareth much longer."

"If I could get him to stay, I would," Jeb told Horace. He knew his promise sounded empty. Only this morning he had found Gracie seated at his desk drinking his bottle of medicine.

"Jeb, you're still quite young," said Horace.

"Thank the Lord for that." Gracie checked his pocket watch. "I've a few things to do before the day is done. Horace, you should know I would not leave you all if I didn't have to. I'm not talking about next week or next month if I can help it. I want Jeb stable and the church ready for the change. If Jeb were not my apprentice, it's likely you all might go a long while without a minister. I know of two ministers who divide their time between several congregations. The way this Depression is going, it's a miracle you all have maintained a minister at all."

"Don't I know it?" said Horace.

Jeb was uncertain that Horace could see God's hand guiding them through the difficulty as readily as Gracie.

"You're not leaving right away, then?" Horace asked.

"Jeb will be handling all the bank matters for the church. But he's done that for me often enough of late. I don't know how long this stomach of mine will hold out. But I'll smooth the waters the best I can."

"Jeb, why don't you come with me, then? I'll have you sign some papers giving you permission to bank for Church in the Dell. Reverend, we'll need your signature too." Horace rose. To Gracie, he muttered something indiscernible to Jeb, as though he was cutting Jeb out of the conversation. Jeb could sense Horace's dislike for him. He noticed Horace did not look at him again for the rest of the morning.

❉

Nazareth had the smell of tar beneath and a thundery day overhead. The town had a September cool that brought a few merchants out onto the walk. Every store window, from Fidel's Drugstore to Faith Bottoms's Clip and Curl, was pasted up with posters and torn-out magazine advertisements for things no one could buy.

A local man with hair jet black, as though he had slicked it on with oil, shouted into a public-address system he had jimmied outside Honeysack's General Store. Jeb knew him from church, a man who checked his watch often during the morning sermon and then leaped to his feet to shake as many hands as possible. The man was yelling about the Depression and his race for a state senate seat. "Vote Bryce for Your Next Senator" was emblazoned in smart red-and-blue lettering across a wooden sign he had placed on a type of home-fashioned stand. The slogan beneath his name was pungent with a Depression-year promise: "Let's End This Thing Together!"

Out in front of the bank Jeb and Gracie shook hands, Gracie with more assurance than Jeb. They agreed to meet once more before Sunday to get Jeb ready for a turn behind the pulpit, the first time with legitimacy. Jeb watched Gracie amble toward his parked car. As he went, several people, some churchgoers and others not, stopped to greet him with a "Hello, Reverend" and "Sure hope you're praying for rain, Preacher." Respect for Gracie in

Nazareth had spilled over into the hilly provinces beyond the town limits, bringing families from as far away as Whelan Springs and Camden to hear him preach. Church in the Dell had grown with new faces since Gracie had taken the pulpit, although the offering basket had yet to reflect that growth.

Down the street, Will Honeysack waved his arm, his sleeve rolled up and pinching at the elbow. Jeb met him at the doorway of the general store. "Afternoon. Wish that thunder would turn to rain."

"Freda said it sounds like a dry thunder. Come inside. Got them banjo strings you ordered. Had to send clear to Cleveland for 'em. Those Cleveland folk know about musical instrumentation and the like."

Will had cranked the radio loud enough to split melons. Kate Smith trilled out "When the Moon Comes Over the Mountain." Two girls not any bigger than Ida May and wearing hats too hot for September basked in the light of the window and sang every word as though it were the last song to be sung on earth.

Jeb inspected the strings and then let Will slip them into a bag.

"Say, you know how to string a banjo?" Will asked.

"Like stringing fence wire. Can just about do it in my sleep."

"Louis, come up h'yere!" Will yelled to a man in the sugar-and-flour-sack aisle. "Jeb, this feller's been looking for a man who could string a banjo."

Jeb vaguely recognized the man as someone he had seen on occasion around the barbershop.

"This is Jeb Nubey, Louis," Will said.

"I been looking for somebody what could string a

banjo for my boy. He got it from a peddler, and his momma thought it weren't good for nothing. Kin I bring it by your place and let you give it a look?"

Jeb did not know if the news should be spread around the county that Church in the Dell had a banjo-picking preacher. Some folk—womenfolk anyway—did not take to banjo picking.

"I'll pay you two dollars if you kin get it ready and tuned. Cash on the barrelhead."

"Bring it by my place. Saturday latest. I'm up around the creek that runs north of Marvelous Crossing. John Long's old house," said Jeb.

"I heard of the place."

They shook on it.

"Seems I'm always learning something new about you."

The woman's voice came from behind Jeb. Without turning around he said, "Afternoon, Fern."

Fern Coulter came to the counter with a sack of brown sugar and a spool of white thread. "This is all I need today, Will."

She had tucked her hair into a Crest hat, a blue knit with a soft brim that sat at a slanty angle across her forehead. Even though Jeb often tired of her constant hat-wearing, he had to admit she looked good in this one. The blue against her blonde hair reminded him of a butterfly that had landed on a white delphinium, stunning but elusive.

He had not spent a decent moment with Fern since that day in August when she had dropped him like hot rocks. School had given her reason to pour every minute of the day into her work. She still showed up at their house every Sunday, as she had done for over a year, to help the

Welby children dress for church. But she always came after Jeb had already left to open the chapel windows and doors. She arrived at church with the children just before the opening prayer and disappeared after the last amen to avoid an exchange of words between them. And overnight she had developed a diplomat's gift for avoiding Jeb's offers for dinner, even the offers attached to helping the Welbys with schoolwork.

Jeb reached for the bagged strings.

"You play the banjo," Fern said. "You're a surprise a minute."

"Not since I was a boy. Charlie sent it to me last month after he found it up in my daddy's attic. You remember Charlie. Thanks for ordering these for me, Will."

"Why'd you quit playing?" she asked without looking at him.

"Everybody makes a bad choice now and again. Seemed right at the time."

"Ida May has some reading tonight. I just say that in case she forgets. Angel can help her with it." Fern pulled two coins out of her handbag and pushed them across the counter as though they were not too hard to come by. She did not flaunt her daddy's money and had chosen to teach to escape the socialite escapades of her other siblings. But she had never gone without like the other girls who had moved away from kin. Her father would not have stood for it.

"Want to meet me for coffee at Beulah's, maybe a slice of her pie?" Jeb asked. His invitation sounded forced, wooden—not at all like he had rehearsed it.

Fern lifted her eyes and looked at Will. Will handed her the bag and said, "He ain't talking to me."

"I'm busy for a lot of weeks, maybe even more than that." Fern had yet to turn and face Jeb.

"How about three tomorrow, after you're finished with your school duties?" Jeb felt the thin thread of his luck tangling around his throat. The conversation wasn't going as he had imagined.

Will polished his counter a third time.

"I meant to tell you something I noticed about Angel," Fern said. "She's not been herself, and you know how transparent she is when she's troubled. Has she mentioned anything to you about her friendship with Asa Hopper's son Beck?"

"Angel's friends with everyone." Disgusted with himself, Jeb gave up on a direct answer to his offer of pie. He turned to leave. But before he could step away, Fern spoke.

"I could go for pie, I guess."

3

White Oak Lake spawned the brooks that fed into the green waters of Marvelous Crossing with its algae-crowned city of minnows and catfish. Yesterday Angel and her siblings had taken one last swim beneath the bridge before the first frost came and browned the landscape and chilled the lake waters to an icy tea. As they swam, Jeb had studied sermon notes out on the front porch while his angst over coffee with Fern ate at him. Then, for the second night in a row, he had not slept. While Angel packed Willie and Ida May out of the house the next morning to walk to school with the neighbor girls, Jeb stood bent over the back steps and poured a bucket of water over his head.

"I know there's something wrong with you." Angel appeared at the corner of the pine-timbered rental house with Ida May swinging on her skirt.

"You'll be late for school. Mrs. Henderson will give you extra work for that," said Jeb. With an old cotton rag, he toweled his hair and then slicked it back behind his ears.

"Every time you get riled up again over Miss Coulter, you mope around the house like some kicked hound."

"You don't know nothing."

"I know you like I know that when I lift a stump I'll find grubs. I never see you changing shirts after you've fed Bell, like you used to so you'd show up at the school-yard with a fresh shirt and smelly hair slickum. The more times Miss Coulter turns you down, the worse you look."

Jeb stared at his face in the kitchen window glass. "I don't remember wearing a fresh shirt to take you varmints to school."

"Not anymore. And now you make us walk. I know when I'm bein' used, Jeb Nubey!"

"Besides, just because I stop wearing hair jelly don't mean I've lost my self-respect. I may have lost Fern, but I still got the charm in me; don't wager I don't, Biggest."

"When you hide things from us, it's all over you, like the way you hold yourself in a hug with both hands and stare out the winder like someone's up and run off with your mind." Angel scooted Ida May back around the house. "Stop listening in, Big Ears."

Jeb followed them a few steps and yelled, "Don't you be shooting off your mouth at school that I'm moping around over some bookworm schoolteacher. It ain't even true!"

Angel ushered her sister forward and then smacked Willie for touching her hair.

"If I'm not here when you get back from school, just get Ida May and Willie on their school lessons."

"Where you going?" Angel asked.

"Town. That's all you need to know. Go on, now."

He listened as their voices chimed in with the girls who walked with them to school and then faded into the birdsong of early morning.

Inside, he made fast work of throwing on a clean shirt that matched as well as anything with the only good pair of brown trousers he owned. He muttered to himself, "Nothing wrong with wearing a fresh shirt. A man has a right to change his shirt if he wants. No big-mouth kid has a right to dictate my toiletry habits."

His back still ached from his last day at the lumbermill, and he couldn't remember if Ida May had done her reading lesson. And now Angel, just as Fern had prophesied, had gone and gotten a sour manner about herself of late. He sighed. He had to watch her mouth like a snake charmer watched a cobra. The more he tried to be father to her and the other two, the more he remembered what his life as a bachelor had been like.

After coffee with Fern, he needed to meet Gracie at the church. That gave him most of the day to look for work. He headed for town, figuring he could ask Will Honeysack for any extra loads he might need delivered. The last paycheck from the lumberyard would last another week at best.

❈

Jeb drove into town. With most of the town children back in school, Nazareth's streets held a quiet morning lull, like a churchyard at sunrise. None of the shops had seen a new coat of paint in years. But the clearness of day brought out the barn reds and sage greens of the shop fronts. Today, state senate hopeful Bryce had planted his campaign on the courthouse steps. He passed out leaflets to the few passersby before heading out for bigger fish in Hot Springs.

Jeb dropped into Beulah's and she scrambled an egg

for him for two cents and then threw in the coffee to boot. He chatted up FDR with Deputy Maynard, the same cop who had locked him up and then let him go, and sat long enough to have Beulah fill his cup twice.

"I thought the old lumbermill was closin' down," said Maynard. "Good thing Hayes Jernigan had the sense to take on that out-of-state job. Boys like you done down on your luck. I feel for you'uns. I hear Jernigan may lay off another string of men next week. Those boys been with him since 1925 and then they daddies before them."

"Guess I better get to old Will Honeysack's before the other fellas make a line right out of his store," said Jeb.

"Maybe so. Reverend Gracie says you took to your studies like a regular college swell. I bet you make a preacher after all, that's what. I don't care what anyone says." Maynard sipped his coffee, brewed hot and black enough to pave Main Street.

"Maynard, you think anyone in this town could ever think of me as a minister?" asked Jeb.

"Not many preachers I know of spend time in jail, but you could be the first." He set down his cup. "Reckon I better take a drive around town, make sure no one's loiterin'."

Jeb wanted to say he was not the same man as a year ago. The fact he had taken in the Welby waifs had said loads to his brother, who had known the old Jeb—old cotton-patch Jeb, who had left a man for dead down in Texarkana. Fern, on the other hand, had not forgiven him entirely, and no matter how much he reinvented the new-and-improved Jeb, she still looked at him as she would a termite. But he said none of that to Maynard, having tired of trying to prove himself to every taxpaying citizen of

Nazareth. Instead he said good-bye to the deputy and headed to Honeysack's store.

❉

Will had not needed any deliveries. He sent Jeb to Woolworth's, where the Whittingtons had just gotten in some boxes of ladies dresses, winter woolens, and shoes. Jeb unboxed them for Evelene and moved a dress rack around until she was satisfied the dresses could be seen from all the way across the street. He stacked shoeboxes, packets of buttons, socks, and winter union suits until the calluses on his hands from the lumbermill work turned red. At noon, Floyd Whittington split corn bread and molasses with him and then Jeb swept up the back room to pay for the food.

Evelene Whittington met Doris Jolly at the front door, where the new tweeds hanging in the window had seduced the church organist into a look inside. "I could see my Josie in this plaid," said Doris. Evelene cooed her agreement.

The two women jabbered until their chatter turned to church matters. "What did the doctor tell the reverend?" asked Evelene.

Jeb checked the clock over the store counter and figured he had a good hour's work left before he had to meet Fern. He bent to straighten a tangle of sewing needles and threads behind the counter.

"Reverend Gracie wouldn't say, but I heard from my cousin who does business with this doctor that it's a serious matter that cain't be treated here." Doris fiddled with several price tags, turning each over to ogle the cost and then drop it.

"Doris, you don't think we'll lose him, do you?"

"I don't know nothing beyond what I told you, so if anyone tells you more, it didn't come from me," said Doris.

"Church in the Dell has never had such a cultured preacher in the pulpit. I can't imagine anyone being able to fill that man's shoes, not by any stretch of the imagination. That one family—what's their name, Mars or Lars—they come all the way from near Hope to get in on Gracie's preaching." Evelene touched the marcelled rows on the back of her head, running her fingers over tresses that bowed like ribbon candy.

Doris saw her daughter Josie's friend Florence across the street and waved her over. "Florence might know if Josie would like this knit dress. They're the same age and about the same size, exceptin' Josie's waist is smaller."

"Could be that Reverend Gracie knows more than he's telling. I'll bet I know who knows. We got Jeb Nubey working in the back of the store," said Evelene.

"I wouldn't involve that man at all. What the reverend's done for him is kind and all, but that's just the kind of preacher he is. We can't expect too much out of a feller with Nubey's kind of background." Doris pulled the knit dress off the rack.

Too late, Evelene lifted two fingers to Doris Jolly's mouth. Doris grew stiff and then turned to look behind her.

Jeb lifted from behind the counter. His eyes met with the organist's. He dusted the knees of his trousers. Doris had done a good job of hiding her dislike of him until now. He decided to say nothing to the two women except to excuse himself and walk past them out onto the sidewalk. Once there, though, he turned right around and planted his feet in the doorway of the Woolworth's.

"I'll be preaching this Sunday, ladies. Hope to see you both in church." He made for Beulah's.

Jeb waited in a booth rather than at the counter where he had talked with Maynard. Beulah tried to take his order once, served him a soft drink, and then left him to stare through the café windows. He spent the time sounding out in his mind what he would say to Fern. But after a half hour of waiting for the schoolteacher to show, he realized he'd been stood up. With a sigh, he paid Beulah for the Coca-cola and headed back to his truck.

"I'm sorry for being so late." Fern could say anything without sounding apologetic. She wore a beret as dark as wine and adjusted it to tumble across one brow. She kept walking as she spoke to him, as though she knew he would follow her back into Beulah's on an invisible leash.

Jeb's resentment of her hats was an anomaly to him. But the dislike was evident, bubbling up like gas from a well, every time she showed up wearing a new one. It was the thing that made her different from the rest of the poor girls in town, as though she served the town willingly but not because life had offered her no other options. It was another of those reasons he felt she had no need for him, however childish it seemed. He hated this beret and wanted to tell her so, but instead said, "You look smart today, Fern."

She picked out a booth.

"Reverend Gracie and I have our meeting, but—"

"Understood. I don't really have time, either."

Fern would have left him standing alone, but Jeb finished, "I do have an hour if you could spare one for me."

Nonchalantly, as though she didn't know she'd kept him waiting for a good thirty minutes, Fern seated herself where Jeb had just gotten up. His booth seat on the other side was cold.

With her looking at him half expectantly, all the words he had put together in the languid stretch of night now escaped him. If he said too much about taking Gracie's place, she might believe he was trying to prove he was legitimate. But even telling himself to keep a lid on matters did not quell the desire to spill his guts about taking over the Church in the Dell pulpit. Neither he nor Fern had ever discussed how the fact that one day he would be a certified minister might improve relations between them. Fern had never promised Jeb that his rise to a secure position would interest her in the least. She had always talked more about her self-confidence in her own job at the school and of her desire to raise up a prodigy or two from the impoverished lap of Nazareth—she had told him that at least twice during their few dates over the last year. Fern had left in the dust her identity as the daughter of Francis Coulter III from Ardmore, Oklahoma, and created a Fern that left her mark on Nazareth like a nun in an African village. It was no wonder that every man, woman, and child in Nazareth admired her. Jeb found that as annoying as her endless collection of hats.

He determined to try to chat things up with her without spilling out so much admiration for her, or at least to try to give off the same cool-as-a-cucumber qualities she displayed around him.

Beulah eyed Jeb from behind the counter, being as how it was his third visit to the café. He held up two fingers. "Coffees, Beulah. One pie for Fern."

"I had to keep a boy after school today. That's why I was late," Fern said. "Poor boy doesn't have good training at home. I hope I helped him. But they've laid off two more teachers, and with this extra load I'm afraid this student's going to fall right through the cracks." She looked past Jeb in a manner that said she was still in the classroom with the neglected child.

"Fern, things have gotten better—better than last year." Jeb did not see a flicker of approval from her. "Now, things is changing again, and I just thought I should tell you. I wish that I could erase my mistakes . . ." He had mentally rehearsed what he planned to say, but somehow it sounded foolish with Fern blinking at him over her cup of coffee. He knew the use of the word *plan* or *vision* might set well with her. But by being too talkative, he felt more like he was digging himself a deeper hole from which to emerge.

Fern's mouth parted slightly. The one brow not hidden by the beret lifted in a questioning little arc.

"Not that you've expected anything from me. You haven't asked me for anything or to fill you in on things like this." Jeb had spun a circle around himself and knew of no way out.

"And you're wanting to tell me what?"

A voice from somewhere told him to change the subject. "No one knows but me. You have to keep it from everyone. Not even Angel or Willie knows anything yet." He ignored the voice in his head that shouted for him to stop dead in his tracks.

"So this is about the children?"

"Not about the children, no."

Fern removed the beret and let it drop beside her.

"Reverend Gracie may have to resign from Church in the Dell."

Fern's brow furrowed. "He's the best thing that ever happened to Nazareth. Don't tell me anything else. I don't want to know."

"It's his health. Not that he plans on staying sick, on account of some doctor he wants to see up in Cincinnati."

"Good news, then," she said, relieved.

"Reverend Gracie has to leave, Fern. He has asked me to take his place." Jeb wanted to turn back the minutes that had just passed. He felt like a fool for looking for her approval. "I shouldn't have told you."

Finally he'd said something that made sense.

Fern kept looking down at her hands or the table in front of her. "I'm glad you told me. Never have liked surprises."

"I'll be preaching this Sunday."

"So you're accepting his post, or whatever you call it?"

"In the coming months, Gracie plans to prepare me to take his place." Jeb watched her pick up her hat and handbag. "Fern, I need to know how you feel about it. I want to be the preacher for Church in the Dell. That is, I'd rather have Gracie as minister over Church in the Dell myself. But he can't now. I'm going to do it, Fern. Tell me how you feel about that."

"It doesn't matter what I feel, Jeb. You're the one who has to take on the responsibility." She looked at him more directly than she had in weeks. "It's not like you haven't done it ever." Her legs slid around to the outside of the booth.

He knew she was referring to when he preached as a con. "But it's different now. This time I'm the real McCoy. I love this place and the people here."

"Since when do you need my approval?"

"I'm doing this for the Welby kids and for myself."

"Then you should do it." Fern came out of the booth and took a step away from him. "Beulah, cancel my pie, if you will. I'm not hungry after all."

Jeb listened as her pumps tapped against the floor all the way to the café door before he climbed out of the booth and said, "Are we finished?"

He watched her leave without an answer. She vanished beyond the window. When he turned around, Beulah was looking too. "You can trust ol' Beulah, Jeb. I won't tell a living soul."

4

Jeb found Gracie bent over the back steps of the church. Gracie spat red onto the ground and then wiped the sweat from his thinning brow.

Jeb clamped his hand over his mouth, pinching his lips together, shocked at finding Gracie in such a state. He tried not to look so shaken when Gracie straightened slightly and looked up at him. "Reverend, what I can do? Get you some water or something?"

"Jeb, for mercy's sake! I hate like everything for you to find me in such a state!" Gracie righted himself. "Since you're here, though, tell you what I need. I left Philip inside. Could you go and check on him? The girls had so much schoolwork tonight, I told them I'd bring Philip with me over here so they could get a thing or two done." Gracie's youngest had another year to go before starting school like his sisters, Emily and Agatha.

Jeb helped Gracie to the steps to sit and gain some strength. "Philip's fine, I'm sure, but I'll go inside and check on him."

"And while you're there, give a yank on the church bell, will you? I swore I saw something sifting down from the belfry when I rang the bell Sunday morning. Did I mention that on Sunday?"

Jeb shrugged. "Not that I recall."

"Could be we have a loose bell. You're better at knowing things like that."

"I'll check on it. I may just need to climb up into the belfry and give the bolts a turn or two."

Jeb found Philip on the front row of the church. He had a toy soldier in his hand and was using it to aim invisible gunfire at the vase of flowers on the altar. "Philip, you watch that flower vase. Greta Patton donated those mums for Sunday, and she'd have all our hides if it turned up broken." He reached for the bell rope and gave it a yank. It tolled and just as Gracie had said, fine particles floated down like sawdust or some such thing. He made a mental note to borrow a ladder that reached as high as the belfry.

"Daddy said you were coming, Jeb. Play soldiers with me."

Jeb joined him and picked up another soldier. He let Philip spear his man a time or two. The entire time his thoughts were on the boy's father. Finally, he felt he'd spent enough time with the boy. "You killed me two times now, Philip. I guess that's all the life left in me."

"Cincinnati is bigger than Nazareth," said Philip, catching Jeb by surprise. He hadn't really thought of how this situation would affect Gracie's children.

"Every place is bigger than Nazareth, I expect."

"Emily says that she never liked it here anyway." Philip had picked up the slightest trace of a southerner's accent. Emily and Agatha favored telling everyone they met that they were from up north. "But as long as I get to know people, it doesn't matter to me where we live."

"Philip, I sometimes think you are older than you look."

Gracie's rubber heels could be heard clomping up the church steps. He entered through the open door, color in his cheeks, robust, like he had sipped from the fountain of youth. "If we can finish before dinner, I'd like it very well. Philip and I are being treated to apple pie tonight." Emily cooked as well as anybody's wife in town. As Gracie's oldest, she had taken on the homemaker role when her mother had passed away.

Philip gathered up his soldiers and dropped them one by one into a tin box, *plink, plink, plink.* "Sorry I had to kill you, Jeb."

"We'll have us another battle soon, General. You'll see how mean my aim is."

They all locked up the church and walked through the grass to the parsonage. Inside the house, Gracie had set up the record book on his desk with pens and extra paper. "Take my seat, Jeb, if you will."

Apple pie slathered its scent throughout the parsonage. Emily and Agatha made kitchen noise along with an outburst now and then of teenage glee.

"Philip, go into the kitchen and ask your sisters to give you a slice of apple. They always have extra," said Gracie.

Philip made mouth music all the way into the kitchen.

Jeb tallied up the offering from the week and compared it to the last. "Reverend, I've studied this matter of me taking your place. I could not tell you for certain that my time has come."

"Offering was down this week."

"Not that I don't have the ability. I believe I do, but it

could likely be that my past could cause a bit of a snag in the minds of a few," said Jeb. "I thought that studying under you would give me the chance to redeem myself in the eyes of the families here. But instead, they look at me like your charity project."

Gracie opened the satchel where he tucked the Sunday offering every week until he or Jeb could make it to the bank. "Bless this offering, oh Lord, we pray."

"The way I figure it, first I ought to ease into the pulpit, like I am just standing in for you. Over time, they might grow used to the idea." Jeb finished his sentence with a confident smile. "But if they don't, maybe that would give you time to find a real minister to take your place or give you time to get well and come back. Maybe if everyone thought you might come back, that would be better, wouldn't it?"

"Jeb, you ought to think about the repercussions. We can't deceive the congregation into believing I'm coming back. Deception backfires."

"Not deceit. No way, sir! That's not at all what I meant to say. What I'm talking about is a waiting period. Everybody knows I'm an apprentice, so I'll take the pulpit as an apprentice. When that Cincinnati doctor makes you well, then I'll just step aside and you're back where you belong."

"While I'm gone, who will lead the church? Will Honeysack? Horace Mills? The members come to the minister for counsel. Perhaps they should drop by Will's place at the general store, drop a penny in a cup, and get a shop owner's advice." Gracie leaned back in his chair.

"There's a lot to think about. Got a lake baptism coming up. The Ketcherside boys haven't been baptized.

Their momma planned on you doing the dunking, Reverend."

"That's a good thing for the people around here to see you doing, Jeb. You've done it with me a half dozen times. You give the person a chance to profess their faith and then you douse them. I can announce that for you Sunday and then I'll officiate at the baptism, but let you 'dunk,' as you say, the Ketchersides. As a matter of fact, I should do just that." Gracie scrawled it in his blue book of reminders.

"To my recollection, I don't know if Arnell and Roe Ketcherside have stood and professed anything. We can't dunk them just on their momma's say-so."

"You'll be the one to counsel their mother. Now you're thinking like a leader of a flock. So you'll have a baptism, and then I know it's pretty far down the road, but there's the Thanksgiving dinner, and the Christmas social. The Whittingtons volunteered their house last year. You'll have the choir singing down at the court-house steps and then give a brief Christmas message. Brief, mind you, because it is, after all, Christmas. The mayor expects that every year from Church in the Dell."

Jeb felt like Gracie had tucked kindling all around him and then lit it. "So you're saying it's now or never."

"Don't forget to ask Horace to examine your records now and again. Bankers have a good eye for mistakes. Too, when he finds we need a little help from time to time, he can be counted on."

Jeb remembered how Horace had not given him much of a look after Gracie told him the news about his leaving. "The one thing I don't want you to do is sit up in Cincinnati worrying about Church in the Dell."

"I believe you can do it, Jeb." Philemon's smile made him look more hopeful, even though his peaked stare gave away his illness. "I heard you had coffee with Miss Coulter today. Tell me about that."

❄

Angel had Willie in a chair outside trimming the hair around his ears and across his forehead. Until the cold weather blew in with frost and ice, haircuts were best done outside where the breeze would carry the errant tufts into the woods.

"Jeb, tell Angel I don't need no haircut," said Willie.

"If you keep on wiggling like that, I'll nip your ear. Stay still, Willie." With a comb handle, Angel measured the hair above each ear and found one side higher than the other. "You been needing it shorter anyway."

Ida May played with a hand-carved doll that was fashioned to dance atop a board. When she yanked the wire, the jointed doll's limbs flailed all over the wooden porch, making it look like a wild dance. "Dub, my doll's a-dancing like a tap dancer," she said, using her pet name for him.

Jeb said to Angel, "Come inside when you finish with Willie." He entered the near-empty rented house. It only had three rooms—two for sleeping and a big room with a stove for cooking, although the stovepipe spewed smoke. The parsonage had a lot of comforts, including an outhouse with a shorter walk. Gracie and several men had even dug and fitted pipes to bring running water to the kitchen.

None of them had many belongings, making things simple for a move back to the parsonage when the time came. The first time Jeb had slept at the parsonage had been as a fraud and a charlatan. He had slept with one eye open, knowing his con as a preacher would some day be found out. The day the real Reverend Gracie had shown up was the day Jeb had the realization that good preaching with a bad heart equals rotten fruit.

He rummaged through his belongings, which he kept in a weathered steamer trunk. A good pair of trousers were hard to come by, but he needed a pair for pulpit duty. Once he had a sack of groceries in the pantry, he'd ask Floyd Whittington at the Woolworth's to let him work for a good pair of worsteds. Gracie had always maintained two good suits for Sunday. Jeb's old blue jacket and brown trousers would have to do for this Sunday.

He thumbed through the Bible he'd rooked his way into owning. The Bible showed wear and contained Jeb's marks—the earlier ones from his life as a charlatan and the more recent scribblings supervised by Gracie. Those were the ones he cherished. While the legitimate move back would give the Welbys a better home and him a better place to lay his head at night, he'd pass it all up for the sake of being genuine, respectable.

Angel came in with the scissors and comb. "You needing a haircut, Jeb?" She had trimmed his hair once, boxing the edges around the back of his head.

"Not today, Angel." He led her to a chair and then sat down across from her. "It's time to tell you a few things," he said.

"See, I said you were acting funny. You've heard from my daddy," she said, expectant.

Many a night he had lain awake wishing Angel would get a glimmer of hope through a letter or anything that would tell her her daddy had been looking for her. "Not your daddy, I'm afraid. This is something that could change everything for us. But for it all to take place, we'll have to swallow some bad news. Reverend Gracie has to go to Cincinnati for his health. He's asked me to take his place as the minister of Church in the Dell."

"Emily and Agatha are leaving too?"

"All the Gracies are leaving. They're going to stay with his family so that he can see a good doctor."

Her face did not contort as it often did when something new on the horizon set her off. She folded her hands over the comb and scissors in her lap and, in the afternoon light trickling into the kitchen, her eyes softened to china blue. The curls she had tried to press into her hair had fallen into straight-as-a-board crimped wisps around her shoulders. For once, Angel did not harden and stonewall him with her opinions.

"That's why Emily barely even said hello to me in the school hall. I figured she just had her nose out of joint about that boy she says loves her." She looked straight at Jeb. "He don't though. Hate to tell her, but it's true."

Jeb decided not to lecture Angel again on the pain the Gracie children had endured since their momma's death. Angel had experienced enough of her own to fill a library.

"Do the people at church know?"

"We have to let Reverend Gracie tell everyone. That's not our place."

Angel wiped tiny hairs from the scissor blades and then slid them onto the small table where they all had eaten beans for three months. "I won't tell a soul. I swear, Jeb. But you been such a mess lately, what with Miss Coulter ditching you and all. You sure you're ready to do some preacherin' again?"

He did not feel like debating again with Angel over his lost love, but he did not know how to answer. So he fell quiet and ignored her.

"I guess that's the way it'll be, then. It don't matter what nobody says about you downtown, neither. Not that I pay any attention." She sucked her bottom lip into her mouth and then said, "Maybe I ought not say."

"May as well spit it out, Angel. You don't let nothing else stop you, once you get it in your head to talk. But tell me first if this is woman stuff."

"Not woman stuff. Not so much in the way you mean woman stuff, if you know what I mean. What with your woman troubles and all, I know better than to hit you with something like that." She clasped her hands in her lap as though she were practicing some poise. "If it got out, someone might not ever talk to me again," she said.

Jeb liked her better sarcastic. "Swear on my own heart," he said, already cynical about the matter.

"There's this boy, my age. You might have seen him once or twice at church with his momma. They don't come much. His name is Beck."

"Seems like I should know him."

"Beck's family is on hard times, same as everyone else. But they're about to lose all they got. So his daddy took everything not nailed down to sell it in Hot Springs. Only it didn't bring in what he needed to pay off the bank."

"Nazareth Bank and Trust?"

Angel nodded. "Beck made me swear not to tell anyone this. They haven't eaten anything, not nary a bite of so much as cold corn bread in two days. I shared my bacon and biscuit with him at lunch today. When he ate it down like he'd been living along the railroad tracks, I just gave him the rest of it. Told him I wasn't hungry anyway. If I could slip some food to Beck, he'd sneak it to his momma and then his daddy wouldn't find out he'd gone begging." She paused and frowned. "Not that he has, actually. That didn't come out like I meant it. Don't tell anyone I said that Beck's gone begging."

"We'll give what we can," said Jeb. His mind wandered back to his last conversation with Gracie.

"His daddy would beat him if he knew."

Jeb cocked his head to one side, trying to read how much of what she said was exaggeration and how much was truth.

Angel added, "I wasn't supposed to say that, neither."

Jeb pulled out two jars of beans given to him by Freda Honeysack. Her garden had come in good in the summer and she had put up more beans than Roosevelt's maid. An old flour sack lay empty by the broom. He slipped the beans into the sack along with a half loaf of bread. "I don't believe I know this boy's daddy and momma too awfully well. How many youngens they have to feed, all told?"

"Five. Three boys and two girls. Beck's the youngest boy. His daddy is Asa Hopper. You know Mr. Hopper?" Angel looked into a single cabinet near the stove and found it nearly empty. She pulled out an apple and tucked it inside the sack.

Jeb remembered the farmer storming mad as a bull out of the bank. "Yes, I know him. You take this to Beck, and don't tell him where it came from. They live pretty far out, away from town. Will you give this to him at school in the morning?"

Angel nodded. "I got some tomatoes to mix in with our beans tonight and a little pepper. When we get some money, I want spaghetti."

Jeb had not noticed the small brown bag on the table until this moment. He pulled it open with one finger and saw the produce. "Someone must have given that to you."

"Miss Coulter. She brought them by while you were gone."

"Fern Coulter came to this house?"

Angel seemed to enjoy his surprise, like she had something on him. "Not for any reason other than Willie ran off and left his jacket on the back of his chair at school. She was afraid it'd turn off cool tonight and he'd need it."

"Beans and tomatoes it is, then." Jeb picked up the late summer tomatoes and peppers and laid them out on the table to chop into small pieces. "So, Fern didn't mention my name, did she?"

"Just to ask where you were. I'll make the beans. You don't salt them good as me." She took the tomatoes to the sink to give them a rinsing and then sighed. "I'd give away my best pair of shoes for spaghetti." Before Jeb could lecture her on appreciating what little they had, she cut him off. "I'll stop talking about it." She chopped the peppers like she had to kill them before they up and ran off. "Nothing wrong with beans."

"We'll have spaghetti as soon as I can get a job to take the place of the lumbermill job, Angel. Here, give the Hoppers half of this cornmeal. They can't have beans without corn bread."

5

The corn rows in tassel by early September rose empty in the husk not many days before October, languishing under the sky's stingy refusal of rain. Farmers complained about the gray sky on Sunday—good-for-nothing blinders for the sun, they called it. Jeb's truck bumped along the snaking road from the log shack to the main road, past the fields that didn't bless Nazareth with even a sister's kiss of autumnal bounty.

In front of the gearshift, his Bible lay thick with so many tucked notes sticking out between the pages it looked as cluttered as his thoughts. Angel stared out at the fields with Ida May on her lap rummaging through a tin box. Angel had clambered from the cot of a bed she shared with Ida May to turn the last handful of pulverized meal into corn cakes. Jeb had eaten his cakes alone while Angel dismissed herself to awaken first Willie and then Ida May. She had been silent as snow since Friday, saying only that Beck had taken the food, but not another word beyond that speck of news. He thought that if he asked her what had been going through her thoughts, she'd only say her usual "Nothing." So he said, "After we get moved back into the parsonage, we won't have this long a drive every Sunday."

She pulled one of her braids from Ida May's hands and tossed it behind her.

Willie had stretched out in the truck bed to chew sassafras, sitting on an old quilt so he could turn up at church in something clean.

"When we goin' to move, Dub?" asked Ida May. She had somehow picked up on a change in the wind, but had not yet pieced all of it together. Jeb knew how fast news would travel if Ida May got hold of it. Neither he nor Angel answered her, so she unknotted the thread from inside her tin box and looped it for a cat's cradle.

Angel made wide eyes at Jeb behind Ida May. Then she laughed. It was the first laugh she'd had in several days. It was the kind of laugh that made her notorious among the boys at school for being the kind of girl that turned to mayhem. By the time they reached the sparsely grassed front lawn of Church in the Dell, Angel was jabbering again like she always had before Jeb told her about Gracie's leaving. Her silence since then had troubled Jeb, especially since Fern had told him of her change in attitude.

Instead of leaping out of the truck to meet the girls she sat with every Sunday, Angel rested her hand on the door handle as she studied the families gathered out on the lawn. It made Jeb look too. Several groups milled around, bunched up like hungry hens in front of the church steps, some women with a posture that lent itself to wagging tongues. The men were all hats and coats in a circle. "Something's up," said Jeb.

"I haven't told a thing to anyone, so don't blame me," said Angel.

Jeb could only remember the talk he'd had with Fern at Beulah's. From that little get-together, a barrel's worth of stories could spread, Thursday to Sunday. He searched Fern out. She stood talking with a few of the single college girls, not much older than one herself. If she had shared Jeb's news with anyone, she did not show it on her face. Jeb walked past her without looking at her or her latest annoying hat.

Willie ran and blended into the group of boys that looked cut out from the same family tree—thrice-mended shirts tucked into pants, kitchen-cut hair, and shoes either too tight or loose as their momma's tongues.

Jeb joined Gracie on the church steps while a third cousin of Mr. Plummer, the tailor, rang the church bell. Plummer, who normally rang the bell, had stayed home three Sundays in a row to tend to Mrs. Plummer's gout.

Gracie touched Jeb's arm and led him through the doors ahead of the crowd.

"More people here than usual," said Jeb.

"Our secret sprung a leak," Gracie whispered. He had never whispered in the whole year and a half Jeb had known him.

"Will Honeysack placed an extra chair behind the pulpit for you, Jeb. You ought to take a seat right now and stay there until after I make the announcement. Otherwise, you might have too many questions to answer." Gracie stopped in the middle of the aisle as though he could plug the leak while Jeb made for the chair. The minister didn't act aware of the few ladies who dabbed their eyes in plain sight of him.

Jeb could not remember why he had taken so many notes or if it was humanly possible to tie the scrawled jumble into a steady stream of thought. A familiar jumpiness worked its way up his arms to his neck, like the day he had first taken the pulpit as a fake, not knowing Adam from Job's pig. Gracie took a seat beside Jeb and smiled his encouragement before bowing his head in prayer. Jeb was not reassured. It would satisfy him to no end if Gracie would stretch his prayers into the noon hour and then call off his morning in the pulpit until a day that Jeb might feel legitimate. As Gracie prayed for the message soon to be delivered, Jeb reasoned it would be good for God to strike him dead. It was the fastest cure to drum up when his good sense took wing. His thoughts tangled like kites.

He had not felt this sick since the time his momma had taken him and his brother to church against their will. Jeb being so young, it was his first recollection of the little church cradled between a cotton field and downtown Temple. Laurel trees had scented the churchyard that day, and he remembered it like he remembered triangles of cold corn bread on the stovetop left out for midnight hunger pangs.

Once inside the small building, a church lady who taught the children and was therefore duty-bound to the whole bunch of them had taken Charlie and Jeb by their elbows and said, "All of the child-ern are going to say a Bible verse in front of the church this morning. You may as well join them." She had not sounded the least bit enthused nor told them her name or asked them theirs. She'd pressed a piece of paper with a Scripture scribbled on it into Jeb's hand, his fingers still sticky with breakfast jelly.

Jeb's abrupt onset of paralysis of the mouth had not allowed him to tell the churchwoman he could not read—

not at age five or ever. By the time twenty or so girls and boys had popped off their verses followed by a sigh of relief, Charlie had taken a step back and hidden behind a tall youth who stood bowed in front of him as though ashamed of his height, leaving Jeb out front. The old woman, who sat with her long dress falling between her knees, pointed at Jeb like she expected a recitation out of Shakespeare's works. All Jeb could see was his momma lowering her eyes. Her cheeks blushed like summer apples on the bough. Charlie gave him a poke and with a loud suck of breath, Jeb blurted out the only thing he had ever memorized by heart.

A lot of people had cordially flattered his mother afterward for the fine way her boy gave the Pledge of Allegiance. Jeb had run all the way out to the wagon with Charlie running behind him calling him things like *idjut* and *ignert fool*.

Gracie brought Jeb back to the present. He must have noticed Jeb's blank stare. "Good crowd this morning. The rumor mill is in our favor this go-around." He read Jeb's anxiety. "This kind of thing always leaks out, Jeb. Best to take it in stride."

Jeb read over again the first of sixty-seven note cards in his Bible.

"I'm going to let you preach, and then I'll announce that you'll preach again in two weeks. I'd like them to warm up to you."

Jeb decided he would step outside when Gracie announced his revisit to the pulpit. The best image he could conjure was of himself running away from Church in the Dell before the town decided to roast him. It had a familiar smack to it.

At the other end of the church, the banker, Horace Mills, waited outside the doorway until his wife, Amy, entered ahead of him. She spoke to two women as she gestured behind her. A young woman with Amy's round eyes followed her into the room. The older women greeted the younger as if they already knew her. She turned and swayed back onto her heels to Doris Jolly's organ playing, a little of the jitterbug in her steps. Jeb thought, *This must be Horace's daughter, Winona.*

Amy included the girl in all the female banter, but some of the older women's discussion must have bored her because she soon turned away to shop around the sanctuary for a diversion. Her eyes fell on Jeb. He swallowed, too aware of the way she noticed him. He wondered if he looked as awkward as he felt. Nothing about her should have caught him off guard. Any local girl around town who had given him a look always got at least a smile back, even with, as Gracie called it, his best minister's decorum on hand. The girl's face relaxed. She hooked her arm into her father's and said something privately to him. Horace glanced at Jeb, shook his head, and escorted his daughter to their customary pew.

Fern, who usually spent every Sunday buttoning dresses for Angel and Ida May, took her seat behind the Mills family. She looked crisp as clothesline laundry and as aloof as if they'd never met for coffee that week at Beulah's.

Angel brought Willie and Ida May in alone now, mothering them into the church even though Willie despised her nagging at him.

Jeb knew the way the churchwomen stared and whispered would prove more than a coincidence. All the gazes drifted from Gracie to him and then back again to the minister.

Gracie did not have to quiet the congregation. The roomful of people fell silent when he took the platform. He bowed his head. A ripple of shuffling followed, and then every head surrendered to the morning prayer. He prayed for Church in the Dell as if he had to keep the devil from the door, his moderate pitch rising and falling. Sun trickled through the eastern windows and across the bowed heads. Particles of dust danced like gold dust in the light, drawn up toward the windows, lifting like God might walk in at any moment upon the light beams.

Gracie wiped his brow. A pale whiteness around the eyes hinted at his illness.

When Gracie spoke of Jeb's dedication to his education as a minister, Fern studiously turned her head and stared out the window as though what was outside was infinitely more interesting than what was in front of her. By the time the minister expounded upon Jeb's scholarly devotion to theology, Fern was smoothing her skirt and thumbing through her Bible—anything to show she wasn't the least bit interested in what Reverend Gracie was saying at the moment. Jeb imagined how he might look out over the congregation every Sunday at a face that refused to acknowledge his existence.

He glanced over at the Welby children. For some reason Angel could not take her eyes off Gracie's oldest girl, Emily, as though her strange mix of jealousy and admiration were interfering with her validation in the eyes of the churchgoers. Since Gracie had rightfully taken the pulpit, Angel had somehow got lost in knowing her place at Church in Dell. She was no longer the minister's eldest girl and had aimed her lostness and jealousy at Emily Gracie.

"After a full year of study as my apprentice, I'm happy to introduce Reverend Jeb Nubey and ask your kind attention as he brings the morning's sermon," Gracie finally introduced him.

Before Jeb had made his way to the lectern, Gracie gave him a firm pat on the back. He wanted to turn and follow Gracie off the platform. The lectern was too thin to hide behind. When he placed the Bible open faced in front of him, his notes spilled out onto the floor. He knelt to retrieve them and found he could not shuffle the cards back into any sense of the original order.

❄

When Jeb gave the concluding prayer he felt as though his feet were nailed to the floor. Not a soul whispered so much as an amen when he finished. But before he could gather his notes and disappear through the rear exit, he felt Gracie grasp the back of his arm and stand beside him.

He thanked Jeb for his wonderful delivery of the morning's message and then said, "For the sake of order, I would like to quell the speculation about my health. For those of you who have already expressed concern to me this morning, I thank you. I can't think of any better place to be but in Nazareth during my time of need. Your compassion for me and my children has not gone unnoticed. I love you all beyond words." His voice broke for the first time since he had divulged his illness to Jeb. "But God did not intend for our bodies to go on forever. A good friend and family member has made the way for me to see a doctor in Cincinnati in the coming months, maybe sooner." He waited for the muttering to fade. "I promise not to abandon the pulpit at Church in the Dell until you have found confidence in my replacement."

Jeb would have liked to leap from the platform and depart without leaving a single track in the sawdust. Gracie, without warning, said the thing that Jeb felt should not be said for months: "I submit my resignation to you but will stay on for the weeks it takes to prepare your new minister for service. Before reacting, I urge you to take this matter first to God in prayer."

Jeb studied reactions. But it seemed he found none. He could not decipher the congregation's assessment of his preaching or Gracie's announcement. Except from Gracie's children. Emily had a stoic look, but her eyes were damp around the lashes. Emily's self-assurance had always deflated Angel, he knew. The instant she was no longer "the pastor's daughter" but instead the con man's conspirator, something had been taken from Angel. Even though the Gracies' kind of community standing never belonged to her in the first place, her resentment toward Jeb had worsened. Throughout the following months Angel's attention had wandered back to Emily every Sunday morning, like a street child who watched a family through snowflaked windows. She wanted what Emily had—the understood respect that came from being a pastor's daughter.

Now, Angel righted herself as though she'd been asked to draw a straw.

"When will you go?" Doris Jolly asked from the second pew.

"If it weren't for God's gift of an apprentice, I'd not

know what to do," said Gracie. "Reverend Nubey has kindly accepted the chance to stand behind this pulpit. When Reverend Nubey and all of you feel he is ready, I will make my departure. If you support him and embrace him as I have, you'll not be sorry."

No one said a word.

Fern Coulter tucked her handbag under her arm and slipped out the back door. Emily Gracie pushed past her brother and sister and ran out behind Fern.

Angel studied the churchfolks' cold reaction, and then, deflated at their lack of popularity, withdrew her approval as quickly as she had given it. She looked at Jeb as though he had robbed a bank.

❋

A delegation of men, farmers, and shop owners from downtown disappeared into the parsonage with Philemon Gracie. That quickly arranged meeting left Jeb in the midst of all the curious women.

While the other ladies clustered in the sunlight of the open front door, Evelene Whittington, the sovereign of the downtown Woolworth's, approached Jeb first. "I know you've been hard at the books this past year. Not a lot of young men want to fool with church matters, what with the country being in such a bad shape. Let me be the first to say that if Reverend Gracie has to go, welcome, Reverend Nubey. God's will be done, I say."

Two other women moved in behind Evelene as Jeb accepted her hand. "Your words mean a lot to me, Mrs. Whittington."

Mellie Fogarty, Ida May's substitute aunt, told Jeb, "Beats all the way you took in these child-ern like they's your own. Don't know how you get by these days, but the Lord will provide, as they say. Glad to know little Idy May will still be traipsing through these church doors every Sunday. I'd have thought you'd have sent them off to parts unknown by now. But no, not you, Mr. Nubey. Or do we call you 'Reverend' now?"

Florence Bernard reached between Evelene and Mellie with her large-boned hands. They felt warm as she clasped his fingers. "I don't know what the men is up to, but we ladies welcome you, Reverend." She said "Reverend" with more ease than the other two. "That was the best sermon I've heard you preach ever!"

Florence's friend Josie kept a yard or two of distance, as did the other women who watched the door of the parsonage through the open back door. Josie and Fern had spent many a Saturday blowing on cups of coffee at Beulah's café. Beulah, who never had come to church until now, talked with Josie. Both of them chatted and paused to glance at Jeb and then out the back door. He was glad to see any alteration in the community's paradigm bring Beulah to church, even if led by the scent of gossip.

Maybe he had done some good already.

The men spilled out into the yard between the parsonage and church. Jeb could not tell by Gracie's stride if he came bearing good news or bad. Before reaching the back door of the church, Gracie caught his eye and gestured for Jeb to meet them all outside. He excused himself through the clusters of restless women.

Gracie smiled at Jeb. "They agreed to consider you as their minister."

Jeb repeated the words "agreed to consider" and then read the worst into its context.

Horace Mills's fingers came to his lips as though accustomed to nursing a cigar. He never made eye contact with Jeb.

"Can you tell if they want me or not?" asked Jeb.

"Trust in God," said Will Honeysack. He looked more worried about Gracie than Jeb right now.

While the men disbursed to collect their kith and kin, Horace said so no one else could hear, "I hope you know I keep close tabs on these matters. I don't throw my money away on lost causes."

Jeb watched him meet up with his wife and Winona. Winona smiled better than her daddy.

6

The old Long house had a strange kind of Saturday pall. The week had flown past, each day another day closer to Gracie's eventual departure. While the minister still fluctuated on his departure date, he reminded Jeb daily of his pending obligation.

Jeb studied for the sermon he would preach the Sunday after tomorrow. The week had passed without too much gossip reaching his ears. But even as he felt the calm tide of his coming responsibility settling into place, Angel had not stopped rattling his cage over how everyone in town knew him to be something other than a man of the cloth. Her words followed on his heels like the scent of skunk.

With only one more week left to prepare, the afternoon crept over him like an invasion of grasshoppers silently eating away the day. Tomorrow afternoon, he and Gracie would pore over his message and remove the weak spots. But it seemed to Jeb the whole sermon buckled in the middle like the old bridge over Millwood Creek. He gave up and went inside.

The Foley bunch had invited Willie to a picture show

downtown, leaving Ida May to pout alone on the front porch. Angel waited at the kitchen entry, holding her most recent letter from Little Rock. Jeb finally said, "Letter from Aunt Kate?"

"Momma's not well."

"At least she finally told you, Angel."

"She's in the nervous hospital. Wonder why they call it that. Like we's all going to believe they's all these nervous people sitting around waiting to do somethin' like get called up to sing in church or some such. Instead, that's where they put a body whose house don't go all the way to the roof, if you catch my drift. Aunt Kate says Momma mentioned my name not long ago and that *encouraged* her. Mentioned my name? What's that supposed to mean anyway, like she just happened to think about me? Besides, this just proves Aunt Kate's not been telling me everything. If I was there, I'd give her a piece of my mind."

"That'd be punishment enough." Jeb escaped to his room, only to have Angel follow.

"Who are you to poke fun, anyway? Somebody's got to get sick or die to make space for you."

"You act like I don't have plans for the future, Angel, like I'm still drifting around. But I got big plans. Jeb Nubey's moving up in the world. If I didn't know better, I'd say you're jealous."

"Jealous? That's a big laugh. You're still nothing but a stray cat hanging on the screen door of life, Jeb Nubey! Last time I checked, nobody's jealous of strays."

Anxious to change the subject, Jeb splashed some cologne he'd splurged on at the Woolworth's onto his hands and then his neck. "You're not dragging me into another of your fights, Biggest. I got better fish to fry."

She sniffed. "That would explain the smell. I've smelt cow patties less potent. What's that you're slapping on, anyway?"

"I'll have you know this men's smellum is sold even in Hot Springs. You don't know anything about what the upper crust is using, so you may as well give up trying."

"Upper crust, hah! The day you turn into upper crust, is the day Wolvertons' hogs sprout wings."

"I don't expect you to elevate your thinking just because things are changing for the better for me." He returned to the kitchen and gathered up his sermon notes.

"Life don't have no elevators, Jeb Nubey; I have news for you." Angel tossed aside her letter and returned to the stove. "If we hear from Daddy, Aunt Kate says I should tell him to send money. Like I'm going to hear from Daddy! Seems like ever since Uncle Wayne left, money's all Aunt Kate ever talks about."

"I guess if you got it, you don't think about it." Jeb put away his Bible and picked up a copy of Augustine's writings. It had been in a stack of books Fern had given to Gracie to give to Jeb when his internship commenced.

"If I were taking care of Momma, she'd be well."

"Did your Aunt Kate ask you to come?" Before Jeb could find his place again in the book, Angel said, "I think I should quit school and get a job. If I could get my own place, Momma could live with me. "

"Girls like you can't find jobs no better than cleaning houses. You want to do that the rest of your life, then quit school!"

"Maybe I should and maybe I will!"

"You always get like this when you want something."

"I see how you look sometimes if we get into a fight or don't seem to have enough food to go around at supper. I know when I'm not wanted."

"I saw you eyeing that dress in the Woolworth's. This is a new dress fight, ain't it?"

"You don't hear nothing that I say. Momma's sick because she don't have real care, not the kind that I can give."

"There you go again, acting like you're going to haul off and leave. Funny how it always happens after Woolworth's opens a new box of goods."

"You think I'm talking about dresses? You lost your mind or something?"

"Maybe I'm not the best provider. But I've seen people in worse situations than us. We got this roof over our head. No one's making us live out of a cardboard box."

Angel started pacing and shaking her head.

"I've been looking for extra work, in case you hadn't noticed. One of these days that lumbermill's going to need another hand again, and I've got my name in for it. All the other mills have gone out because no one is building right now. But everybody needs barrels, and now, due to Hayes Jernigan's know-how, we got the best stave mill between here and Texas. Besides all that, I'll soon have some income as the new preacher. Least I should." He stopped to consider the matter. "Come to think of it, maybe I need to bring that up with Gracie." He came back to his original thought, let out a breath, and said, "Keep your mind on school, Angel, and stop worrying about how you look all the time."

"Are we talking about me or you?"

Jeb shrugged. Angel was complicated. Like Fern. "Can we talk about dinner?"

❋

Jeb slaughtered a rabbit out in the woods away from Ida May's sight. The critter squealed like a girl and then fell limp over his hand. He skinned it and left the pelt to dry on a stump while Angel dressed and cut up the rabbit and stewed it an hour before adding the soup. By nightfall, the stew and hot bread were ready for supper just as Jeb turned on *The Grand Old Opry*.

The headlights of the Foleys' DeSoto shone through the trees as the car rattled up near the front porch. Willie leaped out of the car and nearly fell onto the stone steps before running across the porch and into the living room.

"They's a riot downtown, Jeb!"

Jeb turned off the radio. "Anyone hurt? You all right, Willie Boy?"

Willie could not get his breath. Mrs. Foley eased onto the front porch holding her handbag against her thin stomach. She called out to Jeb, "We're all fine, Reverend. But someone's goin' to get hurt. They set fire to a like-ness of Banker Mills. Not a good likeness, neither, come to think of it. Just some straw man with a sign around its neck that said 'Rich Old Mills.' Wonder who'd do such a thing? It's looking bad down there; talk goin' around like they's goin' to set fire to downtown. I hope they don't burn down Honeysack's place. Supposed to be a good sale tomorrow on quiltin' goods."

Jeb thanked Mrs. Foley for dropping Willie by and then jerked on his boots.

"You're going downtown, Jeb? Now?" Angel held a pan of corn bread with two stained mitts.

"Somebody's going to get hurt. It's best I go see about things."

Willie tried to follow him back out the front door.

"Not you, Willie Boy! Back inside with you. Your sister's got supper fixed. You stay behind, keep an eye on the girls, and have your dinner."

"Beck Hopper said something like this might happen," said Angel.

Jeb's eyes darted to meet Angel's. She started to turn away, but before she could, Jeb said, "Things like that are best not kept a secret, Angel." Jeb did not like the fact she had been hanging around with the Hopper boy anyway. His daddy was getting a bad reputation of late for starting fights.

"He didn't say exactly, just that people was tired of seeing their kids go hungry, and someone was going to do something about it. Beck don't see his daddy as mean like the rest of us do. Kind of like he's blind to his daddy's ways. I kind of see his side of it."

Angel called Ida May to the table and sent Willie to wash up. She wrapped two pieces of corn bread in a napkin and handed them to Jeb. "Eat these on the way and we'll save stew for later."

❄

Even before the truck could reach the main street of downtown Nazareth, the intensity of the fire could be seen—red and billowing black smoke from one of the buildings, although Jeb was not certain about what building had caught fire. Several screaming women with babies or older children in tow ran down the street away from the mob of men lining Front Street. Jeb slowed and parked several blocks down the street to keep the Ford away from the fire.

One building on Waddle had been torched. Several men who had been in the middle of a shave and haircut at Lincoln's Barbershop waited bewildered on the corner of Waddle and Front, their bodies still swathed in the barber's white capes. The barber, Hal Lincoln, tried to pass out buckets of water to the patrons to help him douse the front of his shop. Too stunned, the men watched mesmerized as the flames reached the old warehouse next to the barbershop.

Tom Plummer ran past Jeb's truck.

"Tom, has the whole town gone crazy?" Jeb opened the truck door.

"Don't know how things was started. Some say Asa Hopper riled up the bunch of jobless men living down by the railroad tracks, but I can't say as I know for sure. Asa's two oldest boys has set fire to one of the buildings, but they's fifty or more men out in front of the bank. I heard one say they were going to break into Will Honeysack's store and take all of the food. Will don't deserve that kind of bi'ness at all." Tom ran off.

Jeb left the truck parked on the side of the road and ran down Front Street toward Will's grocery store.

In the middle of Front Street, Asa Hopper swung a lantern. He shouted Horace Mills's name. Some of the men with him shouted too and threw fists into the air. One hurled a rock at the bank; it hit the brick and fell to the walk. The blinds had been pulled down on all the bank windows. Jeb figured Mills and his staff might have slipped out the back way.

Inside Honeysack's Grocery, Freda and Will thrust an iron bar across the inside of the doors. Jeb tapped on the window and Freda shrieked. He mouthed instructions telling them both to meet him at the back door.

A Coke bottle hit the walk and shattered next to Jeb's feet. Dolittle's dairy truck had been left in front of Honeysack's store. For the time being, the milk truck seemed protection enough. Jeb ran between the truck and store and into the alley. Will met him at the rear exit.

"Hurry, come inside before you get clubbed," said Will.

Freda kept pacing behind the display of canned chili while their clerk, Val, locked up the day's cash in a safe in the back storage room.

"They're burning down the whole town, Will!" Val's voice quivered. "This'll give Nazareth a black eye for shore!"

Deputy Maynard ran past the storefront and then disappeared behind the milk truck. A pistol shot rang out in the street, and Freda screamed and escaped into the storage room.

"Maynard's shot off his gun, Freda! Nobody's firing back. Just a cop-firing-in-the-air kind of thing, you know, to try and scare off the old boys." Will cracked open the storage room door. Val crouched under a table wearing a World War I soldier's helmet. "Val, you all right?"

"You'd better take cover, Will!" Val had dragged a heavy sack under the table with him and made several attempts to build a barricade with twenty pounds of chicken feed.

"What if they set fire to our place, Reverend Jeb?" Freda was near hysteria.

"I think I should take her home, Reverend," said Will. "Not going to do any business around here anyway."

Jeb nodded. "The barbershop appears to be the next to go. They could be working their way up Waddle. Any guess as to what set them off?"

"Asa Hopper, is all I know. A big lot of men is mad about losing their land. Hopper's family bought that land sometime back around the middle of the last century. Says he'll not lose it now after all this time. They need a body to blame, I reckon, for this Depression." Will pulled a string on the last light to extinguish it. "But if it's food they want, I'd be surprised if they burned my place. Coming in and taking what they want might be the next thing on their minds."

"Let's get Freda and Val out to your Ford, Will. No use taking a beating over canned beans. Maybe if you get on out of here and let them have it, they'll not set fire to your place." Jeb coaxed Freda out of the storage room. A loud explosion outside sent Val reeling out of the room. It sounded like someone had lit a stick of dynamite and tossed it onto Front Street. He crawled over the chicken feed and followed Freda out the back way.

"Can't let them take from my store without paying, Jeb! It's the principle," said Will. He handed the keys to Val. "Please see the missus home, Val, if you will. You're welcome to stay on our couch tonight. Freda will see you get fed."

Freda argued with Will, but finally gave up and headed for the Ford. "Reverend, you keep an eye on my Will."

Jeb said, "If you could take a drive past my place to check on the Welby youngens, I'd appreciate it, Val." He waited for Val to take Freda out of earshot before he said,

"Didn't want your wife to know, Will, but that mob is on its way here. Let's you and me slip out the back."

Val gave Jeb and Will a nervous wave and drove with Freda down the alley and away from the mob. He still wore the green helmet of the American Expeditionary Force. World War I had been over for years.

❄

Political hopeful Bryce threw his campaigning signs into the back of his pickup after a day of stumping in the next county. He was packing up to head away from the mob. When Jeb tapped on his window, he threw his hands up over his face and yelled, "Don't shoot, Mister!"

"It's me, Bryce. Jeb Nubey. You still got that tin thing you been politicking into every Saturday?" Jeb had hunkered down in the alley and crawled out to the walk, where he'd spotted Bryce.

"It's all put away, Reverend. You needing a ride out of town, I'll give it to you. But I'm not sticking around with things this hot. If they'd burn old Mills in effigy, they'd not think a minute about lighting fire to a politician. Mobs like their kind don't take nicely to my kind, I'm afraid."

"Can you string together your contraption for me so's I can talk into it? Maybe just right in the back of your truck like you do when you give your speeches?"

Will had crawled up the alley behind Jeb. He sat on the ground with his back against the wall, panting. Down the street the rumblings and shouts grew more agitated as men swarmed through the growing crowd.

"Trying to yell at these men'd be like planning your own funeral, Reverend. Sorry I can't help you out." Bryce gunned his engine.

Jeb reached into the cab and turned off the gas. Before Bryce could protest, he'd tucked the man's keys into his pocket. "Help me set up your stuff, Bryce. Then you can hide with Will here in the alley."

Bryce hesitated until he saw that Jeb would not give in. "I'll hook it up, but then you're on your own."

Working quickly, Bryce and Will ran the juice to the public-address system through a window in the front of the store. The tops of their heads peeped over a cracker barrel. Jeb stepped up onto the truck bed, where Bryce had a wooden platform wedged into the end. The public-address system squealed like corralled hogs when Jeb turned on the switch.

Asa Hopper hurled a rock through the bank window to the mob's cheers.

"Boys, have a look this way!" Jeb yelled. More squealing from the ringing loudspeaker caught a few of the men's attention. They stopped their rock throwing for a split second.

Hal Lincoln and several men ran with buckets down Waddle Street. Six more followed. A brigade spread out, starting from Front stretching down to Lincoln's Barbershop, a fast-moving bunch of local boys not so in-clined to run from Hopper's mob.

"Fellers, have a listen!" Jeb tapped thrice on Bryce's microphone.

"Stone the bank, boys!" Asa hurled another rock at the window and watched it ricochet right off the bank's front door. Glass shards splintered and tumbled into the shrub-bery. "Come out, Mills, and face the ones you stole from!"

"Mr. Hopper, you want to give us a listen?" Jeb had

not seen Hopper since the day he had stormed out of the bank.

"You don't know me," Hopper yelled. Loaded to the gills with home brew, he stumbled back and then forward to throw another rock that missed the building altogether.

"Sure I know you. Know your wife and kids. Seen some of them in church," answered Jeb. "I'm Reverend Nubey, and I work alongside Reverend Gracie at the Church in the Dell." He had not called himself by that title until now. It caught in his throat like a moth.

"You just another old boy in Horace Mills's back pocket. I seen you with him at the bank!"

A young boy no more than ten years old drew back to hurl a brick through Will and Freda's window.

"Please, wait," Jeb pleaded with the youth. Then he saw the soft curve of the boy's face and said, "Roe Ketcherside, you don't have no business with these men. Your momma's done planned for your baptism down on Marvelous Crossing. I hope I don't have to tell her you hurled a brick through good Will Honeysack's window." When he saw Roe hesitate, he said, "I don't know how many grocery deliveries you'd have to make for Will to pay for what you're about to do."

Roe let out a sigh and said, "I hadn't been baptized yet, Preacher."

Will stepped out of the store and around the milk truck. When Roe saw him, he dropped the stone at his feet.

"Any of the rest of you want to throw rocks at your neighbor, here's Will Honeysack in the flesh. Best grocery man from here to Hot Springs. You think one of those meat vendors from Hope would give you extra in your sack like he does, you should think again. No one I know of is as generous as Will and his good wife, Freda." Jeb could not tell if Asa Hopper was listening to him or not.

Asa stumbled forward but then righted himself.

Jeb said, "Asa Hopper, maybe you been drinking again. You think? Maybe it's that liquor that's got you riled up more than Mr. Mills."

"They all been drinkin', Reverend," said Roe. "I seen them out back behind that warehouse. One of them set fire to the place with a cigarette. After that, they all let loose like nobody's business. They said they wanted food. Momma, she needs help with that, so I waited around to see if I could get a share."

"You shut up, Roe!" A woman ran out of the tailor shop across the street where she had been hiding. "A-fore I box your ears!"

Jeb tipped his hat at the woman, who came up behind Roe and then grabbed him by his large right ear. "You needing food, Mrs. Ketcherside, I'll give you some of what I got. They's others that will help out too. Help you too, Asa, if you'll allow it."

Roe blanched at his mother's presence. "Momma, I didn't know you was downtown!" His mother turned him around and led him by a fistful of shirt to her old Chevy parked alongside the street, fussing the whole way.

Several men dropped their bricks in the street.

Asa threw another rock at the bank. Then he fell backward and passed out. A breeze of reason seemed to sweep over the crowd as Maynard and Floyd Whittington lifted him by the arms and pulled him toward the jail. Jeb could feel the tension lifting. By ones and twos, sheepishly or sullenly, the men began to scatter.

"Rest of you men want to help Mr. Lincoln put out a fire, he'd appreciate it." Jeb took off his jacket and tossed it in the back of Bryce's truck. He climbed out of the truck to run and help the bucket brigade at the barbershop.

"Wait, hold up!" Horace Mills stepped out of the bank. Two of his clerks embraced in the doorway behind him.

"You did a good job, Reverend Nubey!" said Mills.

Jeb liked the sound of *Reverend* rolling from Horace Mills's tongue. He liked even more how Mills looked him in the eye and shook his hand before he returned to the bank and locked the door behind him. Jeb caught a movement at the window by the door. Mills's daughter, Winona, offered Jeb a gentle wave before letting the blinds fall back into place.

7

Dear Lord,

*I pray my boy gets well from this fever. If he does, I will
give him to you. That is my vow. He has a speshul look
about him for a baby. I saw a redbird on the churry tree
branch this morning, right outside the winda where my
child is sleeping. If sines tell tales, this baby will live and
be marked for your good use, O God. I give my baby boy
to you, Jochabed Nubey. I know he will live poor as you
lived poor, my Savyur. So hep him, if you will, find
riches beyond mony. It comes to me that sech thangs com
high priced. Keep him well, Lord. Keep my Jeb well. He
is yorn for your aposul or whatever you see fit for him.*

Geneva Nubey

No one had ever called Jeb "Jochabed" except his
own momma. It was her given name for him, even
though his daddy never liked it. But until Jeb had un-
wrapped the parcel from Charlie, he had never known
she kept a diary. Charlie's wife, Selma, had found a
trunk filled with Geneva's belongings. When she read

the passage about Jeb, she made Charlie wrap it up and send it off to him.

The place where Geneva had prayed for Jeb to be healed of a fever was marked with a strip of lace. Jeb held it next to his face. It smelled faintly of lavender and cloves. Jeb could imagine his mother now, standing beneath the cherry tree, the blossoms falling around her like snow.

He'd always believed that she held little hope for him to make anything good of his life. He read the passage again.

Ida May bounded down the hallway. "Dud, you awake?" She had wrapped Angel's heavy cotton sweater around her and buttoned it all the way up to the neck. It made her look caterpillarlike. "Is Reverend Gracie going to die?" she asked.

"I'm awake, Littlest." He reached for the Bible on the table next to the bed. Not too long ago he had not been able to read a single line in it. Now it was the first thing he went for every morning.

He pretended to read. But she hovered right in front of him and kept a bead on him until he looked at her. She repeated her question.

"Did Willie tell you to ask that, Ida May?"

"Not Willie. It was Philip told me about it. Philip said his sister told him she was skeered about her daddy dyin'."

"Run take a look and see if your brother and sister are awake."

"God wouldn't let him die. Not a preacher." She climbed onto Jeb's bed and looked at the letter in his lap.

"Everybody dies. Even preachers, Ida May. But

Reverend Gracie's going to be fine. Don't you go off and tell anyone what Philip said. That's gossip."

"You got a letter. I'm the only one that never gets letters. I can read now almost good as Willie. Who wrote you?"

"My brother, Charlie." Jeb closed Charlie's letter up inside his mother's diary.

"Want me to read it to you? I can."

"Go about your business and don't worry about mine, Littlest."

Ida May slid back onto the floor and ran out calling her sister's name.

Jeb came to his feet, stretched, and then sniffed. The stench of charred barbershop lingered in the room, a smell that only Mrs. Bluetooth's lye soap would leach from the clothes he had worn when he helped put out Lincoln's fire. Sunday had so filled his day with the excitement of quelling the gossip that had been tossed from pillar to post around church about his single-handedly facing a mob that he had forgotten to open the mail he had picked up before coming home Saturday evening. The smoke-suffused clothes he had dropped on the floor Saturday night still lay untended. He stuffed the shirt and trousers into a burlap sack and tied it tight, then shivered as he pulled an extra shirt on over the union suit in which he had slept. It felt stiff against his neck, like newly woven cotton.

The morning had turned off cold, near bitter. The frost turned the blades of grass outside as crisp as a boy's whistle. A fog rolled through the forest, low and crawling on a misty belly. Jeb stuffed a rag along the windowsill to try to keep out the cold. Sliding back onto the bed to pull the covers over his feet, he opened the Bible and read a passage until curiosity drew him back to the diary.

He could not imagine his momma thinking about him in such lofty ways. He had a picture of her in his mind, one painted by someone else. An aunt, her sister, was the only family member who had spoken about her. She'd rambled one evening about one thing and then another while canning beans. She told Jeb about how he had nearly died of scarlet fever, but matter-of-factly, like the matter weighed less important than storing up grub for winter. He wanted to recall her face in that afternoon sunlight and glean from the sight of it. But all he remembered was his aunt's stooped posture and the way her low man's voice softened whenever she spoke of her sister, Geneva.

Angel peeped inside Jeb's doorway. "I can't believe you've not made coffee yet. I still have to do everything around here, I guess."

"You look rough, Biggest." He stopped short of saying the redness in her eyes looked like she had cried for half the night.

"Nice thing to hear first thing of a morning, Jeb. You still don't know nothing about women. It's no wonder you can't get one."

"You look like a horse rode hard and put away wet."

"We got a history test right after the bell. I can't be late. So get up!"

"Angel, there's a bag of fresh bar soaps setting on the kitchen table. Mrs. Honeysack gave them to us along with some eggs after church yesterday. I forgot to tell you. I thought you'd like those; they smell like women's soap. Not something I'd want."

When she stared back, Jeb said, "Or I can give them to someone that needs them."

"I'll take them, for Pete's sake! Freda must have been happy you helped save her store."

"That's just a rumor."

Angel paused. "Ida May said Reverend Gracie is about to die," she whispered, even though she was the last person in the house to hear of it. "His kids was talking about him, like they was afraid of what would happen if they left for Cincinnati and all. I don't think they wanted him to hear."

"It appears their imagination's got the best of them. Don't pay them any mind." Jeb didn't want to think about it. Gracie had never told him that he was dying, but the thought had come to him on some of Philemon's bad days. The preacher had never been one to tell much in the way of personal business. Jeb figured that if any bad news cropped up, he'd surely let him know. But Gracie's poor appearance did not speak well of his health.

"I'm riding home with Beck Hopper from school."

Angel did not get far down the hall before Jeb yelled, "No, you ain't!"

"He's sixteen. Nothing wrong with catching a ride with somebody you know, Jeb."

"Everyone knows the Hoppers started the riot."

"No one that matters. Besides, Beck would never do that, even if his daddy told him to."

"Angel, I'm asking you nice not to run with the Hoppers—Beck or any of them."

When she didn't answer, Jeb said, "How you think that looks anyway? Asa Hopper starts a fire and I help put it out and then let you run around with his boy like we're all just good buddies."

"You never cared before what anybody thought of us. I don't know why you care now. Jesus said to love your enemies."

He stared at the rug as Angel returned to the kitchen to feed Ida May. Between Charlie's parcel and Angel's comments, a melancholy crept up inside him and nested. He pulled the banjo out from under his bed and closed the door. Not knowing how people would take to banjo music, he had not even played it when the kids were underfoot. It would be like Ida May to say too much to someone like Florence Bernard, who thought the least amount of lace in a girl's hair was a sin.

All that came to him was a song a Nigra man had taught him, the first song he'd ever learned. He played until the smell of coffee gave him a reason to climb out of bed. He hid the diary under the mattress.

When he stepped out of the room, he found an audience of three had listened to his jazzy tune. He made them swear they'd not tell a soul.

❋

Jeb drove Angel, Willie, and Ida May to school, even though Angel warned that something bad had passed between them when he would not give in to her complaining. He did not want to risk Angel hooking up with Beck and somehow never making her way to the schoolhouse. Boys like Beck talked girls like Angel into things they ought not to do.

Angel did not give a care what anyone thought about Beck, she had said more than once. So to prove it, when she entered the schoolyard she made straight for the youngest Hopper in plain sight of Jeb.

Jeb had thought for sure the Hoppers would keep their youngens home from school, if for no other reason than because everyone knew Asa had started the riot. Asa had gall, and everyone knew that about him. But Jeb figured Beck's momma must have had her hands too full to fool with getting him back to school.

He watched the two of them until the school bell sounded. Before disappearing into the schoolhouse, Angel gave Jeb a glance that said she didn't care a bit about what he thought or said.

❄

Before driving back to the church, Jeb stopped downtown for a paper out in front of Honeysack's Grocery. He stepped inside with the fifty cents he had saved to pay down his bill. "Morning, Will. I owe you some money." Jeb laid the money on the counter.

Will pushed the coins back across the counter. "Your money's no good here."

"Will, I know we've run up a bill, what with our regular business and Ida May's bottles of pop. And do tell the missus that Angel appreciated the bar soaps."

"Your debt's settled here at Honeysack's, Reverend. If you have your grocery list, I'll get Val to fill it for you, though, and you can pay for it with your spending money."

"Will, you know our debt can't be settled yet. Last month we run up a good five dollars at least, plus what we still owed from the month before."

"Freda and I sat up all night figuring out our sitchyashun.

Lot of men been having trouble feeding their kids, but they didn't stoop to pillaging yesterday like a lot of those old boys did. I know I'd not be able to set back and let my grandchild-ern go hungry. Them men ain't crooks that nearly burned up Lincoln's place. Maybe if we'd done something sooner, those men'd not have broke the law. But we—Freda and me—decided the Lord wanted us to forgive those debts of the ones who helped put out the fire. Them and a few others that've been needing relief. You know how many families been waiting for Red Cross? I heard of a hundred fifty in our county alone, sitting and waiting with not a crumb in the pantry. But it's not relief they want to put in their pockets, but money they earned. If these fellers can get a break, maybe they can catch up and get the town back on its feet."

Jeb stuck out his hand to give Will a handshake, then changed his mind and leaned over the counter to grab Will in a bear hug.

Edward Bluetooth entered with a batch of soaps to sell to Freda. When he saw Jeb he said, "Reverend Jeb, you're a hero! It's all over town."

Jeb patted Will's arm once more and tried to downplay his part in the fire to Edward. With a grin and a shrug, Edward drifted off to look at some nearby candies while he waited to speak with Will.

"Reverend Jeb, you take what praise is give to you and thank the Lord for lookin' out for you while he uses you for his own good purpose," said Will. "No charge, by the way, for the paper."

"Will, while I'm thinking of it, you got a long ladder I can borrow? I forget it every time I come into town. Reverend Gracie's asked me to try and repair the bell in the church bell tower. Seems it's getting a little rusty around the bolts."

"I don't have a ladder that tall. Try Ivey Long. He's the only farmer around with ladders that long."

"I'll remember that, Will." Jeb pulled out his grocery list. "I'll take care of these few things. No need to call Val away from his radio show, though. I can gather these few things myself." Jeb glanced at the front page of the *Nazareth Gazette*.

Will tapped the newspaper. "On page three, the Ku Klux Klan took out a whole half-page advertisement telling young folk about the dangers of sitting in parked cars. I think all parents ought to read that page to their young people tonight. It'd make this town a better place to live for everyone. Up near White Oake Lake, Maynard run oft three carloads of youngsters just last Saturday night. One boy and girl run oft together, God knows where, although probably into the mountains. They weren't found until last night, I hear. That girl's daddy nearly whipped her all the way home, and she had to beg him not to shoot the boyfriend. I know that oldest girl of yours is at that age. Without a momma around to set her straight, you got your hands full. Everybody admires you for taking in those kids like you have."

"Angel does need a momma. But there doesn't appear to be one to be had." Jeb was already feeling guilty pangs about the trip to school. He knew he had no right to tell her how to pick her friends. He wasn't her real daddy. She'd told him often enough that he ought to stay out of her business. But he couldn't just sit back, either, and act like Beck Hopper was no big deal. It all just had a bad smell to it and could only lead to ruination.

Maybe if Fern would talk to the girl, she'd be more likely to listen. But he'd seen how Fern looked at him Sunday over the top of her Bible, like she loathed sight of him. If she had heard the talk of him being the town hero, it affected her like Tuesday's laundry. It would not surprise him at all if she didn't up and become a Catholic.

He folded the newspaper in half and then sacked up some peanuts to roast after supper. "Mind if I pick up the rest of those things later, Will? I told Floyd Whittington I'd stop by to check on things with some work crew he had in mind for cleanup."

Will set his sacks behind the counter. "Say, Jeb, while I'm thinking about it, my brother's boy, my nephew Herschel, he's gotten into a fix. He's been big into poultry and such since yay high." He held his hand waist high. "But what with this Depression and all, he's been trying to collect on a poultry deal that ain't paying off. If you know of some farmer in need of about two hundred chicks, he needs to get them off his hands real quick. It'd make a good deal for someone with room to raise some laying hens."

"I'll spread the word, Will. You know I'm glad to do anything for a friend." He shook his hand, waved goodbye to Edward, and headed for the door.

Jeb felt smiles following him all the way out the door.

❃

Several men were gathered out in front of the bank. Jeb took his newspaper and peanuts into the circle of onlookers. Barney Hewlett was there. He had invited some of the out-of-work boys to Floyd Whittington's meeting to help get the bank windows put back in and then set up a work crew to rebuild Lincoln's Barbershop. The barber had been at the doctor's house all morning, one fellow said, with a sick headache.

"You can put me on that list," said Jeb. "I'll work the first two days for free."

Several men agreed as Floyd came over from the Woolworth's with two buckets of paint and a sack of nails for Barney.

Barney thanked Jeb and the others and then passed out some work details. Jeb was delegated the job of measuring for the new bank windows.

"The talk is," said Floyd, "that Horace Mills ordered the bank reopened this morning in spite of the food riot and his straw likeness being burned in effigy. So we need to work around customers and such but get them secured before nightfall."

Jeb and Floyd teamed up to examine the broken window and measured it for the nervous clerk, Finn, who wanted the damage fixed the same day. He and two other male bank clerks had slept inside the bank all night with Deputy Maynard, each man taking watch so that no one entered the bank through the boarded windows, even though Asa and at least half the rioters had been rounded up and thrown into jail.

As they measured, several women employees waited outside on the walk, still timid about going to work. Faith Bottoms and Beulah Winters gabbed with them about Saturday's lollapalooza of a fire and how lucky they all were that only two businesses got burned. Faith, talking loud enough for the men to overhear, offered the bank girls a deal on permanent waves. She singled out Jeb and gave him the slightest hint of a smile.

"Reverend Nubey, I know you don't want no beauty shop deals, but you drop by after hours and I'll give you a private cut." Two of the girls, along with Beulah, whistled and rooted Faith on with her bold proposal.

Jeb had heard a few of the boys hanging around Lincoln's on Saturdays call Faith a hot cha-cha hairdresser. "I just had a good trim," he told her and then acted like he didn't notice the bank girls' swooning.

By noon, the men had finished the estimations and set to work hauling the charred lumber from Lincoln's burned-out building. Jeb joined three of the fellows for peanuts and a Coke and then dropped by Whittington's to see if the glass had been cut for the bank. He then had to return and deliver the news to Finn that the glass would not be in for another week.

"I'll tell Mr. Mills myself, then. Say, he just called and told me he'd be out to see you before coming in this afternoon," Finn told Jeb. "Mrs. Mills wanted him to stay home but he wouldn't have any of that. No one can threaten Horace Mills, I guess."

"Don't say? I'd better get to the church, then." Jeb handed the list of materials they would need to Floyd. He stopped back in at Honeysack's, stowed his food in the truck bed, and left for a meeting that left him a mite nervous.

❊

Horace Mills, who had a newspaper tucked under one arm, waited in the shade of the church overhang. His hair and face gleamed like he had come fresh from the bath.

The whites of his shirtsleeves extended crisp and perfect, one inch from his jacket sleeves.

"You seen the paper, I guess," said Jeb.

"Asa Hopper started this whole mess. He's been threatening the bank for too long." Mills slapped the newspaper against one palm.

"Floyd's working on getting the glass for your windows."

"If you hadn't stepped in, Reverend Nubey, I'd say the whole town would have been burned to the ground. Hopper's politics are dangerous. Maynard would do well to keep him locked up for a long time."

Jeb invited him inside, out of the cool morning air.

"I can't stay long. I just wanted you to know that heroism is rewarded in Nazareth."

The title of "hero" left Jeb feeling restless. "Looks like Doris Jolly left a plate of cookies here on the desk. Take a few for yourself and those girls at the bank. They looked hungry."

Mills pressed an envelope into Jeb's hand. "This is for the church." He pressed another envelope into Jeb's hands. "This one's for you to use any way you see fit, for your sacrifice and for—" Mills drew in a deep breath and then said, "For any hard feelings I've had or conveyed to you. You're a good man, Nubey. I'm glad to call you our future minister."

Jeb had never heard anyone speak of him using such noble language. He sounded like Roosevelt himself.

"I've been thinking, it's time we put a real floor in this place and maybe a lock on the door. Put a man or two to work, for one thing. Another thing, if it were to get around that the church had cash laying about, someone might get the idea to help themselves to a little charity." Mills inspected the sanctuary through the church office door.

"I'll take the money for the church, but please don't pay me anything, Mr. Mills. That wouldn't be right. It's best you give this to Reverend Gracie. He's home in bed this morning but I'll see he gets it." The envelope was thick. Jeb turned it over and looked at it. "A lot of heroes helped put out that fire yesterday, bigger fellers than me."

"Gracie would take it if it were meant for him. He understands the value of a gift. But this is strictly for you and your little family of orphans."

"Not orphans, exactly."

"You know what I mean." Horace grinned.

Jeb knew Gracie had accepted donations of free medical attention or extra scoops of beans from the Honeysacks. Reluctantly, he took the money—a wad of bills, it seemed, that would pay the grocery bill for weeks.

"I know I've been the only thing between this pulpit and the poorhouse some weeks. Take this as your back pay that's been coming to you." Mills kept patting Jeb on the back the whole time he talked, soft but repetitious, like when Jeb led mulish Bell each morning from her stall. "I'd wager that you're going to be a man of influence in these parts, Reverend. You bring goodwill with you, and people need that these days. Men like Hopper sow bad seed in a town. A man like him could make everyone else think that if they have a bone to pick, they should just haul off and burn down the institutions that keep Nazareth alive. I can't help this Depression or the ones that didn't plan for hard times. It's not good business to turn my back when someone like Asa stops paying his bills. If I did that for him, we'd not have a bank in this town or any other business."

"Wonder how long they'll keep Asa locked up?" Jeb slid the money into a desk drawer and locked it.

"At least until the judge comes through. Could be two weeks, but that's a good lesson for him. It'll give him time to cool off and think about what he did."

"His wife and kids might need a visit from a few of the families. I'll ask around among the women in town."

"Let it go, Reverend. Best way to rid a house of cockroaches is to lock up all the food. The next thing we need to hear is that the Hoppers have disappeared. That wife of his would do better on her own, in my estimation."

Jeb did not answer him.

"Salvation Army's setting up a soup kitchen by Friday, if it makes you feel any better. The Hoppers aren't too proud to knock out my windows; they can stand in a bread line like everyone else."

"I'll see that Mrs. Hopper's told about the Salvation Army."

"I know what some think. That I'm the rich man around town. But it isn't true. Not since 1929. I lost as much as anyone else. But I came from hard stock myself. My brother Freddie and I know suffering just like the rest of these Joes. If I can climb out of bad circumstances, anyone can." The entire time he spoke, Mills read Jeb's every move and the tilt of his head. "Don't feel guilty about taking the money. Church in the Dell hasn't paid you much, just like it hasn't paid Gracie much. You put that away somewhere, and it will last you a good long while. That oldest girl, Angel, she's been wearing the same dress all year to Sunday service. My Amy, she notices those things. Take her down to the Woolworth's and let Evelene fix her up with something new. Those two littlest ones too, while you're at it. I'll see myself out. But you can rest assured, Reverend Nubey, that you took the right stand yesterday. You proved to me and the whole town you know the side of right and wrong. Keep it up and I'll see you never go without." He left.

Jeb sat at the desk and unlocked the drawer. He counted the money from the envelope marked Church in the Dell. It came to fifty dollars. He weighted this contribution against the less than charitable words Mills had spoken about the Hoppers. The thought of Hopper's wife and children being run out of town affected him worse than seeing drunken Asa hurl a brick through the bank window. He remembered all Gracie's speeches, but now he felt conflicted about how he was supposed to feel about a man who had almost burned down Nazareth.

He opened the thicker parcel. Someone, maybe Amy Mills, had written his name across the front in elegant script. He counted the money twice. It came to one hundred dollars. He held the cash—the most he had ever seen at one time—in his hands. His fingers felt cool and wet around the bills, clammy, like he had just taken a bootlegger's money. He remembered how Gracie had told him to keep away from town politics. By one measly act of charity, it seemed he might be neck-deep in it.

Something shuffled in the sawdust floor outside the door. When he turned the swivel chair around, he saw Fern watching him count the money. He dropped the cash onto the desktop, a hot potato. "Been here long?" he asked.

She could not take her eyes off the wad of money. She stammered out, "I had a break and thought I should drop by and tell you . . ." She continued to stammer until Jeb started trying to fill in the words for her. Finally she said,

"You did a good thing on Saturday." Except she did not beam like Freda Honeysack had beamed at him from her pew left and center on Sunday. Her countenance dimmed and she kept inching backward.

Jeb stared down at the money. When he looked up again, she was gone. He could not pull himself from his spot on the sawdust floor. Fern was thinking things about him again that would cast him in a less than perfect light. He should be used to that by now.

❋

Beck looked like a boy who had lived on maple syrup and corn bread for too long—skinny as noodles. But brown eyed and tanned too, giving him texture like a boy cut from burlap. His arms were sinewy, hard from keeping wood stacked for his momma's stove.

He always made straight for the woods behind the school at the last bell.

Angel told Willie, "I'll meet you and Ida May out front. Wait for me by the drive." She didn't want Willie telling Jeb that she had met Beck after school, so she went up the school steps, through the building, and then out the back way.

Beck had deposited his books next to the fence post. Angel left hers next to his and climbed over the fence. "You taking a smoke?"

Beck held out his cigarette. "Want to try it?"

Angel said, "I've tried them but they burn my throat. You look good with a smoke, though. Kind of like Clark Gable, only a different haircut." Beck's hair had been snipped around the top in an uneven ridge, most likely cut by one of his sisters.

"Yore old man don't like my daddy now, I guess. Daddy wouldn't have hauled off and started that mess if he hadn't been drinking so much. If they knew that about him, maybe they'd not send him off to prison."

"You really think they'll send him to prison?"

"Whole town's mad at him. Momma's afraid to show her face downtown. That banker'll take away what we got left now for sure. We won't have no choice then but to move on."

"Wives always take the punishment for their husbands' sins. My granny told me that once. My momma was the same way about my daddy, taking all the guff for what he caused. She used to be anyway." Angel took the cigarette out of his mouth and put it to her lips. "Why these things make you look so good anyway? Something about them." She coughed and then held the cigarette next to her face, posing. "I hear that boys wonder things about girls that smoke."

"Wonder if you're loosey-goosey is all." He took it away from her. "You don't need it, Angel. If Reverend Nubey smells it on you, he'll know you been around me. You don't need my kind of trouble follering you home."

"We got some groceries give to us. I brought you something." She ran for the sack she had left beside their books.

"I don't need charity, Angel."

"We take it all the time. May as well take a little of what's been give to us, Beck. If your momma's afraid to go downtown, maybe this'll help her out."

Beck looked into the bag as though something might jump out. "Your daddy know you bringing us this good grub?"

"Jeb's not my father. He's my keeper."

"He keeps an eye on you. I know when he's giving me the eye, like 'Keep away from Angel, or else.' I think he'd like it better if me and my family'd just stop coming to that church altogether."

"I never known Jeb to give anyone the eye. Except me. But he can't tell me what to do and he knows that. I do for myself."

"Why you live with him, then?"

Angel sighed and it quieted him.

"You ever been kissed?"

"Why you asking me that?"

"Ever been parking?"

"You think I'm afraid of boys, Beck Hopper. I'm not."

"Want to take a walk, back in the woods?" Beck walked backward with his arms spread open.

Angel leaned sideways to see if Willie had rounded the corner of the schoolhouse. She didn't see him, or any of the schoolkids, for that matter. "We can take a walk." She followed him around the oaks and past the evergreens that completely hid them from sight.

8

*B*eulah had placed two chairs and a small table on the walk outside the café. Jeb had spent the afternoon with some of the men downtown, framing out the barbershop front for Lincoln. Before heading back to the parsonage, he stopped for coffee and took Beulah's outdoor seating as a sign that he needed a break. Beulah appeared at once with the coffeepot and a cup, pleased that someone had noticed her new seating. "Coffee, black, Reverend. About time for school to be out."

"Angel's walking them home today."

"I guess you're not too happy with her seeing that boy of Asa Hopper's."

"Beulah, how's the pie today?"

"I'll mind my own potaters, Reverend, but my oldest girl followed after the wrong boy once and it liked to have killed us all in the long run. It's one thing to pet a stray. But quite another to let it in the house. You wont peach or lemon? That's all we got left after the lunch hour today."

"Peach is fine." Before she could disappear inside, Jeb said, "Beulah, Angel's only fourteen. And I'm not her real daddy. I do best I can by her, but after all, what harm could a girl as young as her get into?"

Beulah gave him a look like one who felt the worst pity for him. "Peach pie is on the way. I'll warm it up for you."

"Mind if I take this other chair, Reverend? Sky's too blue to stay indoors." Winona Mills toted three shopping bags, one bundled under one arm and the other two hanging off her slender arms like saddlebags.

Jeb came to his feet. "You need some help with your things, Miss Mills?"

"Just a place to drop all this before my arms fall off. Momma's got it in her head to have a party before the weather turns completely cold. Then in eight weeks she'll have another just because it turned cold." She took the chair next to Jeb. "Last thing I want to do is try and find good linens in this town. I knew that if I took time off from school, I'd turn into her errand boy again. I told her we'd do better to shop in Hot Springs. At least there you got the bathhouses and a decent massage. But with her it's always now or never."

"I've heard your momma gives the best parties in town, though. I never grew up with such goings-on. You ought to be thankful you got a momma that can bring folks together during times like this."

Winona was writing on an envelope the whole time he talked. She slid it over to him and left it under his hand. "Here's your invitation, then. Wear something like what you wear to church and you'll be fine."

"Miss Mills, I'm sorry, but I wasn't inviting myself to your momma's party."

"I invited you myself."

Jeb pushed back against his chair and then said, "Maybe first you should run that past your folks."

"Horsefeathers. My daddy thinks you're the best thing since sliced bread, Reverend. They don't care who I ask. They don't put on airs, anyway, and if they did, inviting the minister in town would still work. I want you to come. You'll give me someone to talk to."

Jeb assumed she had plenty of attentive acquaintances hovering around waiting to catch her eye, but all he could think to say was, "I'll see if I can come."

He noticed a shadow had fallen across the table. Winona glanced up and shaded her eyes. "Fern, how are you? They must have let school out already."

Fern acknowledged Winona, but only in a brief greeting. "I'm glad I saw you here," she said to Jeb. "Willie and Ida May walked on home without Angel. They were hoping she had just gone on ahead without them. So I told them I thought it would be fine. But it's not like Angel not to walk them both home. I thought maybe you'd know something that I didn't know." She allowed her eyes to veer left as she took one more look at Winona and then said, "Not that it's any of my business."

Beulah stood behind both women, holding the peach pie slice on a plate. She looked troubled, and managed to do that with hardly a trace of expression. She handed Jeb the pie. More silent than usual, she placed a fork on the table, filled up his cup again, and then went back inside.

"I'd better head back home, then," said Jeb, directly uneasy and conjuring ideas about Angel and Beck Hopper.

"I wish you wouldn't go. You're the only entertainment I've had all day," said Winona with a laugh.

Fern pretended she didn't hear Winona. "Maybe going home is best. I can see how all this would have you more than a little worried."

Jeb slid aside the coffee and pie and tossed some change onto the table. He gestured toward the pie. "May as well eat this, Miss Mills, or have it wrapped up to take home to your daddy. Hate to see it go to waste."

He said his good-byes to both women and started to excuse himself. But Winona stopped him, holding out the envelope she'd given to him earlier. "Don't forget your invitation, Reverend. It's this Friday night at our home." She gathered up her sacks to leave. "And Winona's fine with me, Reverend, if you aren't breaking any minister's rules by calling me by my given name."

He appeased her in the manner she wanted before he ran to the truck. Whether or not he should head straight home or proceed down the road that led to the school, he would decide along the way.

He had driven less than a rock's throw when he realized he had neglected to say much of anything at all to Fern. But surely she understood that he could forget all his manners when he got his head caught up in matters about Angel. A quick glance back at Beulah's showed him Fern was no longer standing out on the walk; Winona had disappeared too.

He sighed. Encountering the two of them at the same time had left him with a peculiar feeling, as though the three of them had met at a crossroads somewhere and then passed without incident. Yet it seemed like an incident had taken place, like a train wreck that he had driven by, looked at but not seen.

But women could make you feel like that without cause.

❄

Angel was nowhere in sight. Jeb drove from the road that led to the school and then traced Angel's route all the way back to Church in the Dell. The weather had turned cold and the landscape had faded to match the color of earth. The summer drought had dulled any hope for a multihued autumn. He imagined Angel's thin body camouflaged by the browning leaves, tucked into some unseen hideaway with a boy too old for his years.

He pulled into the drive and parked just beyond the porch to keep the dust from coating Ida May, who sat on the front steps. She did not have a look about her that said she'd been abandoned after school; she was not mad or huffing like she did when Angel wanted to walk alone with the older girls. An oversized green sweater draped her like a woman's coat and she'd buttoned it from the neck all the way to the knees. She looked less thin, as though she'd gone off and stayed with someone who knew how to better care for her. Her eyes were deepening in color and Jeb hated that he could not tell her she looked more and more like her mother every day.

She sipped something hot from a cup. When Jeb approached her she offered him a sip. "Angel gave me coffee, Jeb. I kind of like it."

Jeb knew Angel was not likely to pour coffee for her sister. He asked, "What made her give you that, Ida May?"

She shrugged. "Ask her, I guess. She's in the kitchen." When Ida May had been bribed she was obviously evasive.

"She's making coffee kind of late. I guess because she just got home herself," said Jeb.

Ida May pressed her lips together and wouldn't look at him.

"Miss Coulter already told me you and Willie walked home without her," said Jeb.

"She gets in our business a lot, Angel says."

Jeb stepped around her and went inside. The parlor light had been left on and the radio blared loudly with band music. He shut off the radio and the lamp. A pounding hammer of a sound broke the quiet, like the thump of knife through a potato.

Jeb entered the kitchen. He said nothing to Angel at first. Instead, he poured a glass of milk as though it were the only thing on his mind.

"Willie ought to be in here peeling potatoes. I'll go and find him. I think he's out by the creek, even though I told him the water's getting too cold for wading." Her voice held a charm that made her sound almost compliant.

"I smell a cigarette," said Jeb.

"Maybe just coffee is all you smell. I tossed some grounds out while ago. I just made a fresh pot. Want a cup?" She peeled another potato and kept her back to him. The kitchen window faced away from the sunset, so only a trickle of light as pale as peaches colored her shape. "I'm tired of potatoes. Maybe I'll just mash these for potato cakes in the morning." She talked as though Jeb were not in the room, as though she talked to no one but herself.

"Willie and Ida May walked home without you."

She huffed, "Ida May's not telling it right, Jeb. I came home right afterward, right behind them. I like to walk with my friends, you know, have someone to talk to besides babies."

Ida May had walked up and stood behind Jeb. "I'm not a baby, Angel, and I didn't say nothing at all about you and that boy!"

Jeb listened to them argue and then said, "Ida May, why don't you go get on with your studies? I need to talk to Angel."

"I have to go look for Willie." Angel threw the knife into the sink, pulled a towel from around her waist, and dropped it onto the countertop.

"You can storm out the door mad as bats, but sooner or later you'll have to come back. May as well have a seat." Jeb turned a kitchen chair around and sat down in it, facing her. He pulled out a second chair and slid it across the floor in her direction.

Angel looked washed out, tired, like she'd been living a life she didn't want for too long and was sick of it. She plopped down in the chair as though someone had pushed her into it.

"No use in fighting about this or blaming your sister for telling on you. It's not the truth anyway, and it's not the point. First off, we got to stop acting like we're getting in one another's business when we talk about these things. People live together and take care of each other, and it always puts folks in one another's business. So let's get it said straight out that I'm in your business, and I'll be in it until we find your momma or get you someplace else you'd rather call home."

The back door opened and Willie entered holding a freshly cleaned fish. He grabbed the door before it swung back completely and hit the banjo standing against the wall where Jeb had left it that morning. He laid the fish in the sink and covered it with water and a little milk to leach the smell from it, then salted it. He saw Angel in the chair and the way she pouted and said, "Don't blame me, I didn't tell him anything. That's what you get for skeering us half to death, though." He rinsed his hands, shook them dry, and went to the bedroom.

"We both know you got to keep an eye on your brother and sister, or at least tell them where you are so they won't worry. I just think that if you were as innocent as you like to act, then you wouldn't be so worried about hiding all this from me. I think I know who you were with. Beck Hopper. Am I right?"

She didn't answer.

"It's one thing to offer charity to the Hoppers. But that boy has more troubles than just an empty belly."

"I want to ask you something, Jeb," she said.

He waited.

Angel turned and straddled the chair back to face Jeb exactly as he faced her. "You ever been in love?"

"I believe I will have some coffee."

"Being in one another's business goes two ways, Jeb. You in my business, I'm in yours. Just answer me if you think you've ever been in love."

Jeb did not know how to answer. The only woman he had considered in a matter as important as love made it widely known how much she loathed sight of him. "Not when I was young as you. But you can *think* you're in love at your age. Feelings about love can blind you to the real thing."

"If I'm in love with Beck, I don't see it matters that his daddy's in jail or that they're losing the farm. If I'm in love, then love is the thing that makes everything else not as important. Like it's against my will. Isn't that something you don't have power over, Jeb?"

It seemed she was close to right. "I don't think so."

"What are you saying, that I can't ever talk to Beck in school or sit and share my lunch with him?"

"Or kiss him out in the woods," said Willie from the hall.

"Willie, shut up! You don't know nothing about me!" Angel nearly fell out of the chair trying to lunge for Willie, but Jeb stopped her.

Willie evaded her and spoke to Jeb matter-of-factly. "Some of the kids saw them clinched like two bears and run and told us when we was walking home. Are you going to cook that fish or just leave it for the flies?"

"Willie, I'll call you when I need you," said Jeb. "Back to your room, boy!"

"I wouldn't sleep too sound tonight, Willard!" said Angel.

"You kissed him, Angel?" Jeb imagined holding Beck Hopper's head under water.

She returned to finish peeling potatoes. Whatever had just transpired between her and Beck, she had not lost the faint power of naiveté that kept Jeb from wanting to thrash her. As much as she thought she knew about this boy, she really knew nothing at all, and that is what caused Jeb to pity her.

"You ought to save love for later, Angel. That's all I'm going to say about the matter. But you can do better than Beck for a friend. I can't sit back and let him lead you along. I've known too many boys like him." He knew that he'd been one of them once. "Just give some thought to what I'm trying to tell you."

He left her to mull in silence. Taking the banjo along, he went out the back way and then wandered out to the stream. The last light of day trickled downstream, coloring the water blue green like the Pacific. He remembered that this was the first place he had seen Fern, before she had known the lies he had spread to hide his real identity. But she had liked him as the man he pretended to be, and it seemed like love.

He picked another tune the Nigra player had taught him and he realized he could not remember that man's name, only the way his music made him feel.

9

Jeb decided the next morning to drive the children to school, telling them that the mornings had turned cool. But after he dropped them off, he watched until Angel disappeared inside the school with her two friends, Sadie and Jane Bernard, nieces of Florence Bernard. Angel had spoken little that morning, except to say she had an exam and needed to be at school early to study with friends.

Jeb joined Will Honeysack early for coffee at Beulah's. He asked him how he was doing spiritually, to which Will replied, "I had a shave this morning. First one Lincoln's given since the fire."

"That was a mess to clean up," said Jeb. "Glad we got him up and running. Val tells me you're hanging some new shelves. If you need some help, I've got my hammer in the truck."

"Always need help. We got a load of blankets in, so figuring it's getting cold nights, we'd best get some shelves up for blankets." He thanked Jeb for the offer. "Not too many preachers give me that kind of help."

They walked to the store and found Val counting ten-penny nails on an upturned crate. Will added a scuttle full of coal to the potbellied stove while Jeb carried in the new lumber for the job.

Once they started, they quickly fell into a system. Jeb and Val held the brackets while Will hammered.

"Freda stay home today, Will?" asked Val.

Will drove another nail into the wall.

Jeb saw Freda's receipt pad still tucked into the slot next to the pens and pencils. The store smelled of produce and feed sacks. But absent was the lingering violet of Freda's toilet water.

Mellie Fogarty stepped into the store with her shopping list. "I heard you had a sale on canned chili, Will? Best to stock up before winter gets here." She stood in the middle of the aisle and looked around. "Freda here today?"

Will sneezed. "Home cleaning out closets."

"In the fall? What did you do this time, Will?" She wandered up another aisle and then yelled, "I don't see the chili. You think you could call Freda and ask her where she put the display?"

"Excuse me, fellers," said Will. He laid aside the hammer and hobbled up the aisle to find Mellie a can of chili.

"I think Will's made Freda mad at him this morning, that's what," said Jeb.

"Second time this month," said Val.

"One of us is always in the doghouse with women." Jeb leveled a plank onto one of the sets of brackets.

"You talking about Fern Coulter?" Val laughed.

Jeb measured the distance for the next bracket. "Fern hates me too much to be mad at me. I'm talking about Angel. I don't want to tell you what she's done, though. She already thinks the whole town's in our business."

"Shame to see her get mixed up with that Hopper

boy." Val slid the plank for the first shelf onto the brackets, eyeballed it, and then pulled it off.

"So much for keeping things on the hush-hush," said Jeb.

Will bagged Mellie's items and then joined them again with his hammer. "You talking about Beck Hopper? I saw him walking Angel to the soda shop after school one day this week."

Jeb gave a handful of nails to Will. "I guess I'm the last to know. Will, you and Freda raised girls. How you get a strong-headed girl to understand a little reasoning?"

Will and Val both laughed.

"The last person I'd want her to be seen with is Beck Hopper. And what does she do but hatch some romance with the worst boy in town."

"He's not the worst boy," said Val. "Ever meet Beck's brother Clark?"

"I know I'm not her daddy," said Jeb. "If I could find him, I'd give him a good talking-to, though."

"Angel comes in here every Saturday hoping for a letter from her momma," said Val. "Breaks my heart to see a girl like her torn away from her mother."

"Her momma ain't right, Val," said Will.

"Can't imagine her not asking for them kids." Val drove another nail.

"It ought not to be so." Will shook his head.

"Let's get the next bracket up." Jeb made several pencil marks and then held the bracket up to the wall. "Hold this in place, will you, Val?"

"You and Miss Coulter could make a family out of this whole sitchyashun if she'd come off her harsh opinions of you."

"Wouldn't matter. Angel doesn't want a substitute family. She wants her own momma back. I've been thinking on something. Even if that aunt in Little Rock would take her in so she could be close to her, that would be better than living among strangers," said Jeb.

"Nazareth's never known a stranger. This whole town treats those kids like they was our own. You watch and see if that Angel doesn't up and marry and settle here among us."

"Can't see that happening, Val."

"Maybe a girl like her would settle old Beck Hopper down. Sometimes a man that can't be tamed can be settled down by the right girl."

"Val, I don't think that right girl's ever found you. You still the wildest bachelor in these parts." Jeb handed the hammer back to Will and excused himself to fetch a bottle of pop.

Val looked at Will. "You think he was making fun?"

❄

Angel rode into town with Beck Hopper only because Willie needed pencils. Beck swore his momma let him bring his daddy's truck to school so no one could say they were doing wrong. Willie needed pencils, and Beck had the gas to get them to town. That was all.

Willie rode in the back but had ushered Ida May into the truck to sit between Angel and Beck. He had given Angel a look and said, "I don't think Jeb'll like this."

Beck parked in front of Fidel's Drugstore not two cars away from Horace Mills's car. Two boys wiped down the Mills car with chamois towels.

"Willie, take this nickel down to the Woolworth's and

buy your pencils. Then meet us back here at Fidel's." Before Willie could walk away, Angel said, "Take Ida May with you." With her hand at the back of Ida May's head, she propelled her forward.

Beck tilted his head to one side to invite Angel into Fidel's. She let him go in first and then glanced up the street before following him. Beck took the booth at the farthest end of the drugstore. Angel sat across from him, her back to the front of the store. Beck took off his coat, a ragged and oversized woolen that had most likely been passed down from one of his older brothers. "I'll order the malteds," he said.

"Wait." Angel slid a nickel to the edge of the table. "Here's my share."

Beck hesitated with his hands in his pockets and then palmed the nickel.

Angel half-smiled at Fidel, whose gaze connected her to the youngest Hopper. Beck, who ordered one chocolate malted with two straws, said to Fidel, "I could use me a job if you could use the work."

Fidel kept looking down where he wiped the counter. "Jobs is scarce these days," was the only reply he gave to Beck. He set to work on the ice-cream shake.

"Fidel, I heard you were needing a boy to work your soda fountain," said Angel.

"Here's your shake, boy." Fidel slid the malted down the counter to Beck.

Beck paid Fidel and took the malted without looking up at him. He walked back to the table with his hair hanging over his face.

"Beck, you ought to stand up straight when you talk to

Fidel. If you want a job, you have to act like you're the best one for it."

"Here's your straw. That test Mrs. Garvey gave us today was a killer. I was never so glad for school to be over."

"She tests hard. But she makes me think about things like the past." Angel saw the way he studied her hands and waited while she plunged her straw in first.

"I just think about the day I'll wake up and realize I'm not going back."

"I thought about quitting, just so I could go to work and try and get my little brother and sister over to Little Rock. But Jeb thinks it's a bad idea to quit school."

"Maybe we all ought to take off for Little Rock," said Beck.

"You and me, you mean?"

"Beats you being told what to do all the time by someone that ain't your daddy."

"Jeb knows he's not my daddy. He tries hard to act like one. I think he's trying to make amends for his past."

"I heard about that too. Never heard of a preacher with his kind of past."

"Everybody has a past, Beck."

"Here comes your brother and Ida May."

"Where did you get the nickel for that malted, Angel, and did you think we might want one too?" Willie slid next to Angel and made her move toward the wall.

"Here, take it, but go get your own straw," said Angel.

"I don't want any of it," said Ida May. "It's had boy's lips on it."

"Jeb's truck's down in front of Honeysack's." Willie

counted out six pencils, divided them three ways, and gave two each to Angel and Ida May.

"Did he happen to see you?" Angel asked.

"Dogged if I know."

"We'd better go. Beck, we'll catch a ride home with Jeb. I'll just tell him we caught a ride to town from school." Angel pushed Willie to leave.

"Who gave you a ride into town?"

Angel looked up, startled by the sound of Jeb's voice. "Willie needed pencils and . . ." She trailed off, realizing it was hopeless. Jeb's face said he knew exactly what she'd done.

"Let's go," was all he said.

"See you at school tomorrow, Beck," Angel said. She watched Jeb walk back down toward Honeysack's with Ida May holding his hand before she grabbed Willie and retrieved their books from the back of Beck's truck bed. "Jeb has no right to talk to me like I'm two," she said to Willie.

"I like Jeb. He treats us better than our own daddy," said Willie. He ran and left her to complain alone.

10

Torches glowed all around the backyard of the Mills's estate. Ancient cherries towered like elder statesmen with drooping beards plucked of all summer foliage. Jeb sat beneath a nearly roofless gazebo, pruned of its seasonal covering of ivy, and watched the sun set. Before the crowd wandered out to intrude on his oasis, he listened to the wind. Like the usher of autumn, it started at the back of the woods behind the estate and surged through the trees, making great oceanic sounds as though the sea had found its way through bough and brush. But the cherries and the ivy-entangled oaks guarded the grounds and kept the wind outside the garden's gates.

He watched the back door for any sign of Fern. He had heard that Winona had been asked by her banker cousin Oz to invite the schoolteacher.

Two water gardens—one to his left and the other a distance behind him—brought a quiet kind of music to the private grounds. The liquid patter mingled well with the women's talk from inside the kitchen. It seemed a shame to pluck a tune from the banjo, but he had promised one song to Winona. His fingers felt cold around the neck. She waited at the rear door, finishing a conversation she had started with one of the kitchen girls. Seeing him tuning under the tree, she joined him. Jeb twanged the first string and tightened it until it rang true and then tuned the others.

"You did bring your banjo. Can you play anything besides hymns, or is that all you're allowed to play?"

"Been so long since I played anything, I can't say as I remember what I did know. There's a song about a river in heaven I like," said Jeb.

"A hymn on the banjo. I don't believe I've ever heard anything but jazz music on the banjo."

Jeb plucked a tune he had learned in Texas, a song that had the Hot Springs musicians gathered on the lawn turning to listen.

"That's no hymn."

"Sure it is." He changed the words to fit a psalm and then sang it to her. One of the fiddlers and the guitar player from Hot Springs, unable to resist, joined in.

Three young women waved at Winona from the backyard porch. She yelled, "Come and listen." So they walked across the lawn in their Sears and Roebuck party dresses. Jeb's fingers were warmed by now, so he segued into another song. When he finished, Winona clapped and asked him to keep playing.

Jeb played two more tunes and then laid aside the banjo, nodding his thanks to his impromptu bandmembers. The sun had disappeared and put the torches to work, yellowing faces like the opening games in Rome.

"We'll have to let the musician have his supper, I guess," said Winona. By now most of the party had spilled out into the gardens. The fiddler and guitar player rejoined the band from Hot Springs and helped set up on the lawn. They played in the final light of evening. Although the air was brisk, several older couples began to dance a waltz that had soft bluegrass undertones.

"I don't guess preachers can dance," Winona said to Jeb.

He considered her offer. "Best I don't." He noticed her dress had come to fit her straight from the box.

She introduced Jeb to her three friends, all girls from campus about to graduate, like Winona, but unsure what they would do with their learning. Two had become engaged and showed their rings to the other two. They tried to entice Winona aside. She gave them an excuse and joined Jeb again.

"You look cold. You want to go inside?" he asked.

"The music's not so great, is it?"

"Nothing wrong with it." He alluded to her bare shoulders. Her dress had an off-the-shoulder cape sleeve. "You look a little chilled, is all."

"The advertisement promised I'd look like a Hollywood star. Instead, all I look is cold. Mother's got the food prepared. Had to hire two extra girls to make it all. I guess it's safe to go back inside." She rose, pulling him with her, holding on to his arm with both hands.

Jeb followed her into the house.

Somebody had started a fire in the den's fireplace. A group of guests from Church in the Dell sipped punch as red as forest berries by the fire. Winona led Jeb to the buffet table. Four large stuffed hens, legs covered with white paper boots, decorated each table like cancan girls. In between the meat platters were more platters filled with roasted vegetables and large green bowls full of potatoes. Winona handed Jeb a plate.

"A preacher in our midst. Tell Uncle to hide the booze." Oz Mills, Winona's cousin from Hope, picked up a plate, turned it upside down to read the label, and then greeted his cousin.

"You're back in town," said Jeb. He had first met Oz at a church picnic, and then again downtown before his less-than-inspiring debacle as a charlatan. There was no love lost between the two—Oz had been dating Fern when Jeb hit town.

"I heard you were still here," said Oz.

"Reverend's got a knack for music, Oz," said Winona. "You ought to hear him play."

"Did you bring anyone along, Nubey, or are you stag?" asked Oz.

"I hear Fern might come." Jeb did not want to imply he had committed to a date with Oz's pretty cousin. That would be untrue and leave him without options. He wanted all options open with Fern in the house. He reached for a hot roll and could have sworn he saw two schoolteachers wrap food in napkins and stash it in their handbags. The word around town, that anyone who could do so finagled an invitation to the Mills party for the free eats, might be true.

Oz didn't comment any further except to say, "You two look like you'd make a good couple. Nice touch with the hair, Winona." He excused himself to wait near the front door.

"I'm sorry for my cousin, Reverend. Oz was a good boy when his momma was alive. That stepmother of his lets him get away with murder."

"He has a thing for Fern."

"He'll never get her."

"What makes you think so?"

"Fern doesn't know what she wants."

"I once thought I knew what she wanted."

"You don't. No one knows. Especially not Fern."

❊

Mrs. Mills kept the platters filled all night even as she complained that Horace had limited her hiring of servants due to the Depression. One of the girls—Mrs. Mills called her Joyous—who was hired from south of town, managed to keep the candles lit and the punch bowl filled, even though Horace had told her to be stingy with the rum in the second bowl.

Jeb stood by the wall chatting with several acquaintances while Winona spoke with her school friends. Through the window, he saw four youths creep across the lawn, having come through the woods and over the south garden gate. They wandered past several guests, who glanced at the boys under the miserly glow of lanterns then returned to dancing and eating. One boy looked something like Beck Hopper, but Jeb decided he'd imagined it.

He crossed the sitting room and went into the kitchen. Joyous was complaining to the other servant, Thea, that Mr. Mills was making it impossible to keep food out for everyone with his stingy rules. She finished making a sandwich from a bread roll and ham and stuck it in a bag for later. Then she said, "Did you hear a knock, or am I imaginin' things?"

Before Thea could go to the back door, Jeb said, "I'll answer." It was a heavy oak door, painted the color of milk, including the metal around the knob and hinges. He opened it to find the four youths staring at him from the dark. "You boys need to move on down the street," he said.

"We heard there was food here, mister. You got a handout?" The tallest boy, lean faced with long wrists hanging out of his too-short sleeves, begged while the others stayed back in the shadows. Even with the shadow of twilight graying his face, his eyes had a begging look about them. Hunger no longer coupled with embarrassment.

"We can't give them a thing, Reverend. Mrs. Mills is keeping an eye on us, and she'll know if food is missing." Joyous stepped into the doorway and glanced out at who might be listening.

"You're that minister from the Church in the Dell, ain't you?" said the lanky boy.

"You boys go on and don't be bothering the preacher," said Thea.

Jeb's plate was filled and he thought of handing it to the boy. He opened the screen to get a better look at the youngest one. When he did, the youth moved farther into the shadows. "Let me see your face," he said. When the boy evaded him, he asked, "What's wrong with your brother?"

"He ain't our brother," said the tall, lanky boy. He bowed his head, suddenly evasive.

The other two moved aside to let the youngest come forward. But he turned and ran behind the cherry trees.

Jeb handed his plate to the tall boy. He took two steps after the boy until his toe tripped against the bottom step. He righted himself. "I know you, don't I?" he yelled.

"Don't let Mrs. Mills see you givin' away her food," said Joyous. "You boys take what's on Reverend's plate

and hurry on out of here. Reverend, you all right? You
need anything?"

The other three boys followed the first, loping like
calves after their momma. Jeb could not say for certain
that any but one of them were Hoppers; only one Hopper,
besides the boy's mother, had ever set foot inside the
church. He watched the blackened glen, the sway of tree-
tops in the wind the only movement. The nerve it took
Beck Hopper to show up at the banker's party made Jeb
wonder about his good sense—that or his guts. He'd
have to watch Angel more closely. That kind of guts
might beget dangerous ideas in a young girl.

❈

As Fern arrived, a clap of thunder pealed like someone
had torn the clouds from the sky. She ran through the
front door with her coat hanging off one shoulder and her
handbag gaping open. Oz met her first and offered his
help with the coat and purse. Jeb felt about twelve,
watching the two of them shoot the breeze and waiting
for a way to step in and draw Fern's attention away from
Oz. He turned and realized Winona had appeared with a
full cup of punch, no rum. She held it out to him. "Looks
as though we're going to get that rain we've been needing," she said.

"I don't want any more punch." He declined the
punch without looking at her, his sights still on Fern,
who dripped on the Millses' doormat and yet looked so
Hollywood about it, like the storm had followed her
into the room to herald her arrival. She ran her fingers
through her hair and with the other free hand was led
away and out of sight by Oz.

It came to Jeb that he might have slighted Winona, but by the time he turned back to thank her for the punch, she had vanished. The sitting room filled up with the couples and the musicians who had stumbled inside to dodge the storm. Mrs. Mills ran around the room handing out towels to the damp guests from a bundle carried by Joyous.

Winona returned and replaced a platter on the buffet table, but she either averted her eyes or saw straight through Jeb, distracted by a chore that bored her. So he worked his way through the crowd and around two tall Ming vases in the entry to see if Fern might be looking for him. On the other side of the house he came upon a long banquet hall with white painted floors. The musicians had toweled off their instruments to set up in the far alcove and prepare for the next set. Horace gave them a list of song requests and then waved for Jeb to join him. At the first piano chord, he could see Oz Mills move behind a group of women, swaying in a slow dance. He spun Fern slowly around and then back. Her skirt was red and twirled like a parasol in the hands of some Japanese geisha. Jeb joined Horace next to the band and turned his back on Fern and Oz.

"Reverend, is there a song you'd like to hear? These boys know a little bit of everything," said Horace. Jeb couldn't think of anything; he was too busy trying not to watch Fern and Oz.

When the song finished, Fern saw Jeb. She left Oz but he followed her. "I didn't see you," she said to Jeb.

Jeb couldn't tell if that mattered to her. "You can dance," he said, "better than most."

Oz greeted his uncle.

"I haven't seen the missus or Winona in a while. I'd best go see what they're up to," said Horace.

"Reverend, you going to take a turn on the dance floor?" Oz asked.

Jeb wanted to take the man's clammy banker's hands, peel them off Fern's delicate arm, and take her for a spin himself. Instead he turned his attention back to Horace.

"I'd rather sit and visit. I haven't eaten," said Fern. "There's a table. We can sit if you'd like," she said to Jeb.

"I'll get you something," Jeb said.

When he returned with the food for her, he saw that Oz had taken the only available seat next to her. "Thanks for warming my chair, Oz."

"I'll pull you up another." Oz fetched another chair.

"Your cousin looks lonely, Oz. Maybe you should offer her a dance." Jeb waved at Winona on the other side of the room with her uncle.

Fern clasped her hands over her plate. "Or we could invite Winona to our table."

Jeb said, "Winona is coming our way."

"I'm still dripping wet," said Fern.

Jeb stood and gave his chair to Winona. He dragged another to the table and sat closer to Fern, resting his banjo against the window frame. He hadn't been there long before Horace reappeared.

"Reverend, there's someone I want you to meet." Horace rested his hands on Winona's shoulders. "If you dear folks can part with our minister for a minute or two."

Jeb pushed away from the table and excused himself. He followed Horace into a library. Amy Mills had decorated the room with red-papered walls and red rugs.

Several men smoked cigars next to the bookcases in the corner of the room.

"Boys, I'd like you to meet our minister of Church in the Dell. Reverend, this is Jonathan Steele, Morris Lepinski, and Jefferson Watts. Steele and Lepinski are railroad men. Watts owns several timber operations in Texas, from Houston down to Texarkana."

Jeb shook the hand of each man.

"We've put together a few land deals in the past. These boys are interested in buying up some of the land through Nazareth."

Jeb said, "I don't know much about land. I wish to goodness I did."

"I told them we had a few bad eggs that was about to lose their places. One being Asa Hopper," said Horace.

"I know his wife's been dealt a bad blow," said Jeb.

"I tried to send him the legal papers about his foreclosure to the jailhouse, but he's gone violent, you know. These boys here would like to help him out—buy him out. But Asa's boys won't let anyone on his place, not one foot. He's gone off and lost his mind entirely. Tried to pull a gun on my clerk the night before the riot, but we let him off on account of his missus. You know what a good man my clerk Finn is. His missus had sent a loaf of bread along as a sign of goodwill. But it didn't do any good. Hopper boys nearly shot him before he drove out of there." Horace kept his eyes on Jeb.

"Finn didn't deserve that," said Jeb.

"We had us an idea," said Horace. "That wife of Asa's thinks the world of you. If you'd deliver this offer out to the Hopper place, it could be the very thing that would get him out of at least his money troubles."

"Me deliver it?"

"If you think it's a bad idea, I'll drop the whole matter," said Horace. "When the fellows asked me about hiring the delivery done, I tried to think of a needy family that could use the work. I thought of you. But it's a job I can pass off to anyone."

"Preachers can't be the bearer of bad news, is the thing, Mr. Mills." Jeb rubbed his hands together. He could use the work and knew the lumbermill had laid off another man yesterday.

"Bad news? Oh, no, this is what will get Mrs. Hopper out of her troubles. I heard that as soon as she heard her husband had been locked up she started asking neighbors if they'd like to buy her out. It's really her land, after all, and right now a noose around her neck."

"Then she wouldn't mind Finn bringing her the offer," said Jeb. He couldn't believe he was turning down easy work.

"Finn can't deal with those Hopper boys after staring down the barrels of their rifles. We thought you'd have a way with that crazy bunch. You got the peacemaker in you, Reverend. What with you being not just a minister but a regular guy, those boys would let you pass onto their land."

Jeb pondered "regular guy."

"Then you could ask Mrs. Hopper if she was interested in the offer. If not, she could turn it down and you could be on your way."

"Easy in, easy out," said Lepinski.

"Make things easy on the woman," said Steele.

"Want to give it a shot?" asked Horace.

"Just ask her if she'd be interested?" asked Jeb. A sigh wheezed out of him.

Horace slipped an envelope into Jeb's hands. "Easy as pie."

He nodded.

"Oh, and one more thing. You know how the tithe works. In case you bring us back a signed offer, come next Sunday you'll see a nice contribution in the offering plate. In one trip you've helped the Hoppers and Church in the Dell."

Jeb hesitated. He could imagine Gracie's pale face in the morning light as he patiently waited to see how Jeb might answer.

"I know you've been living hand-to-mouth since you took over this post." Horace stuck out his hand. "Glad to pass this work on to you."

Jeb shook it. "What's in the envelope?"

"It's the deposit on your work for us. Come by the bank Monday morning, and I'll have the papers ready to deliver to Mrs. Hopper. When you return, you'll get the rest of your pay."

Jeb squeezed the envelope. It felt bulky.

"That's only half now." Horace grinned.

Jeb excused himself, wanting to return to the party to see if Fern was still being pestered by Oz. As he exited the library, he shoved it into his pocket, where it lay heavy against the side of his leg. When he looked back up, he saw a flash of blonde hair disappearing around the corner. Blonde like Fern, who was always around to see but not fully understand. He knew she had seen him with the envelope in his hands.

Winona met him at the end of the hallway. He joined her for the rest of the evening. She was less complicated and laughed easily. He needed that tonight.

11

By Sunday, Ida May had caught a cold. Angel fixed a poultice for her chest and bundled her in quilts to help her sweat it out the pores. Ida May dragged herself to the breakfast table but only ate a few bites of stone-ground grits. Willie dressed and went out to bring in the bottle of milk Angel had left on the back porch. The night had chilled it well. He poured milk for Ida May and then a glass for himself.

Jeb felt Ida May's forehead. "You're cool, at least."

"Just sniffles. I'm going to church," she said.

"You ought to stay home," said Angel. "I'll stay with her, Jeb."

Ida May noisily ate several bites of grits, talking between swallows. "I want to go to church."

"I'll walk you back to bed, Ida May." Angel tried to pull out her chair.

"If she feels like going to church, then let her." Jeb drank the last cup of coffee. "I hope the church offering is up today. Mortgage is come due on the building, and the church bell is needing some new bolts. Almost came loose last Sunday when I yanked on it." He pulled his tie off the back of his chair and started knotting it around his neck.

"Who pays you, Jeb? Reverend Gracie or Banker Mills?" asked Willie.

Jeb saw the way Willie looked at him, sincere and not like he was pulling his leg.

"Gracie paid me a little from the offering plate when I preached last Sunday. And I've done a bit of work here and there around the church that he's paid me for. I never feel right about taking the money; I know the church doesn't have much. If the offering is too low, Gracie pays me in chickens or coffee. Only I haven't seen coffee in a while. But things will change soon." He could not mention the land offer to the Hoppers with Angel's big ears tuned to every word he said. "Why did you ask if Mills paid me?" Unsatisfied with his tie, he looked in the mirror and then yanked out the knot and started over.

"I heard you was in his back pocket now that you saved his bank," said Willie.

"Don't you ever say anything like that again, Willie Welby! Who said that to you anyway?" Jeb wanted to slap someone.

"Don't tell him, Willie! He'll kill him!" said Ida May.

"Shut up, Ida May!" Angel smacked her on the back.

"You don't have to tell me." Jeb yanked the knot of his tie loose yet again. "All we've had is trouble ever since Beck Hopper started planting his lies in your stubborn head, Angel!"

"I'm sick of everyone blaming Beck for everything!" Angel stormed out of the kitchen but yelled over her shoulder, "Next you'll be blaming him for this Depression!"

"When's this Depression going to be over anyway?" Willie saved the rest of the milk and put it in the icebox.

"Willie, I didn't see you studying for your memory verse," said Ida May. "Help me study mine."

"I studied. It's easier than anything. Get me the Bible."

"All of you go dress yourselves. I need a little quiet."

Jeb spent a few moments reading his Bible. When he realized he'd read the same sentence several times, he gave up. All he could think about was Beck Hopper spreading lies about him. If he handled this land offer wrong, Beck would spread more tales, and, it appeared, with Angel's help.

From the bedroom, Angel yelled, "I think I'll stay home. Ida May needs to sleep. I'll sit with her."

"I'm going to church!" Ida called out from the bedroom.

"Angel, just get dressed and let me worry with Ida May," said Jeb.

"I don't want to go!" Angel appeared again in the kitchen and collected the breakfast bowls from the table.

"What's wrong with you, Angel?" asked Jeb.

"Would the world come to an end if I missed a Sunday of Doris Jolly's organ playing?"

"You're going to church. What would I tell everyone?"

"I don't care what you tell them."

"Nothing's wrong with you, Angel. You're using your sister to get out of your duties."

"Since when is church my duty? It's not mine. It's yours!" Angel rinsed out the dishes and left them to soak.

Jeb placed his Bible on the kitchen table. "This is all about Beck Hopper, and you may as well admit it."

"That's what I mean, Jeb. I stay home one Sunday and you blame Beck."

"I saw him last night."

"So did Angel," said Willie, appearing in the kitchen.

"Shut up, Willie!" Angel shoved the chairs under the table.

"You ought to tell me things like that on your own, Angel. Beck wasn't alone at the Mills place. He ran with a pack of boys. They came begging at the Millses' back door."

"Don't talk about him like that, like he's a lowlife, Jeb."

"I tried to talk to him. He ran off after Mrs. Mills's maid gave him and those other boys some food. Are you telling me a bunch of boys was hanging around here last night with me gone?"

"I didn't see anybody else with him. He came alone," she said. "You're testy as a badger this morning. Someone must have give you a punch in the jaw, or why else would you be so hard to get along with?"

"Why don't you tell him everything, Angel? Jeb, Angel yelled at me and Ida May. Ida May went to the bedroom and stayed the rest of the night. But I wouldn't let her chase me off." Willie had grown a foot and now measured eye level to Angel. He would not back down to her.

"His daddy's been mean to him, and to all of them boys and his momma. I feel sorry for Beck, is all." Angel turned away from Willie. "Nobody cares about them. Nobody cares about anyone. Just their own."

Jeb did not tell her that it was he who had given his dinner to Beck. "Are you telling me that Beck only comes around here to beg?"

"Beck's not asked me for one thing. I just give him food because we have it to give."

"We don't have much to give." Jeb wondered if after Gracie left he'd be begging from the pulpit. Gracie had a way of telling the church members when extra was needed. He didn't think he had it in him to do that kind of thing. He looked in the pantry. Angel had left the door standing open. It was more full than it had been all year. With Mills's contribution after the fire, he had used it to store up food for the winter and fix the truck. And after buying the Welbys winter woolens, a garment each for school, one pair of shoes each, and some stockings, even that money had dwindled. The offer from Mills's business friends had come along at the perfect moment, just before Jeb imagined he would go begging himself, just like the Hoppers.

"Come on to church this morning, Angel. I'll pay a visit out to the Hoppers' place tomorrow. I'll see they have food and even some sugar and flour."

Angel waited with both hands still gripping the chair back. "You'll not embarrass them, though, will you?"

"I'd never do that." Jeb hoped the offer he took to Asa would help them out of their troubles. He still felt strange about the delivery, especially now that the Welbys figured him for a Horace Mills flunky.

Youngens never were good about understanding things over their heads.

❈

Onions left to winter over in the patch behind the church turned at the tops, dried like ropes. Jeb had dug every last potato and spread them under the cinderblock foundation. Sulfur pollinated the air near the back door, the yellow dusting of fingerprints still stippling the crawl space where he had backed out, sprinkling the red potatoes with preservative, weeks ago. He knelt and estimated a spread of fifty pounds of potatoes. He would take ten pounds to the Hoppers tomorrow.

Freda Honeysack was admiring a vase of chrysanthemums she had placed on the communion table. "I lost most of my flowers in last night's freeze." She shivered and pulled her coat closed. "These mums is all I had left when I got up this morning. Better to share them with the church. Another good freeze and they'll all be dead anyway."

Jeb looked around for her husband, Will, still distracted from wondering what had happened the night before between Beck and Angel. He would ask more questions later.

"Will's out front cutting that low limb from the birch tree. Said if he didn't do away with it, it would whack anyone walking up the church steps," she said.

Jeb found Will sawing the last threads of the limb. He bore down on the limb and it cracked and gave way.

"Watch you don't mess up your good shirt, Will. Freda will never let you hear the end of it."

"I wonder if anyone ever noticed this tree limb blocking the way?" asked Will.

"I noticed. I'm obliged to you."

"Seems like only a few folks notice work that needs to be done around here."

"I haven't done a good job of telling people things to do like Gracie's asked me to. That's the hardest thing for me to imagine—me asking others to do work around here."

"Don't blame yourself, Reverend. People haven't had the spare time to donate."

"I feel bad enough Gracie has asked me to pass the offering plate. I can't see myself asking people to give more than they got. Gracie has a way of doing it that seems right. I hope he and the kids are able to hang around a little while longer."

"I wonder if this Depression will ever lift? It's like someone pulled the switch on the country three years ago and left us in the dark ever since."

"Hard times don't ever make sense," said Jeb. "Maybe this old world has seen its end."

"They's some folks up around Hot Springs meeting in a tent revival and waiting for the Lord to come back. Could be any day, they say. You think they're right?"

"If he does, it'll get us out of our troubles. If he doesn't, we've got work to do. Like cut this limb out of the way, right, Will?" Jeb helped him carry the wood around to the back of the church.

❋

By the opening prayer not everyone had arrived. A few families crept in looking apologetic during the hymn singing. From the front pew, Jeb read the hymnal as though he did not know the words. But it gave him an excuse not to look around and see who else might disapprove of his taking Gracie's place. The last family to file in was Asa's wife and, to Jeb's surprise, Beck, along with two of his brothers. Angel walked in with them.

Jeb felt his ears redden. He had known by Angel's reaction that morning that she and Beck had planned to meet again while they were away at church. At least he could keep an eye on her during the service.

Willie held Ida May by the hand. Her face was sallow

and her body and limbs thinner than usual, a walking twig-girl. Fern bent to look at her. She led Ida May to her seat and gathered her into her lap. She had woven ribbons through Ida May's braids and made big bows at the tips.

Oz Mills slipped in late too. He tipped his hat to his uncle and then sidled in past two women to sit by Fern.

Jeb felt like he was walking into a tide, fighting to move ahead with a decision that made sense in his head but came out like something dragged into Church in the Dell from a mud hole.

Jeb turned to answer a hushed comment from Florence Bernard and saw Angel and Beck. Beck kept leaning and whispering into Angel's ear. Jeb wanted to come down the aisle and take that Hopper boy by his protruding ear. Angel returned the boy's attention, cupping her hand to her mouth to stifle a giggle. The two of them chatted with no mind to those seated around them. Beck's momma never seemed to notice the flirtation going on two sons away. She sat staring with her brows pressed together like the doors were closing on her life.

The service was sparsely attended, with the two front pews empty except for Jeb, who sat alone. His mind wandered from Gracie's preaching to Angel.

He was tiring of her meddling in all matters concerning the Hoppers. She made him feel as though the harder he paddled to make things right, the more zealously she worked to topple the load. To hear her tell it, he had failed the Hoppers, her, and the whole town of Nazareth. Her way of always wanting to make him out to be the heel would make a mess of things even were he already the Church in the Dell preacher. She had brought up heading for Little Rock more than once in the last week. Both times he had headed off her threats with thoughts of a summer visit.

Today it seemed that Little Rock might be a good idea sooner than summer.

❋

Horace Mills's Buick idled next to Jeb's truck. He had not said a word to Jeb about delivering the investors' offer out to the Hoppers' place. But Jeb could see him riffling through a stack of papers and watching Telulah Hopper walk alone to her husband's old truck.

"It's difficult enough rearing girls without their mother. But trying to train them up and keep up ministry duties is like having the whole world watching through your windows, Jeb." Jeb had finally divulged his fears about Angel to Gracie as the two of them shook hands with the last families from the front porch. "Take care, Jeb, that you don't make decisions about these children based on what others might think. It's not important. Best thing to do for girls is make them feel secure. My wife told me that before she passed away." Gracie passed a stick of gum off to Agatha, who ran out into the churchyard to join her sister. "I wonder if I made Ellen feel secure?"

"Every time I see Angel talking with Beck Hopper, I know what everyone is thinking," said Jeb.

"Only God knows what everyone is thinking."

"I don't know what I'm doing, Philemon, when it comes to that girl. Before you leave for Cincinnati, I should at least try and find Angel's momma. Even if she's not well, she'd do better with her own daughter than I've done."

"Reverend Nubey! Join us for dinner today," Winona

called from the rear seat of her daddy's car. "You too, Reverend Gracie."

"I've got to pay a visit to the Honeysacks. Freda's cooked up something special for the girls and Philip." Gracie balanced his weight between the porch railing and his cane and made his way down the steps. He thanked Winona and returned to the chat about Angel. Jeb followed him out into the churchyard where his girls sat in the minister's automobile with the doors open.

"I agreed to deliver an offer to the Hopper place. The Hopper boys pull a gun on anyone from the bank that steps on their land, so Mills asked me to do it."

"An offer?" asked Gracie.

"Some investment friends of his want to make Hopper an offer before the bank forecloses. Mills says it's a way to help Hopper out of his problems."

"The man that tried to burn down his bank? Strong gesture of forgiveness, isn't it?"

"Mills is all business, I know. But he seems to want to help out Asa's wife. I, for one, think it's a good idea."

"But they want you, a minister, to deliver the offer?"

"If you don't think I should, I won't."

"Mrs. Hopper sat in church this morning. If it's so helpful to her and her family, I wonder why Mills didn't hand her the offer this morning?"

"Maybe he thought it wouldn't be proper in church," said Jeb.

"All of them seem to be waiting on you, including that pretty daughter of Horace's. Be careful with Horace and Asa Hopper. You never know what you'll get when you run your hand down a hole in the ground." Gracie's eyes steeled for the first time all morning.

"You look tired, Reverend. I hope you get some rest this afternoon before church tonight."

He waved as the Gracie family drove away, then spied Ida May's red dress disappearing into the shadows of the woods behind the parsonage. Before he rounded up her and Willie and chased down Angel, he would question Mills again about the offer, just to be certain he was doing the right thing. They hadn't yet driven away. "Morning, Mr. Mills. Winona," he said.

"We've more food to eat than an army," said Winona. "Can you come?"

"I've got to work out something this afternoon with my oldest charge, Winona."

Winona gazed out and saw Angel and Beck talking under a poplar tree. "She's a handful, that one. I wouldn't blame you for wanting to take them all off to Little Rock or wherever their family is staying. They're not your worry, you know. You ought to get an award for all you've done for them so far."

Jeb blinked, surprised that Winona would say out loud what he had been pondering himself. "I wish I could join you for dinner," he said. He tipped his hat at Horace. "Telulah Hopper was at church this morning. It's good for her to be in church with those boys."

"In case you're wondering, we won't have the offer ready until tomorrow afternoon," said Horace. "Think you can drop by the bank then and take it out to her?"

"I hear the Hoppers are suffering from an empty pantry. I sure hope this will help them with their troubles," said Jeb.

Horace pulled out his billfold and handed Jeb a ten-dollar bill. "Buy them whatever they need."

"I'll tell them this is from you."

"Good, maybe she'll listen."

Jeb could hear Ida May shrieking. "I should go."

"Reverend Nubey, you're always so bound to those Welby children. You know the whole town would understand if you gave them up." Winona smiled at Jeb.

"Give them up to who?" asked Jeb.

"They aren't your problem. Let their family deal with them," she said.

"I admit Angel's a handful, but their daddy's nowhere to be found. Their momma's locked up in the sanatorium."

"They have an aunt, I hear," said Winona.

"Getting them back is not as easy as all that, Winona."

"If you need help getting those kids back where they belong, you let me know and I'll help out," Horace said.

"You ought to take advantage of Daddy while he's in a generous mood." Winona never took her eyes off Jeb.

"I'll keep that in mind." Jeb backed away from the Millses' car. "I'll see you tomorrow afternoon, Mr. Mills."

He turned and saw that Angel and Beck had disappeared. He could not figure out what interest Horace had in seeing the Welbys returned to their family. But he had seemed so genuinely concerned that Jeb felt it was a brotherly bearing of a burden. Or God's way of showing him the next leg of the journey.

Ida May ran out of the woods as though a bear chased after her. When she saw Jeb, she met him out of breath, clutching her doll around the throat. "Dub, you won't be happy with what I seen. But you can't tell I told you, neither."

"Calm yourself down, Littlest."

"That boy is kissing Angel on the mouth like Daddy kissed Momma sometime." She corrected herself. "Or maybe more like when he kissed Aunt Lana."

Jeb saw Telulah Hopper seated in her husband's truck. Her head was bowed over the steering wheel. She appeared to be crying.

12

You can't tell me what to do, Jeb Nubey! What if I love Beck Hopper? He can't help who his daddy is. His momma's too worried about her husband to be any good to Beck. He needs me," Angel argued from the front seat of the truck as Jeb drove them back to the Long shack.

"You don't know nothing about love, Angel. I admit I don't know anything about being your daddy, neither, but I do know a boy like that will get you into lots of trouble if you let him," said Jeb.

"What do you know about Beck, anyway, except what his daddy's done? He's the kindest boy I know, and he doesn't see any bad in me, neither." Angel's voice rose to a harsh pitch.

"We all got some bad in us, Angel. A boy like Beck paints you perfect and makes you feel better, but it doesn't make it true. People in love see the bad in one another and love each other anyway. Falling in love gets better every time you have to forgive one another."

"Like Miss Coulter's forgiven you?"

"Miss Coulter doesn't make any claims on loving me, Angel. And that boy's not in love with you. Is Beck making plans to find a good trade so that he can care for you? Has he saved any money so that he can take care of you?"

"No one is saving money, Jeb. Not these days. Everyone just makes do with what they have. So you can't lay that on Beck."

"I don't want you seeing Beck Hopper ever again, Angel."

"You can't tell me what I can and can't do, Jeb!"

He heaved a sigh. "You're right. That's why I can't do for you anymore."

"I don't know what you mean," she said, batting back tears.

"I think it's time that I take you to at least try and find your momma. I just can't do right by you, Willie, or Ida May. I've tried to treat you like you was my own, but all I see ahead for all of us is more trouble."

"You don't mean a word of it!"

"We'll pay a visit to your Aunt Kate first and then take you to your momma in the sanatorium or wherever she is. Who knows but what the sight of you will help her." Jeb parked the truck next to the shack beneath a sprawling oak and turned off the ignition. He yelled through the open truck door, "Willie, help your little sister out of the truck. Storm's blowing in, and Ida May's still got a cold." He glanced back at Angel. "You coming inside?"

"In a minute."

Angel sat alone in the truck for a long time.

❋

"Don't you know that if I could have joined Momma in Little Rock I would have already done it?" Angel stood looking through the window, wearing an apron a size too large for her thin body. The afternoon storm had darkened the house so she cleaned the floor by lantern light to save on the light bill. "I know I've not told you all that Aunt Kate's said, but she doesn't want us to come, Jeb." Angel set aside the broom to show Ida May how to pour the batter for corn pone. "She can't feed her own kids plus one cousin that got dropped off with her, and that was after her husband left her high and dry."

"Ida May, fetch that letter from your Aunt Kate. I want to know where she lives," said Jeb.

"If Momma wasn't so bad off, she'd have her to take care of too. But she says Momma will be in the hospital for a long time." Angel leaned over, elbows resting against the curling facade of the countertop, and covered her face with her hands. Her hair dropped around her eyes and she whimpered, "I miss her so bad."

"If your Aunt Kate at least saw you three, she might have a change of heart. You're old enough to help out with her children."

"Her four plus Willie and Ida May. Aunt Kate's oldest two boys favor lighting matches and setting fire to things—like the ends of girls' braids."

"I don't know how to take care of you, Angel."

"We're not so bad, are we, Jeb?"

"The last thing I want for you is to end up like me."

"You're not so bad, either, you know."

"Only by the grace of God I'm not."

"Us too, Jeb. We're all just where we are by God's grace."

"I want to see Momma, Angel." Willie had walked into the kitchen with a burlap sack of potatoes he had brought home from the church.

"She won't be like she was, Willie," said Angel.

"I want to know how she is, even if it's bad." Willie dropped the sack at her feet.

"Don't you want to at least know for yourself about your own momma, Angel?" asked Jeb.

Angel pushed aside the potato sack with her foot and then sat down at the kitchen table. She let out several shallow breaths before she said, "Jeb can drive me to Little Rock, Willie, but not with you two. Jeb, I'll see if Mellie Fogarty or one of the other ladies will watch these two while we're gone."

"She won't stop giving me baths," said Ida May. "I do like her cake baking, though."

"I'm going with you, Angel," said Willie, his irritation plainly showing in the way he drew up his mouth.

"Why can't we all go?" Ida May mewled.

"Willie won't keep up with his schoolwork on the road, and I will. I want to see Momma first, and then I'll send for you two. How would that work, Jeb?" Angel asked.

"Your sister's right, Willie. You'd get too behind in your schoolwork. If things work out with your Aunt Kate, I'll be back to get you both."

"I hate school," said Willie. "But if I'll be home soon, I'll tolerate it."

Angel slid the pan into the oven. "Little Rock's not home, Willie."

❋

A layer of frost coated the windows in a slick blur. The moon sat enthroned in a ringed halo with the sky a gray wash of black and green. The toads had fallen silent and an autumnal cold surrounded the Long shack, seeping into the cracks and whistling past the glass into the bedroom where the Welbys slept. Angel turned several times in her sleep, restless and mumbling things that Jeb could not decipher.

When he had confessed to Angel about taking her to Little Rock, he thought a calm would settle over the house. But instead, the idea of packing Angel off to see her unstable family had left Jeb with a sick feeling. He could not imagine what had possessed him to blurt out such an idea. When Horace and Winona had urged him to return the Welbys to their kin, it seemed reasonable—the best thing for Angel, Willie, and Ida May. But now driving them to Little Rock made Jeb feel like another person in their life had casually decided to throw them away.

He lay listening to the quiet breathing sounds that children make when they are content. Alone, the shack was nothing but nailed-together scraps with no one inside but him. With the children inside it, the old Long place was a warm womb, a happy place for dreaming and pondering. He would wake Angel at dawn and tell her that Little Rock was a bad idea.

The rain turned to sleet, pebbling off the glass and sill like a sack of buttons thrown at the house. Winter would soon settle upon Nazareth. Arkansas cold weather was hard on kids and old people that didn't have means. Jeb threw the extra blanket from his bed on top of Ida May. His mind kept restlessly cycling through his choices. Maybe, he thought, it might be best to wait another night before deciding what to do about Little Rock. Horace would pay him for delivering the land offer to the Hoppers. That money might hold them over for a week or two, and he could buy extra coal for the stove. He decided that he could sleep with that matter laid to rest. But he lay awake, thinking about Telulah Hopper and whether or not she would see the Mills offer as the best of news.

❄

Jeb had just enough gas to get the Welbys to school and then a trip to the bank to meet with Mills. He would ask Mills for the pay up front for the delivery and then gas up the truck. But first he had to meet Gracie at the church. As was Gracie's custom every Monday morning, they prayed for an hour.

The church was lit by the soft glow of candles. The rain had dwindled into a soft freckling of icy moisture on the lawn. Gracie told him that he was feeling better, and he did have a better flush around his eyes.

"If you can hold out for a week or so, I may drive Angel to Little Rock," Jeb finally told him. He knew that Gracie expected him to preach again the coming Sunday.

"Never felt better. I still got plenty of vinegar in me, so don't throw me on the trash heap just yet. You got the money for the gas and the trip?" Gracie asked.

"Mills has paid me half the money already to deliver the land offer to the Hoppers. Said he'd be making a nice contribution to the church too."

"I don't know what we'd do without his generosity," said Gracie. "But regarding this offer . . . do you know any particulars about what the Hoppers will get in return?"

Jeb had not asked Mills enough about the deal, he realized. "If Mrs. Hopper accepts the offer, or can talk Asa into accepting it, I figure it will help them out of some of their trouble. He's not doing his family any good in jail, that's for certain."

"Mills is shrewd, Jeb. I just don't want you mixed up in any scheme. Not that I'm accusing Ace Timber of scheming."

"I've had my doubts. But at this point it seems I'm nothing more than a bona fide delivery boy. No harm in that, is there, Reverend?" asked Jeb.

"That may have once been true when you were employed to pick cotton. But you'll soon be this woman's minister. You can't be anything else to her, or else when she sees you coming from now on, that's all she'll see— Jeb, the bank flunky. Others have tried to draw me into all kinds of schemes, only because I have a trust with my flock. I can't tell you how often opportunists try to gain access like that. When the people of Nazareth see me come through their door, I only want them to see Jesus coming—not the Bible salesman or the snake oil hawker."

Jeb heard the faint jingle of money from the delivery ebbing away. He had already spent five dollars of it on food from Honeysack's. "I don't know what else to do, Philemon. That old Long house is cold as ice and we've run completely out of coal. The lumbermill turned me down for a job and it looks like they're going to have more layoffs. The church is barely paying you, let alone paying me anything. I thought that if Mills felt like he could trust me, it would go better for the church. I've given him plenty of reason in the past to have his doubts about me."

"Jeb, I'll never make your decisions for you. I like Horace Mills too, and I appreciate your wanting to build a bridge of trust to him and his circle of influence. But he is, after all, a businessman. I'm sure he's told you that he's given a lot to Church in the Dell. But I've turned down anything from him that had strings attached. I want him to learn to give freely to God. Not with controversy tied to it. Nor with a promise of return on his giving. God wants the kind of giving that's attached only to a desire to obey him."

"You've turned down his money in the past?"

"It's a private matter, Jeb. But trust me when I tell you that Mills is in need of a heart change. He can't buy his way into heaven, but heaven knows he tries. I'm not telling you delivering the offer for pay is wrong, but it doesn't hurt to ask Mr. Mills how it will benefit the Hoppers. As for the church benefiting from the delivery, I'll have a lot of questions for Mills before I accept that kind of donation. I want to know if he expects the church to profit off the heads of its suffering people, namely the Hoppers."

Jeb knelt next to Gracie at the old altar built by the sweat of some forgotten set of hands. They stayed and prayed until the candles were all but extinguished.

❁

Gracie had taken two dollars from the week's offering and given it to Jeb before he left. "The church needs to get used to paying you something. And you should grow used to what the church pays you." He did not ask Jeb any more questions about what he had decided to do about the land offer delivery.

Driving home, Jeb saw Ivey Long stacking wood onto his wagon just beyond Marvelous Crossing Bridge.

Long looked weary, and Jeb had paid him for the month's rent already, so he stopped and asked him if he needed a hand. Ivey was grateful for the help. Jeb told the aging farmer to take a seat up front on the wagon while he finished stacking the cord of wood—all that would fit anyway. Ivey paid him two dollars for his help and offered the remaining wood to him.

Jeb loaded up the wood, enough to give them warmth for two nights. It felt good to have a little money in his pocket for once, and firewood to boot. Whatever Gracie had meant by getting used to what the church paid him, he was thankful for the extra. In the end, it was all from God.

❊

At the Nazareth Bank and Trust, all broken glass had been restored with new and every window and door given a fresh coat of paint. All signs of damage from the riot were gone, as though all traces of the farmers' dissension had been erased and forgotten. Even the sign over the bank had been cleaned and restored so that no trace of the hurled rotten fruit and tomatoes remained.

Jeb had visited almost every storekeeper in town looking for work. He finally found his way to the bank and paced back and forth out front until a clerk returning from lunch saw him and said, "You looking for Mr. Mills, Reverend?"

Jeb nodded and followed the clerk into the bank. Mills's secretary immediately left her desk and returned to tell Jeb, "Mr. Mills has been expecting you all day, Reverend Nubey. He'll see you right now."

Mills was not at his desk. He had moved to one of the

two chairs facing his desk and he now offered Jeb the other chair.

"I'm sorry for the delay, Mr. Mills," said Jeb. "But I've been thinking about Mrs. Hopper, and I think I'd like to know how your offer will benefit this family."

"You're aware I can't divulge the details of the offer to an outside party. It wouldn't be ethical." Mills kept his answers short.

"I told Reverend Gracie about delivering these papers to the Hoppers and he cautioned me about being sure that I knew what I was doing." Jeb waited for Mills to react in anger, but the banker remained cool.

"Did you also tell my good friend the Reverend that Church in the Dell will benefit from your assistance?"

"He knows. But he wants to be sure that the church doesn't benefit from the suffering of its people."

"This town has suffered, Reverend Nubey, from this intolerable man's rage and violent behavior. The Hoppers have cost not just the bank, but the town of Nazareth, hundreds of dollars in repairs. This offer to the Hoppers will not only help them out of their bankruptcy, but will send them on their way to another town. They can start over. The Hopper name is ruined here in Nazareth. You know how hard it is to rebuild a good name, Reverend."

"Mr. Mills, I have a lot of respect for you." Jeb hesitated, knowing how Mills occasionally interjected his convict past. "But you should know that I have changed not just on the outside, but inside. That is more important than a reputation."

"Ministers are reliant on reputations, Reverend. I don't know if your dear mentor has gotten that across to you, but you can't run a church without the respect of the people—or without resources."

"Jesus told us we'd lose our reputations for him. He gave up his reputation for the sake of spreading his truth. He placed charity above reputation, Mr. Mills. I have to do likewise."

"So you're turning down my offer for the sake of protecting a criminal? That doesn't sound like good Christian reasoning. Your own charge, Angel, is being drawn into this family's circle and most likely will fall into their troubles as well. You're risking everything for the sake of a family that will not appreciate your protection of them."

Mills stood and offered his hand to Jeb. "No hard feelings, Reverend. But my investors are not going to extend this offer for long. I'll find another to deliver it, if these men decide it's worth the bother. You came to return the pay I gave you, I suppose?"

Jeb pulled out the cash that he had stuffed into his pocket. "It's only a dollar short. I'll have that back to you in a day or two."

"Call it square, Reverend." Horace checked his watch.

"What about the money you asked me to give to the Hoppers?"

Mills straightened. "You still have it?"

Jeb pulled it out of his other pocket.

Horace took it. "I'll take care of that. I have another meeting, if you'll excuse me." He walked Jeb to the door but did not follow him out.

Jeb stood outside on the walk, feeling like a wretch with not a penny left to his name.

13

Angel sat next to Beck in his daddy's truck. He had driven them to Hot Springs and stopped outside a diner just short of running out of gas.

"Let's stop here and get us a Coke, girl," he said.

Angel liked the way he called her "girl," like she was his. "Beck, you got money, don't you? For gas, I mean."

"I got twenty dollars. Let's go." He climbed out and walked inside like he expected Angel to follow him.

Angel knew school was now out, and Jeb would realize that she was gone. She tried to imagine the look on his face when Willie told him she had not walked them home from school.

By the time she sat next to Beck on a stool, he had already ordered a soda and a side of peach pie. "You mind if I ask where you got twenty dollars, Beck?"

"Worked for it—most of it, anyway. The rest I got selling my old man's shotgun."

"Your daddy will kill you for that."

"By the time he gets out of jail, I'll be long gone and living my own life. He'd use it for no good anyway. I'm tired of him living any way he wants and telling me to do differently. 'Get out of bed, Beck. Don't get in trouble. Do your chores and don't be a taker.' That's all he's ever been—a taker. He ain't nothin' but a big ol' hypocrite. Everyone in Nazareth hates us because of him."

"They don't hate you, Beck," said Angel. She picked up the fork and shared his pie.

"Sure they hate me. I'm Asa Hopper's boy. That's like saying I'm the son of the devil in Nazareth."

"I don't hate you."

"You and me, we're going to have us a good life together. I'll work to buy my own filling station and fix cars. You'll be home raising our kids. Everyone knows you're the best cook."

"Beck, we haven't talked about any of that. You shouldn't say things like that without asking me."

"What else do girls do? Raise babies and take care of their man." He paid the waitress for a second Coke.

"I'd like to be a momma some day. After I make my first million."

"Women don't make millions, Angel. Not too many men, either. How you going to get rich on making babies?"

Beck had not made Angel mad until now. "I'm not a babymaker, Beck! I'm going to learn something about business. Maybe I could own my own diner like this place. Then I'd own a few more and have diners all up and down the highway. I'd never want for food again with a deal like that."

"You got to have money to make money."

"It's the same as owning your own filling station, Beck."

"I work to make my way, save up every dime I make, and then buy out some old boy that's ready to give up pumping gas. They's no one that can work on engines good as me. I'll take some dusty old filling station and grow my own gold mine. You know how to cook. I guess you can run your own diner some day. But you got to have a plan."

"Did you plan to take off today with me?"

"'Course I did. I been saving my money so you and me could get out of that hellhole and make us a life."

"Twenty dollars won't last long."

"I'm getting a job, Angel. I told you I'm a good mechanic."

"Down the road I saw a motel."

"We got to save money. I brought stuff we can bed down with. We can sleep under the stars, girl."

His fast solutions were making Angel agitated. "Beck, it's too cold to sleep outdoors. You telling me you think I'm going to sleep in this truck?"

"I'll keep you warm, girl."

"Beck, this ain't what I had in mind. I want to go home."

"Trust me, Angel. You said you love me. You going to quit on me now?"

"Here's your Coke, son. That'll be a nickel." The waitress held out her hand.

Beck paid her the nickel and said, "Where's the closest filling station, ma'am?"

She directed him up the road.

"Let's go, Angel. I'll show you I can take care of you."

❅

Twilight was falling across town, graying the old buildings like blue ash. Jeb had dropped hungry Ida May off with Willie to eat and wait for him while he searched for Angel. He drove twice down Stanton Lane and circled back into town and out to the Hopper place, where he found Telulah seated on the porch steps, red eyed. She answered almost entirely in nods. Her oldest son, Clark, paced on the porch mumbling about finding Beck and stringing him up like a fish. An old Model-T parked next to the house was their only other transportation. It sat out of gas and in need of an engine part.

Jeb promised to return the next day with groceries. He did not know how he would pay for the gas to return. He would have to share from his own pantry, but he was certain that Gracie would offer food to the Hoppers if he asked. He left Telulah sitting in a stupor. She laid her head against her knees and cried.

When Jeb passed Marvelous Crossing, he saw Fern's Chevy coupe slow and then stop in the middle of the bridge. Her face suggested her anxiety. She rolled down her window to say to Jeb, "The Ketcherside boys said they heard that Beck and Angel had run off to marry. I don't know if you can count on the Ketchersides telling the truth. Arnell Ketcherside and Angel don't get along."

"Any idea where they may have run off to?"

"Roe Ketcherside says that one of the Lundy girls heard Angel talking about living in Hot Springs. That doesn't mean they've gone to Hot Springs."

"I should have taken her to Little Rock. She's not going to listen to me. I'm not her daddy and she knows it."

"Angel respects you, Jeb. Don't blame yourself for her running away. She's confused is all. So many of the boys pick fights with Angel. I don't know what it is about her that makes them treat her like another boy. She doesn't flirt like other girls her age, and she misreads the boys when one of them is trying to get her attention. She takes that kind of attention all wrong, like they're against her when they're really just trying to get her to talk to them. I understand; I was never a flirt. It makes sense that she would become so enamored with the first boy to pay attention to her."

"I don't see any other choice. I'll have to drive to Hot Springs. I'll see if Josie will take in the kids for a night and get them to school in the morning."

"You got gas money?" she asked.

Jeb checked his gauge. What with driving all over town and out to the Hoppers, the truck tank sat near to empty. He let out a breath and slumped back against the seat.

"Take this," she said, leaning out the window.

Jeb could not look her in the eye to take the money.

"You don't have time to argue." She tossed it through his window and the bills scattered across his lap. "I'll take Willie and Ida May to Josie's if you want. If she can't take them in, I'll take them home with me. Maybe I'll do that anyway. You can head for Hot Springs right now. Those two'll have to stop somewhere for the night. I doubt they have much money."

"Beck sold his daddy's shotgun. What money they do have they'll not want to spend on gas. I don't know how to thank you, Fern."

"Find Angel, is all."

❊

The drought had turned the road to Hot Springs into a winding ribbon of dust. Jeb stopped at a roadside store and filling station to buy a cold drink, gas up, and ask

around about Angel and Beck. The store owner considered Jeb's description of the Hopper truck but then shook
his head. "Not many folks has passed by h'yere today.
Seems like I'd remember a truck like that."

For a quarter, the store owner's wife bagged up a ham
sandwich for Jeb to take on the road.

Jeb could not beat the night to Hot Springs. Dark fell
before he reached the city limits road sign. He pulled into
the lot of a diner called Sam-Anne's. The lights inside
made the place look green, as though filled with pond
water. Every bar stool was taken, and the noisy clientele
made Jeb's head pound. He saw nothing of the Hopper
truck. A waitress with a slight limp yelled at the cook like
she was married to him. Then she saw Jeb on the last
stool at the counter's end. "Help you, mister?"

"Cup of coffee. I could use some help too." Jeb accepted a small pitcher of cream from her.

"Not too good at help. My husband's more helpful
than me, he says." She filled Jeb's cup perfectly—to the
rim, but stopping short of spilling over.

"I'm looking for . . ." He thought of how he should de-
scribe Angel. ". . . my daughter. She's run off with a boy
her age. Both too young to be out on their own."

"Girl about yay tall?" She held up her hand and made
a knifing motion next to her cheek. "Boy, skinny, with
close-set eyes, dark haired and needs a haircut? Smokes
like a chimney."

Her words nearly took Jeb's breath away. "You saw
them? That sounds like Angel and Beck."

"I heard her call him Beck. Sounded like they was getting into a fight. I don't think she was happy with the
evening accommodations. They's spendin' the night in

that old truck, from what I overheard. Your daughter's a mite spoiled to better sleeping quarters, I gathered." She sliced a piece of pie—rhubarb—and gave it to Jeb. "You got plenty of worry on your hands with your girl run off. Pie's on the house."

Jeb said, "How long ago were they here?"

"Mel, you remember that couple of kids that came through. Split a piece of pie?" she asked her husband.

He checked the rusting clock above the grill. "I'd say they been gone a good half hour. 'Peared not to have had much scratch between the two of them, if you want to know the truth."

"Did they drive into Hot Springs?" Jeb pushed aside his coffee.

"Only one way in. That way." The waitress pointed east. "But the girl did say she didn't want to drive much farther. If I were to take a guess, I'd say they took a side road about a quarter mile up the road and turned in for the night. Up around Carpenter Dam. Kids use that road for parking. Let me box up that pie for you. No need to let it go to waste."

Jeb took the Sam-Anne's box with him and headed east. The night was as black as a cave.

❀

Beck had more on his mind than sleeping. He parked off the road just short of the main road leading to an enormous dam project. They had passed only one other parked car—two teens sparking near Lake Catherine. Beck sat staring at the lake, one arm stretched along the top of the truck seat. He wound a strand of Angel's hair around a stubby finger. "We're finally on our own, girl."

"On our own and tired. I should have brought a pillow. I'll sleep against this door, I guess, and we can share the blanket."

"Come lay against me, Angel. I'll keep you warm."

Angel shifted and then turned the opposite direction and leaned her head against Beck's shoulder. His bony frame felt frail and he had a musty smell like her Uncle Dew after he'd spent the evening tinkering under the hood of their old Ford.

Beck whispered something that she could not understand. His hands came up under her blouse.

"Beck, I thought we were going to sleep." She tried to move his hands, but he was strong from all the heavy lifting he had done for his daddy.

"We can do anything we want, don't you see? No one's around to tell you what to do, Angel. You're my girl now. I love you, Angel. Let's get to what we came here for."

"Beck, stop it! I'm tired and I can't think straight. Let's get some sleep and not rush things."

Beck ran his fingers across the top of her skirt. "How you undo one of these things anyway. In the back?"

Angel tried to pull away, but he pulled her next to him.

"Girls like you are the most fun, my brother says. A bit on the feisty side, but fun in the sack. My brother Clark told me all about how to do it, so you don't have to worry."

Angel jerked forward, but too fast. Her forehead banged against the side window glass. She howled and then felt her eyes tear. "Beck, I'm hurt. Now quit, or I'll get out and walk home."

Beck sat back in disgust. "I don't get you at all, Angel. You came all this way with me and now you're backing out. You're afraid. I knew you'd be like this. You sure talk tough for a girl in your situation."

"What do you mean by my situation?"

"Your family threw you out. You're living with a man you hardly know. Seems like you'd appreciate what I'm trying to do for you."

Angel's stomach rumbled. The half a slice of pie had only made her more hungry. "So I have to be desperate to run off with the likes of you, is that what you're telling me, Beck?" She straightened her skirt and pulled it down below her knees.

"I'm not better off than you myself. I know I'm no catch. Look at me. My daddy's in jail. Momma's about to lose the land and house her daddy left to her. All my brothers are no good, and I'm turning out just like them. I'm skinny and ignorant as a stump. I never knew what you saw in me to begin with."

"Beck, I didn't mean to say you're a good-for-nothing. You're not like your brothers, and your daddy's just fallen on hard times like everyone else. I see a lot of good in you. You're kind and you make me laugh." She allowed her hand to fall on top of his. He clasped his around hers and it felt warm. "You're handsome and you're not ignorant. You just need to work on your reading some."

He laughed and squeezed her hand.

Angel rolled down the window to let in some air. "You kiss good. At least I think you do. You're the first boy I ever kissed."

"You're the second girl I kissed, but the best. I can't tell you who else, or she'd lie and say it wasn't so. But I know the truth."

"Why would she lie?"

"Because I'm a Hopper and her daddy'd kill her if he knew."

"Not Sarah Dolittle?"

Beck's stunned demeanor told Angel she had guessed right. "You're right. Her daddy would kill her and you too."

"I hate being poor. I mean, I could take not having all the things the Dolittles have because they have a dairy farm that's brought in enough to get by on. But I hate being looked down on."

"Ain't no different being a sharecropper's daughter. It's worse. Nobody thinks you're worth a dime unless your daddy owns land and drives a big car. People around Snow Hill all had it bad, though. Lots of families were bad off as we was. But my momma, she took it all inside of her like nobody I ever knew. It affected her mind. You ain't no good to nobody without a good mind. People say things about you and call you crazy. Momma wasn't crazy. She was just looking for a place inside of her that didn't hurt so bad. She started staying holed up in that old shack and quit seeing her friends. She wouldn't go to church with my grandma no more. Granny had to take us kids and she couldn't drive and daddy wouldn't drive us to church. It was a waste of gas. So we rode in Granny's wagon every Sunday to church. Her horse was older than her, and some Sundays I thought that old mare would just keel over. But it outlived her."

"Ivey Long still drives to church in a wagon. Nobody looks down on him."

"It's different when you want to drive a wagon than when you don't have a choice. Ivey thinks automobiles are of the devil. He saves his money for other things besides gas. The Longs never do without. Beck, I'm tired of being hungry. I'm not spoiled. I just want to have a minute in the day that I can have to myself without worry. Not have bill collectors coming around threatening to shut off the lights. I don't need no big house or a big car."

"I want to give you those things, Angel."

Her stomach rumbled again. But she leaned forward and kissed Beck. She wanted to love him and needed to love him. She would settle for the need to love.

Beck wrapped his arms around her—awkward boy arms that had never loved any more than she had but wanted to know love. It was an empty kiss and it disappointed her. She had expected more from it, as though it would flood her soul with love just by the very act. Or rearrange the hurt inside her. But she felt like the old Long house had looked with nothing inside it.

The sound of feet against pebbles had them both sitting straight up in panic. Angel saw the troubled face through the open window.

"Jeb!"

14

Angel shivered, even though she had wrapped her trembling limbs in the blanket from Beck's truck. Jeb had said almost nothing at all to her after he had thrown open the door and marched Angel back to his truck. They had driven less than a mile when he pulled into the same diner where the waitress had told him about seeing Angel and Beck. The parking lot had thinned of cars except for a few farmers who had stayed late for coffee and smokes. "Did he feed you supper?" Jeb asked, even though he already knew exactly what she and Beck had shared.

"I'm hungry," was all she could say.

The waitress put out her cigarette when she saw Jeb walking Angel through the front door. "Hello again," she said to Angel. "Have a seat, sweetie, and I'll fix you a plate of corn bread and beans. Have we still got some of that chicken stew?" she asked her husband.

The cook checked the pot on the stove and ladled out a full bowl of stew. The waitress set it in front of Angel and returned with the beans and corn bread. "Coffee for you, mister?" she asked Jeb.

"Nice and strong. I have to keep awake for the drive

home," he said. "Bring the girl a glass of cold milk, if you don't mind."

Angel shoved a spoonful of stewed meat into her mouth. Then she let out a sigh of relief.

"How long you think you can go without food?" he asked.

"Wouldn't be the first time," she answered.

As she ate, the waitress commented about the ring around the moon and how cold it had gotten and then how the night had grown cold enough to bring sleet. She filled Jeb's coffee cup a second time and then returned to the counter's end to gab with the farmers.

"Angel, you drive your momma crazy too?"

"Don't ever say that!"

He sighed and rephrased his question. "I didn't mean to say it like that. What I mean is did you get into this kind of trouble when you lived in Snow Hill?"

Angel drank nearly half the glass of milk in several rapid gulps. She wiped her face with a napkin and said, "I wasn't trying to get into trouble. I was trying to find my way out of it."

"Beck Hopper can't take care of you, Angel. He up and sold his daddy's gun and took what little cash his momma had stowed away for their meals this week. Nothing he took with him was his to call his own. It was only a matter of time until he resorted to taking from others along the way. He's a messed-up kid. I don't want you getting mixed up with him. With the two of you running out of food and gas in a few days, you think he'd find work at his age when all the qualified men are taking up all the low-man jobs?"

"I don't know what I thought. Maybe I had the idea of a better life in my head and it seemed to me I ought to just try and grab hold of it. I'm tired of waiting for a better day to come. What's wrong with right now?"

"God doesn't always give us what we want right now. He likes to teach us things. We humans are a hardheaded lot. I guess he figures that we learn best under the weight of hard times and waiting."

"You talk more about God now than you used to. I'm kind of sick of it, truth be told."

"I'm not meaning to preach at you. But if you'd learn a thing or two, you'd not throw yourself at boys like Beck. Gracie says that we're all like baby birds sitting in the nest with our beaks wide open. You know how Ida May wants to know everything we know, but if we try and explain the situation, she gets even madder? Her mind can't get all that we want to give her yet. God does that for us. He's so big and deep that he has to feed us a little of his wisdom at a time so we can grasp it. It's like trying to fit an elephant into a funnel. But if we can learn just a bit of what he's trying to tell us through the hard times, maybe some day we'll understand him better."

"It's too late for a Sunday school lesson. I'm tired, Jeb."

"I'm up, you're up."

"I'd like some more corn bread, please," Angel told the waitress.

"You never answered my question about whether or not you fell into this much trouble at home."

"I never ran away. My momma, she did the running away."

"So you're following her lead."

"She never should have left us. Daddy only got messed up with that neighbor lady, Lana, because he was missing Momma."

"Not to hear Willie tell it."

"Willie doesn't know nothing!"

"Willie says your momma left when she found out about Lana."

"He's mixed up about her, that's all."

"Angel, I only know that I've done all I can do with you. I can't make you mind me or do right by me or your brother and sister. You never want to listen to me unless I'm agreeing with all you say. No telling what would have happened back at that lake if I hadn't walked up. You're too young to play house."

"Tell it to the whole diner, Jeb."

"Tomorrow, I'm telling Gracie that I can't preach this coming Sunday. I'm taking you to Little Rock and helping you find your momma and Aunt Kate."

"You're getting rid of me. I saw it coming. If you wanted to do that, you should have let me run off with Beck."

"I wouldn't let my own daughter run off with the likes of Beck Hopper. I wouldn't let you, either."

"We can't afford the gas for Little Rock."

"Horace Mills offered me some delivery work. It pays good, or so he says." He mulled over what he was fixing to say. "I'm taking him up on it in the morning. After he pays me, we're leaving town. You best get up in the morning and pack up all your things."

"What about Willie and Ida May?"

"Miss Coulter is watching them. Between her and Mellie Fogarty, they'll keep those two in good company."

"Aunt Kate won't take me in." Angel's voice trembled. "She can't." She wiped both eyes and pushed aside her empty plate.

Jeb always ached when Angel cried. It was a seldom-seen occurrence, but when she cried it tore out his heart. "She has to try. I won't leave you until you feel settled in, and maybe we'll find work for you."

"You'd give up preaching this week for me?"

"We don't have a choice, do we?"

The waitress lifted the coffeepot above Jeb's cup, but he covered it with one hand. "No more for me, ma'am."

"More milk for you?" she asked Angel, but Angel shook her head. "I guess you're glad to have your belly full again," she said to Angel.

"It was good eats, ma'am."

"You ought to thank your daddy for coming after you," she said.

"He's not my daddy."

The waitress turned and stared at Jeb, her brows lifted in a puzzled stare.

"Here's your money. I thank you for your help, ma'am." Jeb paid out and headed for the door. He felt the woman's eyes on him all the way out to the parking lot. When Angel climbed into the truck he said, "I wish I could have been your daddy. Maybe things would have turned out differently for you and your brother and sister. One day I'd like to deserve a daughter like you."

He imagined for a moment a child at his knee, a little Fern with cotton silk hair and a mind of her own. The dream seemed to unfold inside him, his life and Fern's joining and making another. They looked happy, like the fashionable husbands and wives in the moving pictures. "Maybe her life will be better than ours, Angel. But we haven't been so bad together, you and me."

"What kind of delivery, Jeb?"

"Bank business. Nothing you'd care to know about."

He prayed he had not made Horace too angry to re-consider the delivery job. Gracie would simply have to understand.

❋

The waitress had been right about the weather. November sleet covered every inch of ground and leaf before the sun had a chance to bloom across the Ouachita ridge. Jeb made Angel ride with him to the bank. He dropped by the school to tell Willie and Ida May that Angel had made it home safely the night before. Fern was standing out in the schoolyard ringing the bell. He did not see Beck's truck anywhere. He asked Angel to wait in the truck and met Fern on the lawn.

"Looks like your little bird's flown home," she said.

"It was a long night. I found them parked along Carpenter Dam in Hot Springs."

"Beck hasn't shown up for school. Did you see him home too?" she asked.

"I was too afraid I'd kill him. I told him to go home and give what money he had back to his momma." When he dropped by the Hopper place with the bank offer, he would ask Telulah if Beck had gotten home all right. But he would not worry over the boy any more than he would worry over Asa or the rest of his rowdy family.

"Willie and Ida May must have had full trust in you. They slept like lambs."

"Fern, I need to ask you something. I'm taking Angel to Little Rock. I can't see that I have a choice in the matter."

"You want me to keep them? I'm happy to do it. Are you sure you want to take Angel away? She's a handful, but she has been so happy with you."

"I'm not her real daddy, and she knows it. One thing I can't do is hope that she'll ever pay me that kind of respect."

"How long you think you'll be gone?"

"Long enough to help her get settled. Once we talk their Aunt Kate into making room for them, I'll come back for Willie and Ida May. Will you tell them for me?"

Fern agreed. "I guess we won't get to hear your preaching this Sunday."

"I haven't told Reverend Gracie. I'll tell him on my way out of town."

"God's laid a lot on you since you first came into town, Jeb Nubey. I've never seen a man work so hard as you to prove yourself to a town."

"God's patient with me. Maybe the townspeople of Nazareth will be too." He did not read outright approval in her eyes, but she did seem to soften. She always softened when it came to the Welbys. "I'll leave a message for you and the kids at Honeysack's if I can find a place to make a call in Little Rock."

"I'll check in with Will and Freda, then, in a day or two," she said.

Before Jeb had closed the truck door, Fern waved and called out, "Take care." He smiled at her, and for once it did not seem to make her angry with him.

Fern watched him drive all the way down Long's Pond Road.

❊

Angel waited out in the truck while he dropped into the bank to ask if Mr. Mills would see him. He had waited only a moment when Mills's secretary invited him to step into the banker's office.

Mills did not stand when Jeb walked in. He held a parcel tied with twine. He pitched it onto his desk in the direction of Jeb. "Ready to deliver our offer, Reverend?"

"You act as if you've been waiting for me, Mr. Mills."

"I'll admit I waited longer than I'd thought to. Take a seat. You look awful."

"I had to go off looking for Angel. Drove half the night. You were right about the Hoppers, Mr. Mills. Asa's boy ran off with Angel. It liked to have scared me to death. I don't know what would have happened if I hadn't found her when I did."

"Bad news, those Hoppers. One thing I have is a good judge of character. You should go home after you deliver the documents and get some rest."

"I'm driving Angel to Little Rock. That's why I'm here. I need the work to pay for the gas."

"Winona and I told you we'd take care of you getting those kids back to their momma. Winona thinks the world of you, although I sometimes question her judgment in men." He laughed and held up both hands. "No offense. Just joshing."

"Miss Mills is a fine young woman. You've done well by her, Mr. Mills. Do I need to wait for Mrs. Hopper to read these documents or do I simply hand them to her?"

"Good question, Reverend." Mills opened the parcel. "You get Mrs. Hopper to sign on the dotted line of this document today, and I'll see you're paid a bonus." He shoved another envelope across the table, a long bulky package that looked like the one he used to pay his tithe to the church. "Here's your first installment, the money you gave back to me. Also, here's the money I told you to give to Mrs. Hopper for food. I'm not a louse, you know." He laid down the ten dollars.

Jeb tried not to show the discomfort he felt when he thought of asking Telulah to sign Mills's offer. "I'm grateful you saved the job for me, Mr. Mills. I could not get the Welbys back to their momma without it."

"This envelope has your wages. This extra here is for your trip." Horace pulled out several bills and held them out to Jeb.

"I don't know what to say."

"You're building a life for yourself, Reverend. Most people sit around letting life happen to them, like all they have to do is lift their feet. That's why so many folk are getting swept away by this Depression. But I've been watching you. You studied under Gracie; you took in kids that didn't belong to you and gave them a home. Now you're cutting loose the things that are holding you back from what you want. You plan for life, and life treats you sweetly—mark my words. Nazareth's Church in the Dell's been needing a man like you behind our pulpit. Gracie's getting old and can't see beyond tomorrow. You can take this little church places and build a life for yourself, Depression or not."

Mills made Jeb sound as though he were fulfilling a part of his own master plan for life. Truth be told, he had not thought much beyond tomorrow. He took the money and the parcel and left the bank.

"Where we going to make this delivery, Jeb?" Angel eyed the parcel in his lap as they motored down Main. "Is it far? Sounds like an easy job to me."

"Will and Freda have been needing some chores done

down around the store. I won't be long. I'll leave you in Freda's care until I get back."

"Chores for Mrs. Honeysack?"

"I don't want to hear any of your lip, Angel."

"You don't trust me anymore," Angel said.

"Like I said, I won't be long."

"You're not going to tell me where you're going. I can't go with you. Something's up. Mr. Mills ask you to do something shady?"

"Not at all. Me and shady don't dance together no more. You know better than that."

Jeb left her at the front door of Honeysack's Grocery. As far as he was concerned, Angel had been in too much of his business all along. She would never have to know about the bank's business with the Hoppers.

He felt a strange uneasiness seep inside him again, even though he had accepted honest work. He decided that his guilty past would always follow him around and cause him to question even the best of motives. He turned left on Pine at Sewell and headed the truck toward the ten-mile stretch of road leading out to the Hopper farm. Today would be a day of good news for Telulah Hopper. That made him an ambassador in God's eyes.

❋

The Hopper place, like a speck of gravy on the horizon, might have been a place overlooked, like no one had lived in the shanty for years. It had fallen into the kind of disrepair seen only in a remote foreign hellhole. Past crop rows defined the landscape in strips of brown, shriveled twigs. Soiled cottony tufts clung to the brittle cotton plant shafts as meaningless survivors of the dust storms that had blown across Oklahoma and into Arkansas without remorse.

Two hounds loped alongside the truck until Jeb brought it to a stop right in front of the portals of the unpainted shack. He reached outside the truck and patted both dogs until they rolled onto their backs for more attention, then stepped out of the truck expecting to see Clark Hopper's rifle pointed straight into his face. Instead, Telulah appeared in the doorway with a bowl of apples. She welcomed Jeb with a smile, exactly as Mills had said she would.

"Mrs. Hopper, did your boy Beck make it home last night?"

"I liked to have whupped him for running off with your girl like that, Reverend. He's been raised to know better. I got him out in the barn with his brother Clark cleaning out the bad hay. Seems like we don't have much use for the barn now, but it's best to keep those boys busy." She laughed, but her eyes retained a spark of regret. "Keeps them out of trouble."

Whenever she said her *s*'s or *th*'s her tongue protruded through the gap left by her missing front teeth.

Jeb picked up the parcel and toted it along with him.

"I'm glad to know Angel made it home safe. I don't figure Beck would have been gone long. He can't make a living on his own yet. He wants to larn how to fix automobiles like his brother Clark, but Clark says he cain't do nothin' yet but dream about it. I guess that's a blessing in disguise, as they say."

"Mrs. Hopper, I'm here with some business I want to tell you about," said Jeb. He felt uneasy again.

"Business with me? What business would I have with

the church?" she asked. She laid the bowl of pared apples on the porch railing.

"Not church business. Bank business."

Her smile faded. "You workin' for Mills now too, I guess."

"I wouldn't be out here if I didn't think it would help you all out. I know Asa can't help you from jail. You can't make a living without your husband around."

Telulah seated herself on the front steps as though all of the breath inside her had been let out. She rested her face on one hand, her eyes lifted like the two hounds' heads that panted at her side.

"If you don't mind, open this up and see what the bank has to offer you."

"Offer me? Eviction notice is all they want to offer me, Reverend." She held up her hands, refusing to take the parcel. "Asa'd skin me alive for taking those papers."

Jeb prayed that Mills had not played him for the fool just to deliver foreclosure papers. "You can trust me, Mrs. Hopper."

Telulah took the parcel, pulled out the documents, turned them over, and said, "I never could read too well. Asa used to read the newspaper to me at night and laughed at me when I couldn't say my words right."

"I'd be glad to read it to you, ma'am." Jeb took the documents from her and quickly read the opening lines. "Mr. Mills and his investment group, Ace Timber, would like to buy your land, it says."

"Buy it? Why, we can't grow nothing on it now but dust." She laughed.

Jeb read farther down until he came to the actual offer.

When he read her the price she said, "Why, it's worth twice that even without the crops."

"Would you rather I take this offer to Mr. Hopper at the jailhouse?" he asked.

"I'll let Clark and Beck tell him. Best he doesn't hear it from me."

"But you inherited the land from your family. Is that right, Mrs. Hopper?"

"Free and clear, until Asa took out a loan on it to build up the farm and that barn. Would have been better to build me a new house than make me keep living in this old shack."

"So the land is in your name?" Jeb asked.

She studied the matter and then said, "Come to think of it, it is."

"Would you like for me to take your part of the signed papers to Mr. Mills for you, or would you rather wait?"

"How much money was that he offered me again?" She took the offer and read it as best she could. "Where do I sign?"

Jeb had a fountain pen in the truck. But his feet felt stuck to the ground. "Mrs. Hopper, maybe it's best you wait. You're in an awful way with Asa in jail. You should have more time to think."

"Half the money's better than none at all, Reverend. Can you fetch me something to write with?"

Jeb went out to the truck to do as she asked. But the elation that he had expected never settled on him.

15

The way of an orphan, Angel decided, brought disaster and people into her life that kept trying to fix her. She felt kind of like a Philco radio with a broken knob. Everyone that came her way would try to bang something useful out of her, fidgeting with her wires and tubes and then finally unplugging her altogether. It seemed like everyone wanted her to sing or say something funny or clever, but when she did not feel like performing, they called her broken and sold her away like used goods to the next person who felt like they could help her rise above her clutter of broken wires and tubes.

Her heart had been exchanged like the wares of a peddler, some unseen guy that threw her into his cart hoping to find a home for her soon. Was it God? Didn't God know her parts were jimmied and tinkered with and no longer the original apparatus?

Jeb had driven her away from town with no good-bye to Willie or Ida May, as though he were sweeping her dusty soul away from Nazareth's pristine threshold. Angel felt as barren and leafless as the oaks that lined the dusty road to Little Rock.

"I forgot my pillow," she said.

Jeb inhaled slowly as the truck climbed the next hill and then said nothing at all.

"I said, I forgot my pillow. Aunt Kate would want me to bring my own things for sleeping."

"If Aunt Kate is shy a pillow, we'll buy you one at the Woolworth's. Little Rock's a big place. Pillows are the least of our worries."

"You could have at least let me tell Willie and Ida May I was leaving. What if Ida May can't go to sleep tonight?"

"Fern says she slept good at her place. Besides, it didn't bother you none last night to go off and leave Ida May."

"I wasn't thinking about Ida May. That was wrong. I know that now." Angel was not sure if what she said was true, but she knew that it should be and that Jeb would want to hear her repent. If she recanted enough her running off, he might soften so that she could at least bear to ride with him all the way to Little Rock. As it was, the air was thick between them and made Angel feel even more rejected.

"Angel, this is not about apologies. It's bigger than a single mess-up on your part. You've got to know you're finally home, and maybe when you know that, you'll settle down and stop throwing away your life on people that don't mean anything to you."

"You keep telling me what I'm supposed to be feeling and who means what to me. Beck Hopper meant something to me." Even when she said it, the words seemed to ricochet off her hollow insides like dropped acorns.

"Beck Hopper was your way of saying, 'I want a place to belong. I want someone to belong to me.'"

"You don't know me like you think you do." Angel slid down in the seat, tired of the scenery.

"I need gas. Here's a filling station. Looks like they set up a stand outside." Several itinerant workers gathered around a barn-red stand on wheels buying sack lunches. "Maybe they'll sell us a sandwich. If you get out, put on your coat. It's gotten cold."

The sign across the road from the gas station read "Prescott City Limits." A man and his girl sold harmonicas from a roadside stand. While Jeb pumped gas, Angel talked with the girl. She handed Angel a harmonica. Angel blew on it until it made a wheezing squeal. "How much for one of these?"

"I'll toss in the box it come in," said the man. "For a harmonica and a box, two bits."

Angel only had a few pennies left from her pie the day before with Beck.

"Go ask your daddy. See if he'll let you buy one," said the girl. She was a heavy girl who did not seem to have missed any meals lately. "We had to sell our store, and these harmonicas is all that we have left to sell. Momma was fixin' to pitch them."

"I'll play you a tune," said the man. He picked up his own harmonica and played a song. The men in line next to the stand glanced up and then focused mundanely again on the sandwich line. "Give ye somethin' to play with as you're drivin' along. Bernice plays with hers better than her dolls."

"I don't think I can get a whole song out of it. But I'll see if I can give you the two bits for it." Angel crossed the road, holding the harmonica with both hands and making steam with her breath.

Jeb came out of the filling station and strode across the lot to stand in the sack lunch line. Blackberries and thorn bushes grew up at both ends of the stand as though it had parked in that place for a long time. "What you got in your hands, Biggest?"

"Harmonica. I need twenty-five cents."

"I don't want no squawking harmonica in my truck. Drive's been peaceful so far. No need to add noise."

"I'll learn fast. Please, Jeb."

"I know how it'll be. Youngens get bored and do nothing but make noise with those things. Take it back across the road where you got it. Do you want a ham sandwich or not?"

"If you'll let me have it, I won't eat nothing. I won't cost you a dime this whole trip. Please let me have it, Jeb. I never had an instrument like you have, not in Snow Hill or anywhere." Her daddy, Lemuel, had hated anything, he said, that took food out of the mouths of his youngens.

"You're going to pass up dinner for the sake of that stupid harmonica?"

"They only have a few left. It's like an orphan."

"How much did you say that orphan costs?"

"Two bits, but that includes the box."

"Your Aunt Kate won't want to add noise to the mix of extra mouths to feed."

"Aunt Kate likes music. I heard her say it once." That was a lie. Aunt Kate had never visited them in Snow Hill. But it was a chance she was willing to take.

Jeb handed her the change. "You're still eating if I have to shove it down your throat, Angel Welby."

Angel threw herself against Jeb. "You are the best, Jeb!" She pulled the harmonica out and tried to sound a note. All she got was another hissing wheeze. She ran across the road and handed the money to the girl. Two Mexican men in line laughed and said something to one another in Spanish.

"I'll play it when you play the banjo!" Angel yelled across the road at Jeb.

Jeb turned away, more out of sorts with the long sandwich line than with Angel. She ran and clambered back into the truck, running the instrument back and forth against her lips, trying to mimic the sounds the man had played.

Jeb finally got the sandwich order and climbed in, handed Angel her food, and headed down the rural route. A half mile into the countryside, he rolled down his window. "Either I'm cooped up listening to that thing, or I'm freezing. You're tossing it out the window."

"I'll put it back in the box." Angel did that and then tucked the box protectively under the seat.

"Angel, you beat all. Other girls want a kitten or a puppy. You're the only girl I ever knew that wanted a harmonica."

"I think I'm going to be a natural. You're not the only one in this outfit with talent."

"There's a sign. Not too many hours from Little Rock now."

"You think my momma will want to see me?" she asked.

"Of course," he said without much in the way of expression. Then he said more gently, "She's pining for you, Angel. No telling how many times she's looked out her window and prayed you'd come see her."

"Maybe she is. Aunt Kate never says one way or

another." She thought for a moment. "I wonder sometimes what made Momma like she is. When I was little,
she wasn't like this at all—crazy, I mean. She used to
take me for walks down by the pond that froze over every
winter. She'd tell me, 'Don't walk out on that ice, Angel.
It won't hold up,' and stuff like that to let me know she
was watching over me."

"I remember things about my momma too. But
nothing stays the same. The way this Depression's gone,
it's a wonder everybody hasn't been locked up in the
loony bin."

"Don't call it that, Jeb."

"Hospital, then."

"Your momma only have two kids?" asked Angel.

"Me and Charlie. And we have a younger sister. My
mother died when I was small. Certain things remind me
of her. Cherry blossoms, the smell of preserves bubbling
on the stove on a hot summer day. I remember certain
things about her too, like the way she fell quiet when my
daddy's brother, Festus, came around."

"She must not have liked him."

"No one liked Festus. Not even daddy. But my
momma had a way of calming Festus that set the whole
house at ease. She had that way about her. She called it
'God inside.' "

"Your daddy ever talk much about God?"

"Daddy thinks about God like he thinks about fixing
the roof. If it's raining, it's too wet to fix the roof. If it's
dry, the roof don't need fixing."

"When's the last time you saw him?"

"Charlie says Daddy needs to get it straight that I'm
preaching now and that I'll be a preacher from here on

out. He thinks I'm doing this to get through the Depression, or to bide my time until something better comes along."

"So your family don't want nothing to do with you, neither."

"I wouldn't put it like that. Daddy never could get close to Charlie or me. Probably not Momma, either. He likes it best when I'm doing something he disapproves of. Then he can say that I'm the one that never comes around, like I'm neglecting family duties, not him. Truth is he never stops to think he could come off that porch and go see Charlie or me. Daddy never knew why he pushed people out of his life. He never stopped to wonder why. I used to be like that."

"What is a good family anyway? When I see families at church—mommas looking after their kids or grandmas sitting with their grand-youngens—I feel like I've missed out on the whole show of life. It makes me wonder why some people get their own ticket to a good family while I get a big fat nothing."

"Families aren't perfect, Angel. Not a one of them."

"They're together, Jeb. Not like us. We've been piecing us together a family since we met, you and me, our own little patchwork quilt—here's the Jeb square, next to the Angel square, sewed right next to the corner of Willie and Ida May."

Angel amazed Jeb sometimes with her perception.

"Too bad we keep coming unraveled," she said.

❄

The afternoon did not turn colder as all the old-timers had predicted. It was November and the sun came out to play.

The sky above the road to Little Rock danced with cottony clouds alongside the blue as though a timbrel kept rhythm for the heavens. A field was colored by the faces of fifty men out baling hay as fast as their backs would allow.

The truck cab heated up, making Angel peel off her coat, a donation from Florence Bernard.

The closer they drew to Little Rock, the more Angel's insides churned like an overfilled butter urn. She tried to imagine Aunt Kate's face when she showed up on her doorstep unannounced.

"Downtown Arkadelphia's a busy place," said Jeb, noting the parked cars all up and down the road, parked in front of the shops that advertised everything from laundry soap to foot cream.

"Arkadelphia. Seems like I heard of this town," said Angel. "Is it close to Little Rock?"

"Still a piece from Little Rock. Say, there's a soda shop. How 'bout we stop for ice cream?"

"You got the money for ice cream, Jeb?"

Jeb parked in front of the town soda shop and drugstore. He pulled out a wad of bills and counted them.

"If I didn't know better, I'd say you been bootleggin'."

"Mr. Mills paid me for the work, that's all."

Angel watched him step out of the truck without saying anything.

Jeb opened the door and walked into the drugstore. He had already ordered two ice creams by the time she joined him on a bar stool. "Since I'm almost out of your hair, you may as well tell me what kind of work you're doing for Horace Mills. No harm in telling me. It's not like I could tell anyone, or that you're doing anything that should be kept secret. Right?"

"Asa Hopper's turned his boys on the bank people that have tried to deliver bank papers to them. Mills hired me to do the work so the job could be settled peaceably. I'm a preacher, ain't I? 'Blessed are the peacemakers.'"

"He gave you a wad of cash that big just so he could foreclose on the Hoppers? You got paid for doing his dirty work, that's what," said Angel. She set down her spoon as though she had no use for the ice cream.

"Not foreclosure papers. The bank's buying out the Hoppers to help them out of their worries. You going to eat that ice cream, or you want me to eat it?"

"Beck says his granddaddy paid for that place years ago. How much Mills give them for that place? It must be more than a hundred acres or so. You telling me the Hoppers are in the money now?"

"So to speak." Jeb did not know how to answer Angel.

"Beck must not have known about it."

"No way for the boy to know about it. Until today, the Hoppers didn't know."

"Wonder what the bank will do with that land? Windstorms have about blown everything away that was useful. At least that's what Beck told me."

"Not my business. But Mills wanted the Hoppers to be on their way. Asa tried to burn down the whole town, Angel. It's best they move on, find a new life."

"So you're helping Mills give them the boot, skedaddle, hit the road, Jack." Angel's sarcasm drew the eye of the soda jerk.

"Until Beck talked you into running off, I'll admit I wasn't keen on the idea. To tell you the truth, I can't wait for that boy to leave and never come back to Nazareth."

"That's what Jesus told people—one wrong move and you're out!"

"Eat your ice cream."

"It's not the kind I like. Ice cream shouldn't be green."

Jeb caught the eye of the soda jerk. "Could you please find something large enough to fill this girl's mouth?"

"Chocolate, please," said Angel.

"I'll check on the Hoppers when I get back, Angel. I don't want them to starve any more than you do."

"It's not their bellies that troubles me, Jeb. It's that land. They've just lost their souls to Horace Mills. They'll never be the same. Horace will up and sell off their place to someone that don't know how Beck was born out by that stream when his momma was setting bait for trout. Or how Asa proposed to Telulah under that apple tree near the barn. Bankers like Mills never stop to think that you can't put a price on a body's history."

Jeb shoved aside his ice-cream dish. Angel slid it next to hers and mixed his remaining vanilla scoop with her chocolate.

"You always have to be so smart, Angel?"

"I like it mixed. Not just vanilla alone."

16

Jeb meandered down stretches of country roadways dotted by sharecropper shanties until the main city roadways came smooth beneath the truck tires on Old 67. The country road gave way to Asher Avenue. Little Rock had long strings of streetlights connecting uninterrupted along the main arteries, including all the way down where Asher eventually connected with Main Street and city stores like M. M. Cohn, Blass, Scotts, Woolworth's, McLellan, and the S & H Store. Montgomery Ward and Pfeifer Brothers' Department Store lined the downtown streets with winter temptations. But Jeb pulled the truck up to the corner of Asher and Mablevale Pike where a man leaned against a light pole sipping coffee and catching up on the front page of the *Gazette*. Jeb slowed alongside the curb and asked, "We're trying to find Elm Street. Have you heard of it?"

The man drew up his mouth and said, "You might try pulling into the filling station on this here block. I'm kind of new, but I know of a feller by the name of Gunny runs the place, and he's lived h'yere all his life."

"We could use another tank of gas anyway; thank you kindly," Jeb answered.

The corner station had several customers waiting for fill-ups or tire checks and several Fords in the two oil-slathered bays. Jeb picked up a Little Rock map and let the attendant help him find Elm, which was only three blocks away. He bought two moon pies and handed one to Angel.

"I need you to help me find your Aunt Kate. When I pull onto Elm, you tell me when you see the address 2019. We should be there shortly."

Angel had not said much in the last half hour.

"I think your aunt will be happy to see you."

"I hope so. All I know about her is what Momma used to tell us. She hasn't seen me since I was young. According to the map, we're to turn left on this next street. That's Elm. The way I figure it, not too many kids in our family have had good come to them. The only ones still with their momma is Aunt Kate's kids. I got an aunt and uncle down in Louisiana that parted their ways, and we never heard what happened to any of them. Somehow Aunt Kate's done good by her own, and they manage to get by. Maybe this is the best thing for me and Willie and Ida May."

"Little Rock's a bigger place. Maybe the schools are good too. Not that you could do better than Fern Coulter for a teacher."

"She's not my teacher this year, but she's done well by Willie and Ida May."

"I couldn't get the boy to read, but she's got him reading and writing too."

"I'd hate to see Miss Coulter marry off with that Oz Mills, though. He'd never love her like you do. He loves his own self too much to love someone else the right way." She pointed to a street sign. "That looked like 2019, Jeb. Turn around." She got anxious for the first time.

Jeb stopped the truck and backed into a drive between two old houses.

Angel smoothed her hair around her face and pulled a ribbon out of her sack. She tied it several ways on her head before finally making a thin pink bow that fell sideways across the crown of her head.

Jeb read the name painted across the mailbox, "Butto," and then pulled into the yard. Heavy oaks as old as Arkansas shaded the yards darkly and left shallow ice puddles unmelted. Angel pulled out the envelope again and read the street address several times, counting down the houses until she finally said, "This is it. Butto is my aunt's last name. I see cousins all over the porch. They look big, don't they?"

Jeb slowed the truck and turned off the ignition in front of the house. It had a fairly strong roof compared to some of the neighboring houses—a green shingle overhang dotted with sweet-gum balls from the slanting tree.

Two of the children on the porch ran inside. Their shoes flapped against the wooden porch, which heaved even under their frail weight. One big girl with a baby on her hip stared at them.

A woman appeared with the two youngest boys hiding their faces in her tattered skirt. She peered out at Angel, who by now had stepped onto the lawn.

"We're looking for Kate Butto," said Jeb.

"I'm her," said the woman.

"Aunt Kate, it's me. Angel." Her voice sounded more shy than usual, not like the boisterous schoolgirl marching the halls of Stanton School.

Angel's aunt drew in her bottom lip and sighed. "Angel Welby? Thorne's Angel?" She held out her arms.

Angel ran to her and threw her arms around her.

"I liked not to have known you, girl," said Kate.

Jeb blew out a breath. "Afternoon, ma'am. I'm Jeb Nubey."

"After all these years, I still can't believe it's you," said Kate. She looked up at Jeb. She gave him the once-over and then an approving nod in Angel's direction. "You're the preacher that's been carin' for Thorne's kids, ain't you?" she asked.

"The best I know how," said Jeb.

"You passin' through town?" asked Kate.

"Mind if we step inside?" Jeb noticed several neighbor women had gathered on the lawn across the street to gawk.

"Effie, go and make some coffee. Matthew, you go clean off the couch for company." Kate led them into the house.

The children followed Angel, curious about their big-girl cousin. As they walked into the small parlor, Effie cleared the couch by gathering old newspaper into wads.

"The boys sleep here on this sofa every night, so we have to clean things up when company comes."

Jeb saw bedding strewn down the hallway and around the kitchen doorway. "How many children you keep now?" he asked.

"I got my four and two of my sister's kids. I landed a job as a nurse's aide up at the nervous hospital. It's right up the street on Elm and Markham. It keeps the lights on and beans in the pantry. That, and I can keep an eye on my sister." She yelled at the boys to back away from Jeb.

"I didn't know you worked there, Aunt Kate."

"I do, for a fact, Angel. But she made me promise not to tell you or your brother and sister. If she knew you was here, it would upset her to no end. She has her good moments from time to time and remembers her time with you all. On those days, the doctor says it seems like she could be released at any moment. Then she has a bad day. But you don't need to hear about such things, Angel. Kids ought not to hear and see the things they do in this day and age, anyway."

"I want to see her, Aunt Kate."

"That hospital's not a place for kids, Angel. People with nervous disease, they don't have no control over theyselves. Some days I see things that stands my hair on end. I got some good stories, though."

"Mrs. Butto, is there any way that I could see Mrs. Welby? On Angel's behalf, that is, so that the girl can finally get some answers about her momma. She's come a long way."

"Reverend, can we talk outside?" she asked.

"Jeb, I think I'm old enough to hear this stuff. It's my momma you're talking about." Angel blinked back a tear.

"Mrs. Butto, please speak freely. Angel is fourteen now."

"You ain't a baby no more, that's for sure," said Kate, eyeing Angel's height.

"Maybe if all these kids could leave, that would be best," said Angel.

Kate shooed the children out the door and then closed it behind them. "Drat if it hasn't turned cold." She sat next to Angel on the sofa. "You know what it means to restrain someone?"

Angel stiffened.

"Your Aunt Kate's talking about straitjackets and such, Angel." Jeb decided it was a mistake to allow Angel to stay in the room. "Maybe it's best we talk later."

"I'm not stupid. I've heard of straitjackets."

"They had to restrain your momma this morning, Angel. Today is not a good day. Tomorrow might be better. Are the two of you planning on staying in town tonight?"

"Aunt Kate, I've come to—"

"See her momma. And we'll stay until she gets to see her," said Jeb. "Is there a good cheap room we can rent for the night?"

"Next block down. Follow me outside and I'll point directly to it." Kate took them out onto the porch and pointed to a green house with a sign on the door. "Name's Till Churchill. Good woman. Not the best housekeeper, but she's got two rooms open, and you all can stay for a few dollars. I'll have to walk you down and tell her I know you. She don't rent to strangers. I'd offer you a place here, but we don't have an inch of space left. Even my oldest girl, Effie, has had to turn the attic into a place to sleep. She got herself pregnant some time ago, and now she's got a kid to feed."

"How old is Effie?" Jeb asked.

"Fourteen, same as Angel."

❄

Till's boardinghouse rose two stories above a tangle of ivy and neglected climbing roses that had long lost their bloom. Jeb and Angel toted in one satchel and a paper bag of their belongings.

Till walked with a man's cane and did not look as

though she spent much time upright. The frown lines around her mouth gave her a permanent scowl, so when her voice sounded genteel it surprised them.

"These two rooms is all I have left. The others are taken up by boarders. Some work up at the hospital like Kate, others downtown. I once took in men only, but hard times have me taking in whoever has the money to pay. I hope you don't mind, Reverend."

"These rooms will be fine." Jeb placed Angel's sack inside one door.

"My leg's gone bad on me, so I can't clean things up like I used to do." She opened the door all the way. The coverlet on the bed was sagging onto the floor on one side. Cottony webs undulated from the ceiling, caught in the draft between the door and the ill-fitted windowsill.

Jeb paid the woman and asked if he could pay for an evening meal for the both of them.

"Breakfast is included in the price. For two dollars you can have your dinner thrown in to boot," said Till.

Jeb ordered two meals and thanked her again. Till ambled down the staircase to tend to supper.

"We didn't tell Aunt Kate the truth about me, Jeb."

"We didn't lie, either, Angel. I think we should give her time to get used to you being around."

"Effie's in the attic with a kid in her bed. On top of that, Aunt Kate has a kid sleeping on every square inch of floor, Jeb."

"I'll admit it's not the best of circumstances."

"I want to go to Momma tonight, Jeb. The thought of her bound up in some hospital makes me sick to think of it."

"We should listen to Kate, Angel. She works in that

place. Let's have some supper and get some sleep.
Tomorrow will bring a better day."

❋

The sign out on the lawn read "Arkansas State Hospital
for Nervous Diseases."

Jeb yawned as he drove up the drive. He had awakened several times in the night, tossing around on the
lumpy mattress. He'd found Angel sitting up against the
wall in her room, listening, she had said, to scratching
noises behind the boards. Till had cooked a breakfast of
cornmeal mash and butter for a morning party of eight,
including Jeb and Angel. Two of the borders had been
women and the rest men who complained of the Red
Cross lines running out of bread.

When he and Angel stepped onto the lawn, Angel said,
"They call what Momma's got 'nervous disease' here. I
guess that sounds better than 'the crazy house.' Effie said
we can find Aunt Kate just down the hallway where the
nurses' aides get their orders for the morning."

"That cousin of yours—Effie—she's got herself in
trouble, Angel. I figure some boy like Beck Hopper
sweet-talked her. Now she's in a fix."

"There you go, bringing Beck into matters. I'm here,
ain't I? Beck's a million miles away, Jeb. You can't blame
him for everything." Angel led the way into the hospital.

A janitor, dark as obsidian, mopped the corridor left of
the entry, his sinewy arms reaching out with large circu-
lar sweeps. He acknowledged Jeb and Angel with a
glance and then returned to his floor duties.

The other corridor was lined with mattresses. A patient
lay curled up on each mattress, fetal shaped. At the end of

the hallway, some of the mattresses had been stacked eight high.

"They must be low on rooms," said Jeb.

"I hope they didn't toss Momma out here like some cat." Angel walked quickly past a woman who cried like a baby and reached out for her.

The hospital corridor smelled of bleach and urine. Angel cupped her hand over her nose. "Momma always kept a clean house. She can't like it here."

Two nurses stoked a cigarette outside a duty station. On either side of the doorway a row of doctors' photographs dating back twenty years stared at Jeb like science specimens in a cage.

"You need something?" asked one of the nurses.

"My aunt. Kate Butto," said Angel before Jeb had a chance to answer.

Kate appeared in the doorway. She sipped coffee from a stained cup. "You're up bright and early."

"Is it a good time to come?" asked Jeb.

"She slept good last night," said the nurse, who wore a nametag that read, "Flora Jones."

"This is my niece, Angel Welby," Kate introduced Angel. "And her minister, Reverend Nubey."

The nurse named Flora smiled at Jeb. "Is there a Mrs. Nubey?"

"Don't start up, Flora," said Kate. "Reverend, you and Angel foller me." Kate pushed a cart of food trays, leading them past the colony of mattress sleepers and the janitor, who had set up a "Wet Floor" sign. "I have to drop off breakfast for A Corridor, then we can go see your momma, Angel."

She stuck her head into a room. "Lola, Sarah, Ginger?

I got breakfast for you." She slid out a tray and carried it into the room.

Jeb and Angel watched from the doorway.

Two of the women took the bowls from Kate's tray as though they had not eaten in days. But the other, skinny and childlike in her oversized hospital gown, drew up her knees atop the hospital bed and turned her back to Kate.

"Don't be difficult, Ginger. I'm too tired to fool with you this morning." Kate held out the bowl of grits and bread to the patient. "Doctor says if you don't eat this morning, they'll take you for shock treatments. If they do, you can't blame me. I warned you."

The woman turned slowly and accepted the bowl.

Kate had just turned her back to speak to Jeb when the patient named Ginger drew back her bowl.

"Kate, look out!" Jeb yelled. He shoved Angel out of the doorway.

The bowl of grits splattered across Kate's back. Kate turned around, mad as bees.

"Are you all right?" Jeb asked.

"Ginger, you know you'll be in trouble for this!" Kate wiped grits from the back of her arm.

Ginger began to wail, openmouthed. It made the other two ladies laugh. They fell across the bed giggling. Kate stood watching them laughing like hyenas. Then she broke out laughing herself. Ginger stopped her cries and began to lick stray grits off her fingers.

Behind Angel, Jeb heard a soft moan. He turned and saw a woman staring at them. She had appeared out of the blue. Her soft visage, with dark eyes as round as Ida May's, was sad and deep as a mountain cavern.

Angel followed Jeb's gaze with her own. Her face

paled. "Momma? Momma?" She stepped toward her mother.

Thorne Welby gripped her hospital gown and pulled it together in the front. She backed away and whimpered.

"It's me, Angel, Momma."

Kate stepped out into the hall still dripping with Ginger's grits. "Thorne, don't act like that. I told you it was time you saw family again besides me."

Thorne turned and ran up B Corrider into a room, slamming the door behind her.

A soft sob spilled out of Angel.

Jeb took her in his arms. "You'll get through this, Biggest. Don't cry. I'll walk you to see your momma."

17

J eb sat out on a concrete bench on the hospital lawn. He had taken his Bible out of the truck and read the same Scripture four times before closing it up altogether. The notes from the sermon that he would not be preaching this Sunday marked a chapter in the book of Psalms. Gracie had spoken well of it. It would have to wait.

Kate had had to exercise her influence over Thorne, coaxing her out from under a quilt and out into the room, where she agreed to sit without crying. Angel had tried to put up a good front, but Jeb saw the shine in her eyes that said a small dam was about to break loose. He had excused himself, believing Thorne might behave better if his unfamiliar presence disappeared from her nervous sight.

He felt a tug inside him pulling first one way and then another. If he drove away and left the Welbys alone to work things out, he would not be able to rid himself of the image of Angel sitting helplessly next to her mother, unable to coax even a familiar word from her. He imagined her sitting under the counsel of cousin Effie, who would explain the way of the world to her—do whatever any old degenerate tells you and end up worn out like an old dress and tossed up in the attic like a secondhand relic. Effie's gaggle of friends would no doubt bring with them a philosophy of paper-thin magnitude.

He did not doubt Kate's love for her family—just her naiveté regarding a kid's defenselessness to the world's elements. She was like a mother bear asleep at the mouth of the cave, oblivious to the snakes that slithered past toward her cubs.

Two women sat on a blanket several yards from Jeb. They passed magazines back and forth until they began to argue over one. They jerked it back and forth in a tug-of-war before finally falling to the ground rolling, wrestling, and shrieking. An attendant ran from under a tree where he had stopped to take a smoke and untangled the patients.

Jeb thought of the pulpit that waited for him back in Nazareth. With the pastorate, although meager of pay, came the growing respect of the people. Even the boys around Snooker's Pool Hall who once would not give him the time of day had started waving at him from inside the doorway. His days as a con had started to fade from minds like the evening sky fading on Marvelous Crossing. Best of all, the contempt that had radiated from Fern Coulter for the past year had softened, at least by a small measure, the last few times they had spoken. Fern seemed moved by his intervention in Angel's waywardness.

And then there was Winona Mills, whose interest was growing like a cloud of perch beneath the surface of the lake. She was a fine mess of fish, the way he figured things.

He shook his head at the thoughts stirring inside him. After a year of study and commitment to the gospel, the old Nubey was rising from the dead again. He breathed a prayer and tucked his Bible under his arm. It was time to see if Angel had found any signs of life coming from the general direction of her mother.

❄

Dr. Eisenbein, an import from Germany, examined Thorne while Angel waited outside the door. Angel could hear her mother responding, sometimes with a "yes" or "no" and sometimes not at all. Aunt Kate had remained at Thorne's side only because of her employee status on the floor. When she once ventured to ask Eisenbein a simple question, he barked at her like a guard dog. Kate had fallen silent for the remainder of the examination.

Angel paced back and forth on the green-and-once-white tiles. She hated the smell of the place and the noises heard up and down the hallways. She decided the only other place a person could hear such things was in hell itself. One woman lying out of sight on one of the mattresses down the hallway had a counting habit; she counted everything out loud—the wheels on the medicine carts, the floor tiles, and the buttons on a passing nurse's uniform.

Angel found a window to stand by and watched the passing cars beyond the gate and the birds flying overhead. She decided that no matter how bad things got, she would never end up in a sanatorium. It came to her that her mother had given up on hope. That was what had ended her.

Kate stepped outside the door and called for Angel.

Angel came into the room and found that the German doctor had left. Her mother huddled in a heap on the bed. She looked at Angel, and Angel could not decipher what she was thinking.

"I hate that man. He's like talking to the devil. Maybe he is the devil," said Kate.

"Aunt Kate, if you don't mind, I'd like to talk to Momma."

"Sweet child, you can talk to her now." Kate opened the window shades.

"Just the two of us, I mean."

Kate put her hand to her mouth, apologetic. She quietly left the room. Angel settled herself in a chair, took a deep breath, and said, "Momma, Willie's so big now, you wouldn't believe. Ida May's in school and is learning to read. Jeb helps her to read. Did I tell you I taught Jeb to read? Can you believe it? Me?"

Thorne gripped the neck of her gown with both hands as though she feared it might fall off if she didn't. She spoke suddenly, her face intent on Angel. "Yesterday mornin', first thing, I heard a commotion like I never heard before. They had piled up those old mattresses out there for the ones that they don't have room fer. They was draggin' out one mattress after another, and then I saw her."

"Her who, Momma?" Angel was surprised her momma had finally decided to talk.

"One of the patients. They had dragged her and thrown her in the mattress pile and left her there for too long. No one even noticed her on the mattress when they was stacking them up. I asked one of the nurses if she was all right. But that old nurse just laughed and looked at me like I was a fool for asking. She told me that patient had died. What folks think is funny around here's not funny anywhere else. That's the thing about it."

"Momma, we have to tell someone."

"Won't do any good. I figure they'll toss me on the pile one day like I was nothing more than an old blanket. I'll be the funny story of the week."

"Listen to you, Momma. You can talk."

"'Course I can talk. I'm crazy, not mute." Thorne drew up her thin legs and slid them beneath the blanket. Then she smiled when Angel laughed at what she said.

"I miss you more than you can know. If I was to tell you all we've been through since Daddy sent us away with Lana, you'd not believe it." Angel settled herself on the end of the bed.

Thorne sat up, took two gulping breaths, and said, "Kate didn't tell me that. That he sent you with that Lana. Your daddy knew she wasn't no 'count. But he didn't care about all that. Long's he had someone to keep him warm at night, that's all he cared about."

"What did the doctor say? Can you leave soon?"

"Lana told him lies about me, things your daddy knew to be lies. But he kept seeing her. I tried to shoot her one night, pick her off like a crow on a fence post. But they stopped me."

Uncle Dew had apparently not told Angel everything the morning they took Momma away.

Angel started to ask her again when she might be able to leave. But the distant horizon of the hills drew her mother's attention. She stopped answering any of Angel's questions. The fingers on her right hand began to tremble. "Ssshhh!" She made several shushing noises like a child cowering under a bed waiting for an intruder to leave.

Kate came into the room. "She hasn't eaten since yes-terday. That's the problem. She won't feed herself. It's enough to make me want to yell at her. But that don't do no good, neither. When she gets upset, she won't eat for days. Some of the nurses took to forcing food down her, but I wouldn't have it. So they let me feed her as long as she stays calm." Kate leaned toward her with her hands resting on her knees and said, "Thorne, time for breakfast."

Angel left the room, unwilling to see her mother fed like Ida May when she was sick. Her mother had not asked one thing about her or Willie or even her youngest girl. Angel saw Jeb standing at the end of the hallway. "I want to leave," she said.

Jeb opened the door for her. He did not ask her any questions on the way to the truck or even after they mo-tored away. Instead he drove past Kate's and straight to the boardinghouse. In a quiet way, without looking at her, he told her to go inside and get her things. "We're going back to Nazareth," was all that he said.

❊

The horizon was soda-cracker white, salted with clouds but no rain. The truck blew a tire and Jeb had no choice but to wait for the closest filling station to open the next morning. They walked for two miles and then hitched a ride to an old motel just outside Malvern. The owner of the place told Jeb that for two dollars he would give them a ride back to the truck. Jeb paid him for the night. He gave Angel the only bed in the room, a rickety iron bed made for one sleeper, and made his own bed on the floor out of two thin blankets given to him by the motel keeper's wife. A picture of a farm silo had been hung on a nail on one wall, but Angel peeked behind it to find it was hiding a hole in the plaster. She combed the braids out of her hair and went into the washroom to dress for the night. After she had slipped under the covers and turned off the lamp next to her bed, Jeb said aloud in the darkness, "You doing all right?"

"Tired. Kind of mad, I guess. I lie awake every night thinking about my momma. I always imagined we were thinking about each other." She fell quiet.

"When she laid eyes on you the first time, I saw something. You've changed a lot, I would imagine, since the last time she saw you. But once she knew it was you, Angel, an old spark kindled inside of her."

"I wish I could have been born into a normal family. Like one of those girls back in Nazareth. One where everybody has the same last name in the family and all the kids have the same momma and daddy. They all bow for prayer at dinner and then the momma feeds them all they want to eat."

"Lots of pain in most of the families in Nazareth. Same in Little Rock, Texarkana, and all the way up in Oklahoma. Not too many families have the perfect way of life, Angel. Daddies, sometimes they leave the mommas. Or one of them dies. Kids get sick. Only one place is perfect. It's not here on earth."

"Momma didn't even hug me."

Jeb heard a sniffle. "Be thankful she's got a sister to look after her."

"What I'm trying to say is that life's been so hard for me. For my brother and sister. I can't see any of us turning out well." The bedsprings squeaked beneath Angel's shifting weight.

"You'll turn out better than the whole lot of Nazareth, Angel."

"Sometimes I thought I could hear my mother whispering to me at night. Now I know it's a crock. Every time I have a good thought about how I might turn out, how do I know it's not just another lie I'm telling myself so I'll feel better?"

"You have to decide that from now on you're going to climb out of the past and leave it behind. Every step you take away from the past is a move in the right direction. You can feel good about that."

"Like when you decided to stop conning everyone and be who you said you was?"

Jeb was silent for a moment and then answered quietly, "Same thing."

"You ever want to go back to your old ways, Jeb?"

"All the time."

"But you don't do it."

"It would be like stepping back into my past. That's the place that almost done me in. I want to go away from it, not back to it."

"What if you make a decision and you think it's taking you forward, but instead you go two steps backward?"

"It happens. Once I realize it was a mistake, I turn around and go in the direction that leads me ahead."

"Things aren't always clear, though. Like the way Reverend Gracie talks about hearing from God. How does he know it's not just his own voice, and not God's, telling him how to live?"

"Some men, great men of God, live their whole lives never knowing for sure if they're hearing God's voice. But they have one thing to guide them."

"You're fixing to preach again."

"Jesus left me something of his to read. I learn things that teach me how to live and how to tell if I'm making the right decision or not. When I get away from that and start making up my answers as I go along, then I get in trouble."

"Do you hate yourself for it?"

"Sometimes. Then I get up and go again."

"The good preachers don't stumble, do they, Jeb?"

"Same as everyone else."

"But sometimes you have to live with the trouble you caused the rest of your life." She spoke like a second wind had come into her and she was awake and ready to talk. "Like you and Fern Coulter."

"Angel, it's late. We have to get up and get the truck running again. Don't start with Fern Coulter at midnight."

"Kids in school say you spend your time running after Miss Coulter while Winona Mills spends her time running after you."

Jeb didn't answer. He rolled over and pulled the window shade down to keep the moonlight from striking him square in the face and closed his eyes. When he finally heard Angel's steady breathing, he sat up and went outside for a walk. He could not sleep with women in his head.

❈

A boy not much older than Angel helped Jeb roll the truck the rest of the way into the filling station. The patch over his pocket said "Ralph," even though the station owner called him "Coffee." Jeb figured it might have something to do with the color of his teeth. But Coffee could patch a tire faster than a cat on grease, and as he worked he talked to Jeb about how most of the businesses outside Malvern had been hit hard in the last year or so. He just kept patching tires, he said, and pumping gas, and somehow he had helped keep food on his momma's table. He talked of how his uncle was wounded in World War I and had never been right since. The whole time he talked, a bone-skinny cat wound around Jeb's feet.

"Anyplace to pick up breakfast around here?" asked Jeb.

"All the restaurants around here closed, the last one six months ago. They's a farmer up the road toward Hot Springs. He'll sell you all the apples you can eat and some bread."

"I'm sick of apples," said Angel. "They sell them on every corner in Nazareth and all over Little Rock. You'd think the whole world's gone crazy on apples."

"Take these," said Coffee. He handed a grease-stained brown sack to Angel.

Angel looked into the bag. "Biscuits. I'm sorry to be complaining and carrying on so much. I can't take your breakfast."

"My old lady makes too many as it is. She's trying to fatten me up and marry me off."

Angel handed Jeb a biscuit and ate one herself.

✳

Angel talked all the way from Malvern through the roads that led away to Hot Springs and then as they rolled along getting closer to Nazareth. Jeb finally saw a roadside café busy with automobiles pulling in and out of the parking lot. He pulled in and they found a place at the bar to eat. Angel ordered a hamburger and a Coke.

"Best burger I've had in a while," said Jeb after a moment.

"I want to know why you're all of a sudden Mr. Moneybags. You tipped that boy that fixed your tire a whole dollar. You just the big tipper now, ain't you? If I didn't know better, I'd say you're running liquor, but that would be crazy. People can get their whiskey now in the store."

"I told you I was working for the bank. That should be enough. Nothing wrong with running papers for the bank." Jeb salted his potatoes.

"Depends on the kind of papers you're running."

"Bank papers."

"Things Mr. Mills don't want to handle himself, like foreclosing on people and stuff like that."

"Or offers that they want to make to help people out of their troubles."

"What people?"

"Waitress, could you fill this girl's glass again so she'll stop running off at the mouth?" Jeb let out a sigh that drew the eyes of people seated on either side of them.

"Does Asa know about this deal you give to his wife?"

"I should have dropped you off in Little Rock and drove away."

"I knew it."

"The Hoppers are in trouble, Angel. They missed their payments on their place for too long. Banks can't stay in business if people don't pay their bills. Mills wants to help them out of their troubles, but whenever he tries, those Hopper boys pull a gun on him. How Christian is that?"

"Hopper boys don't claim to be Christian. So are they going to get to keep their land?"

"They're going to get to pay off their bills and have some to live on. It's better than starvation. Asa may go to prison for what he did downtown. What will Telulah do then, with those boys still living at home and all their land half blown away?"

She turned away.

❃

Angel said little during the rest of the meal and the last hour of the drive into Nazareth. Jeb decided to stop by the church and let Gracie know they had returned home early. But when they pulled into the churchyard, several families were gathered on the lawn. Fern Coulter, pale as pearls, came running up to the truck.

"Jeb, thank God you're back! Reverend Gracie collapsed this morning. They just took him to Hot Springs to a bigger hospital. He was so worried he'd not be able to talk to you again. Can you go to Hot Springs tonight?" she asked.

"Angel, I'll take you to the house with your brother and sister. I want you home in your own bed tonight." Jeb let out a sigh. He felt like his soul had just been washed out from under him.

18

St. Joseph's Mercy Hospital was lit up on every floor, no doubt a quiet hive for the Sisters of Mercy who doted on the infirm. Jeb checked in with the nun seated at the front desk. She arranged a vase of daisies with one hand while telling a nervous husband where he might find his wife, who had gone into labor in a nearby Hot Springs grocery store.

Jeb told the sister of his clergy status, just as he had heard Gracie do on occasion. She informed him that because of hospital rules about pastoral duties he could call on Gracie past visiting hours. Jeb climbed a staircase that smelled of paint and disinfectant. When he opened the door out onto the second floor he heard a girl's voice scolding someone. He found Emily Gracie standing over Agatha, begging her to finish her arithmetic problems even though she would not be in school the next morning. It was like trying to bring dust to life. Agatha curled up in a chair with her sweater pulled over the bottom half of her thin frame for a blanket.

"Jeb!" Philip called out when he saw Jeb coming down the hall.

"Philip, you don't call him that. It's Reverend Nubey now," said Emily. She extended her hand to Jeb and smiled, tired and too worn out to care whether or not Philip minded his Ps and Qs. She looked thirty instead of fourteen.

"Emily, I heard about your daddy and came as fast as I could," said Jeb.

"He's better. Or he says he's better," said Agatha.

"Let me take you to him." Emily handed the pencil to Agatha. "Finish in the morning."

Philip collapsed on the rug, tired of their arguing.

"Where will all of you sleep tonight?" Jeb asked Emily.

"The Sisters of Mercy have a room in their convent. When my father told one of them about us, she wouldn't hear of us staying in a motel room tonight."

"She had crossed eyes," said Philip. "And a mustache."

"Don't pay him any attention, Reverend," said Emily. She led Jeb down the hallway and into the room, where they found Gracie with eyes almost closed. His lids lifted at the sight of Jeb. He tried to say something but could only whisper.

"I'll do the talking this time," said Jeb. Gracie's pallor made him look as though someone had let every drop of blood from him.

"Dad, the sister that's taking us to the room for the night is getting off her shift now." She kissed Philemon on the cheek and squeezed his hand. "I love you. Sleep well."

Gracie held her hand for a moment and then let her slip out of the room.

"I shouldn't have gone to Little Rock. It was a wasted

trip, and you needed me here." Jeb took the chair next to the bed.

Gracie slipped his hand around Jeb's and hoarsely said, "No, the little girl needed to see her mother. How was Mrs. Welby?"

"Insane. I brought Angel home."

"After all this wait, you were right to take her. It was best she see for herself that her mother is not well. You'll find her more settled, no doubt, now that she can stop wondering and guessing about her mother's condition."

"I've never known Angel to settle down because of anything. But she is different. I see that in her now. Something has changed. I hope you're right."

"I can't go back, Jeb. Church in the Dell will have to get along without me."

"Don't think about Church in the Dell right now, Gracie. We want you well."

"How do you feel about taking the platform after all?"

"I still have that Sunday message simmering in me. That will do for this week. As for the remaining fifty-one Sundays, I don't know what I'll do."

"You'll do a fine job. I'm proud of you."

"I'd rather see you up there than me, Gracie. Without you around, I think sometimes I'll lose my way."

Gracie's fingers fiddled with something inside the neck of his gown. "May as well get this over and done with, I guess. I've been saving something for you. It's a gift someone once gave to me." Gracie pulled a chain out from around his neck. He opened the fastener and slid off what looked to be some sort of charm.

Jeb took it. He turned it over and said, "It's a gold key."

"My father gave it to me at my ordination. It was no

large ceremony, mind you. The elders of our church encircled me and laid hands on me after I graduated college. Read the inscription. I don't think I wore it off too badly with worry."

Jeb held it up to the dim hospital light. "It says, 'Do Not Lay Down Your Plow.'"

"My father was so proud I had entered the ministry that he wanted to buy me something. He couldn't afford much, and having been a farmer his whole life, he was at a loss for what the key should say. But it meant the world to me. 'Do Not Lay Down Your Plow.' The Scriptures say that, of course, or close to that. But to him it meant that once I had my course set for the ministry I should endeavor to keep plowing ahead, around the stones, through hard soil, and even in drought. He had done so for years as a farmer. Now he wanted me to continue as he had done, but in a different kind of field.

"My wife and I knew many hard fields. I don't know if you've ever tried to plow ground for the first time. It isn't the same as digging up last year's field. You don't know what's beneath the surface, or even if you've found the best soil. That's what it's like when you start that very first church. Church in the Dell has its stones and times of drought. But it's a field plowed long before we came. You'll do well, Jeb. Of this I am certain."

Jeb tried to hand the key back to him.

"I want you to keep it. Here, take this chain and wear it around your neck as I have, if you want. Whenever you feel as though you want to give up, pull it out and read it as a reminder that the man with his hands on the plow is the man most likely to reap a harvest. I know this church has a few thorns in the bunch. But if you practice at feeding them, God's Spirit will fill in where you think you've failed."

Jeb read the key again and then placed it back on the chain and around his neck. He did not want to burden a sick minister with his own list of complaints. But the fear that he would not have Gracie around to make him rewrite a lousy sermon or reword a didactic phrase sickened him. "I love you, Philemon. You're going to be well again." He slipped the key inside his shirt. "I won't put down the plow. I swear it to you on my life."

❉

Jeb checked into a room down the street from St. Joe's and visited Philemon twice a day until Saturday. He visited him once more before he headed for home. Philemon prayed for him and for the Sunday message. Jeb felt for the first time in over a year that he might be ready for the task. Or at least he did when he read the confidence in Gracie's eyes.

The sky had bloomed early that morning but froze in the distant landscape with November bringing an early wintry cold. The few berries left unpicked in the wooded jungles of ivy and oak lay in ice-coated bondage on the vines. The truck slid up over an icy hill and then skidded down into a winding turn of road. Jeb squeezed against the brake, easing the old Ford back and forth until it found its bearing again on the sludged-over highways. He knew when he had arrived at the town limits; every tree of substantial size had been papered with election flyers. Come Monday, the whole town would be out voting and dodging campaigners on the way to the mill or town.

Jeb arrived home in time for a late biscuit and bacon breakfast and then realized he could not shake Angel's insistent accusations against his bank delivery to the Hoppers. He counted out his bills and found a place to hide them in a tin box beneath a loose board. Before the school bell rang he wanted to know exactly how Telulah Hopper and her family would fare after they had signed the bank's offer.

First Jeb drove toward the bank. He sat outside in the truck, deciding whether or not Mills would consider his inquiry as intrusive. He had finally stepped outside the truck and almost walked through the front door when he heard Winona's voice coming from inside. Before he could reach for the door handle a politician slapped a paper fan with "Vote for Bryce" emblazoned across the back into his hand.

The bank door opened. Winona stepped out, fresh as spring. She smiled and sounded surprised to see him. "Reverend Jeb, I can't believe it's you. It's good you came back after Reverend Gracie's illness. How do those kids like living back with their family?"

"They're still living with me. I couldn't leave Angel in Little Rock."

She hesitated and then said, "That sounds like you. Always looking out for others. I hope you can tell us Reverend Gracie's getting better."

"It's hard to say. He's still bent on getting up to Cincinnati to see some doctor, but I think the hospital in Hot Springs is helping him mend for now. Sure put a scare into those kids of his."

"So you'll be stepping into his shoes now?"

"I can't promise I'll fit into Gracie's shoes. But I'll be

assuming his duties as pastor of Church in the Dell. He seems to think I'm up to the task."

"You are, of that I have no doubt." She tapped Jeb with her pointer finger right against his shoulder bone. "Let me buy you lunch today, Reverend. I have something I need to tell you. But it has to be in complete confidence, even though I think it's something you'll be glad to hear."

Jeb hesitated.

She seemed to try to read his hesitation and said, "This has to do with your ministry, Reverend. You'll want to hear it."

Jeb said, "Beulah's around noon, then." Winona looked exceptionally fine in the color blue, he decided. He stuck the paper fan in her hand. "Here, you can put this to better use than I can."

She took Bryce's campaign fan and laughed. Then she wafted away, leaving nothing behind but the better women's way of marking their trail in the breeze—something as sweet as bluebells. Her scent matched her dress. She pulled a fur coat around her frame and dropped the fan into a newspaper boy's open hand.

❈

Horace had left his office door open to allow in the heat from the bank's potbellied stove. Jeb shook off the chill and warmed beside the fire. He could hear Mills's chuckle all the way out into the lobby. When Mills's secretary, Mona, saw Jeb, she greeted him and asked if he had an appointment with her boss.

"I'd like one, if possible," said Jeb.

"Come on in, Reverend. Good to have you back. You must bring with you news of all kinds on this November day." Mills walked a customer out of his office. "What would you like to tell us?"

"I didn't leave Angel in Little Rock, for one thing. I think Gracie's ready to retire, at least for a time, so that he can mend. That's the news from Nubey."

"How fortunate Gracie has you to take his place. Man like you will do well, in my opinion." He invited Jeb into his office and closed the door behind him.

Jeb took his seat across from Mills.

"I have some news of my own. Those Hoppers are leaving town. Looks like Asa's going to be sent to the work farm down at the penitentiary to do some time. Best news we've gotten in a long time here in Nazareth. I never seen this place so jittery since that riot broke out. Best to put things like that behind us and move ahead to better tomorrows, if you know what I mean." Horace had a relaxed demeanor, more jovial than Jeb had ever seen him. "We owe it all to your intervention."

"Telulah Hopper's leaving too? I was hoping she'd have the chance to stay and keep her roots here. Maybe somehow get at least part of her land back. Is there no way she can keep her house?"

"That woman's packing as fast as she can. Don't know where she'll go. Between you and me, I don't care. I don't mean to sound unchristian, but she needs to start somewhere new, in a town where no one knows her name."

"She's a good woman, Mr. Mills. With her husband being sent off to prison, couldn't our town come together to help her out? She's not to blame for what Asa did. If he hadn't gotten so drunk, I don't know that he would have done what he did."

"It's your job to be sympathetic, Reverend. But my job is to make the hard decisions."

Jeb said, "What will happen to the Hopper land?"

"Timber. Those investors you met have cut a deal with Uncle Sam to plant thousands of trees on that place. It will rejuvenate the lumbermill in Nazareth, put a lot of good men back to work."

"At least Mrs. Hopper has a nest egg to take with her."

Jeb excused himself. He thought it best not to let Mills know right off how the news about the Hoppers sickened him. Gracie would most likely tell him to hold his tongue, weigh the matter a bit before spilling his opinions out all over the bank.

He would pay Telulah a visit after lunch and express his sadness over the loss of her land. If she was going to lose the land anyway, she might be glad to see Jeb after all, since he had helped her connect with the land offer her husband had so adamantly refused to acknowledge.

❈

"If ever there was a man who could take the reins after the departure of our dear Reverend Gracie, it's you." Winona spouted on about Jeb so much, it seemed she had more invested in his pastorate than even he.

"I still can't believe it myself."

"What's it feel like?"

"Not too many years ago, I remember breaking my back over another man's field and hating it—I'm talking about picking cotton. I always thought if I could get a little piece of that land myself, I'd not mind the work if it was for the sake of my own land. Church in the Dell's been Gracie's field. But now it's mine to look after. So taking it over for him is like getting my own little piece of land—an honor I don't take for granted." Jeb did not tell her that his faith in himself ebbed and flowed by the hour. "That doesn't mean I think it will be an easy pulpit."

"Your character will prove itself. Everybody'll see. I've already heard the gab around town about you. The women all think you're the best thing to come along since bobbed hair. They like the fact you were a sort of gangster. They think it's kind of exciting having a John Dillinger in the pulpit."

"They do?"

"I think you'll be surprised at the girls who show up on Sunday. But all that aside, you know how soon Gracie will be leaving?"

"I told him that I was in no hurry to move into the parsonage. Most likely, he'd appreciate it if some of the ladies helped him pack up, and then the men can help load his belongings. You can bet his oldest girl, Emily, will manage it all for him."

"I still can't help but think if we can help you find a good home for those Welby children, that will be one less worry. Don't you sometimes think that as you take over the parsonage, it would be best to be free and clear of kids that aren't yours? Church in the Dell's a handful for any man, but managing a brood of chicks that belong in another person's pen, if you catch my drift, has got to be a load."

"I'm not complaining about the Welbys, Winona." Her habit of bringing up the subject of the Welbys leaving was starting to annoy him.

"Don't get me wrong. I don't mean to sound insensitive. I pity those poor babies. What I mean to say is that

I did some checking and if you want, there is a family in Pine Bluff that takes in children put out by their families. Good Christian people, from what I hear."

"I don't remember asking you to find a home for the Welbys."

"Reverend, you know I wouldn't do that without your asking me. I have friends who live all over. I happened to mention your precious charges to a friend, and she knew of someone who knew this family in Pine Bluff. That is all. See, until now, I hadn't mentioned it to you. If you don't want to know about a place that will take these kids off your hands, nothing could drag it from my lips."

"Beulah, wrap my food in wax paper, please. I need to take it with me," said Jeb.

Winona nearly lifted off the booth. "I've made you angry with me. See, my mother tells me that even when I'm not meddling I come across as though I am. Please forgive me." She clasped both of Jeb's hands. "I'd hate myself if I thought I'd made you angry with me."

Jeb was surprised at the way her eyes teared. He had not seen this side of Winona. "You're forgiven." He sat back down. "I'm sorry if I sound testy. I feel like I've been driving back and forth from here to Hot Springs and beyond for days on end. A little rest tonight and I'll be better company in the morning."

"You've every right to be testy. And I owe you more respect. You are, after all, our new minister."

"I'm still plain old Jeb."

"But that's what makes you different from other preachers. Other men, for that matter."

Jeb had to admit Winona had her likable ways.

"But promise me you'll not tell those kids I brought up

this Pine Bluff family. I'd be like Public Enemy Number One in the eyes of that Angel. I really do like her. She's a peach."

"I won't tell her. She tends to jump to conclusions, truth be told."

He assured her that the matter was dropped. He'd decided not to tell Angel about the Hoppers moving away, either. She was much too fiery a girl to understand such things. As a matter of fact, it was best that all the business of the church and any matter she might misconstrue in her confused state be concealed from her inquisitive nature. She could not be counted on to be reasonable. He decided that somehow he would help her rise to such ripeness of judgment over time. He was, after all, a minister.

"Winona, you really wear the color blue better than any woman I know. May I walk you to your automobile?" he said.

She took to the idea like jelly on bread. With the banker's daughter on his arm, Jeb felt a sense of destiny rising inside him. By morning, the pastorate would be his new frontier, a land of milk and sweetest honey. He would savor it with the highest measure of dignity a man of his standing could muster.

❄

The rifle barrel aimed out the front door of the Hopper house confused Jeb. His feet both frozen in the cold, barren Hopper soil, he faced Clark Hopper's assault with a sort of blind paralysis. "Clark, it's me, Reverend Nubey!"

"You lyin' polecat of a preacher! Ain't no one sorrier than you ever walked the earth, not since Lucifer hisself. You never told my momma the truth about them papers.

I'm goin' to kill you dead and bury your sorry hide under all them trees that Mills intends to plant on our land." The way he said "our land" was thrown out like a kind of indictment against Jeb.

"Clark, I'm a little mixed up about things. What do you mean by the 'truth' about the papers she signed?"

The gun barrel disappeared, and Telulah appeared in its place. "Don't matter what he did, Clark. You take that gun out of the preacher's face or I'll bean you with it myself. Just because he done wrong, don't mean we'll make it right with two wrongs."

Jeb dropped his hands at his sides. "Mrs. Hopper, I heard you were leaving town."

She laughed, her lips drawing up like a dried-out apple. "You havin' sport with us, Reverend?"

Cautiously, he approached the front porch, stepping over the two dogs that were too lazy to stir from their warm place in the sun.

Telulah took a seat on the last stick of furniture on the place, the front porch rocker. "Clark, you better go and fetch your brother from town. They's still a bit of gas. I don't want him walking all that way in the cold." She said to Jeb, "H'it takes him pert near to dark to walk all the way home from town when he goes off of an afternoon. They's been a hard frost on the ground the last week. He'd catch his death, and I can't pay no doctor."

"Mrs. Hopper, I don't think I must have known all the particulars about this bank deal." Jeb found a warm spot on the cold porch next to the hounds. He remembered how many pages long the contract had been. He had only skimmed the first page.

"You mean you brought those bank papers all the way

out here without knowin' what was in them? Reverend, I thought you had read them through, or I wouldn't have signed. I told you I'm not the best reader, and God knows my boys can't help me with such things."

Jeb buried his face in his hands. "I was only the delivery boy, Mrs. Hopper."

"But you're the preacher, too. That's what made me sign it."

"What did they give you in return?" Jeb lifted his face to look at her.

"The bank took all our land, that's what. They paid off the past few months' note, the back taxes, but they took all hundred and eleven acres. All they give us was the boot. That, and fifty dollars to help us get out of town and out of their way. You look pale as Solomon's ghost, Reverend." Her face softened around the eyes. "You really didn't know, did you? Banker Mills took you like he took me and Asa."

"I thought since he said he was giving you at least half of what the land was worth, you could at least keep a plot of land with your house, a spot for your garden."

"And here all along I thought you was helping Mills so you could be rid of my boy, Beck. I know he's caused you grief. All of my boys run on the wild side. If I could, I'd make them better men. But Asa, he's not much for knowing about such things. His daddy weren't no good, and his momma died young. I was hopin' you'd help him find the way out of his troubles."

"You thought I was trying to get rid of Beck?"

"Beck's sweet on that Angel of yourn. Blamed fool got it in his head that he could run off and marry a girl as young as her. Many a kid is doin' that kind of thing, I know. But when you came after your girl like that, it made an impression on him. He came home that night and said he wished his daddy would be that hard on him and his brothers."

"I've made a fool mistake," said Jeb. "But it wasn't aimed at you or Beck or Asa. No wonder your boy wanted to bury me out in the woods."

"Don't be so hard on yourself, Reverend. You're a young preacher. People like Mills, they don't think nothing of using a good man like you to get what they want." She rose from the rocker as though it took her last ounce of strength. "Clark, run and fetch your sisters, load up this h'yere chair and me with it. I reckon I'm done with this place. We may as well all go into town and pick up Beck. When this town wakes up in the mornin', I'd just as soon not be here to see it."

She turned and saw several sets of initials scratched in the porch railing. She bent and kissed each one, saying good-bye to the ancestors who had sweated to pay for the land she was now leaving.

Jeb walked her to the old Hopper truck.

"Soon, every person in this town will owe Horace Mills, Reverend. Nazareth won't be the same place it once was. You mark my words. Be careful about his friendship," she told him.

He thanked her and gave her the handkerchief from his pocket, in which he'd hidden twenty dollars. It was the least he could do. She waved good-bye without looking at him. It was better that way.

19

The Long house had more drafty cavities in the walls than Jeb could stuff with paper and rags. He woke up to the coldest Sunday he could remember. Every blanket he could find was piled on the children, with all of them sleeping in the same bed to stay warm.

The evening before, Angel had screamed until she was hoarse about Beck Hopper. Every student in Stanton School knew of his daddy being sent off to the pen. But worse than that, they all heard how the new preacher had helped to run the Hoppers out of town. Around the school, Jeb had become a sort of folk hero, with Asa Hopper as the town foe. The enemy had fallen, in their eyes.

Angel told him that Beck had left school last Friday before the bell just to get away from the mob of kids that had taunted him during the midday break until Fern had shouted from the steps for them to stop. Angel had feared that Beck might face more than just taunting before he got away, so she had helped him slip out between the history lesson and the last math lesson of the day.

Jeb could not figure out how the word had gotten around about his involvement with the bank and the

Hoppers. He didn't think Telulah had a vindictive bone in her body. But one slip from the lips of a bank employee at the teller window would send the tale multiplying and changing each time it was passed.

He padded down the hallway, watching his breath mist in front of him as he went. It would be a relief to move into the parsonage again. The place had been built as good as any house in town, with a good stove and a brick chimney.

Telulah Hopper's gaunt expression had haunted him in his dreams. She had not told him where they would go next, and he knew it was because she did not know. Asa would be sent down to the state pen in two days. His family would not be around to witness the state boys taking him away in chains.

Jeb could not figure out how he could have been so wrong about Mills and his own decision to deliver the ill-fated papers into Telulah's hands. Asa had acted wrongfully. Beck had nearly taken Angel into youthful ruin. Yet Jeb felt like the dickens for helping Nazareth Bank and Trust bring down the Hoppers. He would give the remaining dollars in his tin box to have Sunday's new church duties not weighing him down at the same time. When Gracie recovered well enough to travel to Cincinnati, he would confess the whole matter to him. Gracie always helped him to see clearly when the world was so clouded over with details that nothing made sense to Jeb. Gracie had tried to warn him about entanglements with Mills, but somehow the common sense of it all had not found a landing place until now.

Yesterday he had felt on top of everything. Today he didn't know if he could step foot on the new church floor without it caving in and dropping him straight into the pits of hell.

He dressed early and got Willie up to start a pot of grits. Willie wore a quilt into the kitchen. "Dang, Jeb, if it ain't cold as Alaska in this house. When can we move back to the parsonage?"

"Put some butter in that, Willie. I've been eating too many diner grits over the past few days. I want something that tastes like we're not completely destitute."

"Angel says you got money like nobody's business now that you work for Horace Mills. Is that right, Jeb? Are you rich now, rich like Mills?"

"Your sister's mad, and she exaggerates when she's mad, Willie. You know that about her." He did not feel the need to discuss his personal business with youngens.

"Angel told us about Momma while you were away at the hospital too. Is she exaggerating about our mother being out of her mind? To hear Angel tell it, Momma ain't never coming out of that nervous hospital. She made Ida May cry." Willie stirred the pot like he was mad at it.

"What if that part is right, Willie? I'm no doctor, but your momma didn't look too good to me. Can you live with knowing the truth about her?"

"I wish I could have seen her. Maybe I could have helped her remember more things about us. I don't know if Angel tried hard enough. She gives up on people too easily."

"Don't be putting that kind of thing on your sister, Willie. She spent a whole morning with your momma. I'm the one that decided she should go home. No amount of wishing can make your mother better than she is right now. I wasn't about to leave Angel or either of you in that madhouse with your aunt. She's got her hands too full of problems with that oldest girl of hers as it is."

"We do have butter this morning." Willie stood with the icebox door wide open. "Granny used to say it's a good day when you have butter in the house."

Jeb picked up his Bible and opened to the morning's text he and Gracie had selected together:

> *For I know that in me (that is, in my flesh,) dwelleth no good thing: for to will is present with me; but how to perform that which is good I find not. For the good that I would I do not: but the evil which I would not, that I do . . . But I see another law in my members, warring against the law of my mind, and bringing me into captivity to the law of sin which is in my members. O wretched man that I am! who shall deliver me from the body of this death?*

Jeb felt his knees weaken. He ran into the parlor, yanked up the loose board, and pulled out the tin box, throwing open the lid. The money scattered onto the floor.

Willie glanced in at him and said, "You all right, Jeb?"

He gathered the money back into the box before Willie could see it. It seemed to him he had done both a right and a wrong in taking it. Knowing the difference is what left his insides churning. God was silent at the worst of times.

❋

Hayes Jernigan from the lumbermill was the first to greet Jeb at church, just as he yanked the rope for the tolling of the bell. Hayes had not darkened the door ever that Jeb could remember. He shook Jeb's hand and grinned from ear to ear. "You're the best thing that ever happened to this town, Reverend. Mills had a meeting with me and my boys last night at the sawmill. He told us the lumber business coming our way was due in part to your help."

Jeb gazed up into the belfry. Nothing had happened when he'd pulled the rope. He yanked once more, but heard nothing. In fact, the rope's resistance made it feel as though it was hung up on a rafter.

"Hayes, please don't give me any credit," he said. "Mills's investment group is bringing in the work for the lumbermen. Not me."

"You're a minister like no other I ever met. I told the banker you'd have my support at the first sounding of the bell come Sunday, and here I am! My wife's busting at the seams. She's been trying to get me in church for ten year or more. You helped save the whole town, Reverend. And to think you was once a notorious criminal. In a manner of speaking, that makes you more like the rest of us. Don't God move in mysterious ways?"

The wood rafter from the belfry squeaked, and they both looked up.

"I told Gracie I'd fix that bell, but what with him being so sick and all, I forgot entirely. Now I can't get it to ring at all."

"It appears to me you ain't got a bell, Reverend, if you don't mind my saying so." Hayes laughed. He acknowledged two of his saw bosses coming up the front steps and walked out to greet them at the church portals. His wife joined several women on the porch, all of them giddy with the good fortune that had come to Nazareth in the form of Ace Timber.

Jeb stared up into the steeple. He stepped back so that the sunlight bleeding through the roof would help him get a better look inside. Hayes had told it right. The bell was gone entirely. For the life of him, he couldn't figure out why.

Curious, several women gathered around Jeb and joined him in staring up into the empty belfry. They muttered among themselves about how thieving men were running loose even out in the country now. Then they took a seat. Jeb sighed and squeezed through several churchgoers to make his way up the aisle.

The wad of cash in his trouser pocket felt like an anvil. He continued to greet the people who poured in from all over the county, even the boys who shot pool every Saturday night at Snooker's. Gracie would be proud of who he had brought in this morning. Seeing the pool hall bunch made him feel more easeful. Each person came forward and shook Jeb's hand. The schoolkids gathered at the back of the church, whispering and casting admiring glances at their new minister.

The atmosphere of welcome had Jeb letting out a sigh of relief. At least with support, he could lead the flock as Gracie had taught him to lead.

Angel had not yet shown up. Fern appeared, though, with Ida May, her hair pulled into perfect pigtails and then pinned, making a cinnamon bun on each side of her head. The teacher observed the crowd in attendance with a quiet amazement before she helped Ida May find a place on one of the remaining pews and engaged a few of the women in idle chat. Then she lifted her brows and smiled at Jeb more approvingly than she had in a year.

Winona and her mother, Amy, came in, both wearing something that looked as new as the latest wintry freeze upon the trees. Winona mouthed something to Jeb that he could not understand. Fern read it better. She glanced away, ignoring Winona altogether. Winona said it once more and Jeb read her lips: *"You look good in that suit."*

Jeb relaxed and smiled at Winona, careful not to linger too long over the way she put the shape back into that dress of hers.

Fern had already engaged in other conversation. He remembered the way she once helped him study out on the porch on Saturdays. She could cut through confusion with the precision of a dutiful seamstress. But he was too respectable now to ask the town schoolteacher to tutor him through his latest crisis of the heart—namely the Hoppers. Besides, it seemed that things had turned around for the better this morning. Church in the Dell had not seen a Lord's Day this blissful in a boatload of Sundays. He shook a few more hands and felt his confidence lift.

Horace Mills finally appeared at the church entrance, but he wasn't alone. He stubbed out a cigar on the porch railing and then patted the backs of several of the lumbermen. The two men behind him removed their hats. Distantly, Jeb recognized one of the men with him; he'd been part of the circle of investors he had been introduced to the night of the Mills party, when he had given his plate of food away to Beck Hopper and a pack of hungry youths. Horace met Jeb in the aisle, bringing a whole parade of admirers along with him.

"Welcome to Church in the Dell, Reverend Nubey! Jernigan says someone absconded with our church bell. I'll lay odds it was a Hopper." His smile stretched woodenly as he added, "Looking forward to the morning message." He shook Jeb's hand.

Jeb didn't know how much an old church bell would bring on the market, but he figured if Mills was correct, it might be enough to feed a few hungry children and a desperate momma. Gracie might tell him to wait and see what came of matters first, but it seemed Mills might be right.

The words on Gracie's key echoed in Jeb's ears. He had not known how heavy the plow would become, wearing calluses on his heart so early on.

He returned Horace's greeting and then headed back toward the lectern as though an invisible hand walked him along with strings tied to his hands and feet. He opened the Bible as the last few townspeople standing took their place on the pews. Church in the Dell fell quiet, all eyes on Jeb Nubey, expectant of what their new minister and the most popular man in town might say to them.

"Let us pray," he said. All heads bowed, and he felt the soul of every man, woman, and child in the room delivered into his hands. Where he took them next was anyone's guess.

❄

The songs filtered out into the hollow, churchmen and saintly women praising God to the highest for his great works. A truck had stalled down the hill, overfilled with every earthly spoil a broken-down family owned.

Clark Hopper finally made the right connection under the truck hood that sent the engine humming. "Got her started, Momma."

He let out a sigh of relief. The truck was just about done for. After stalling twice yesterday as they got on the road, it had simply died yesterday evening. The sun had already gone down, so there hadn't been anything else to do but wait for sunlight. The two oldest children had slept beneath a bundle of goods all night to allow their momma and younger siblings the warmth of the cab. They'd awakened to see several families motoring past them on their way to church. The adults had all carefully averted their eyes. The children had stared with unabashed curiosity.

"Listen to that purty music," said Telulah, her ear cocked toward the church. "Sounds like the angels of heaven rising from the frost this morning."

"It ain't angels, Momma," said Beck. "Angels don't hate nobody."

"I don't feel hate from this town, Beck. Not anymore," said Telulah. She'd had a strange dream in the night. She and the boys were driving through Nazareth and they passed a tall building. Suddenly mud dumped onto them from above. As they looked up, they could see the church people hurling dirt their way, covering everything they owned with muck and hissing at them with venomous sayings.

But there had been one man standing in the middle of them all. He had the kindest eyes and was the only one not dropping mud onto their heads. He looked on them with so many emotions, Telulah had to count them—pity, love, remorse, and shame at the way the others behaved.

Telulah had smiled at him and when she did, she saw him for who he really was.

"Don't be mad at these churchfolk, boys. They have no idea what they're doing."

After passing around a loaf of bread and making the

boys say grace, she listened to the singing and organ chording and hummed along, even though she was not sure of the words.

She knew that did not matter to God.

❋

Jeb shook hands with every person in attendance that morning. The sun had finally warmed the front porch enough that Jeb could stand outside and make room for those departing for home. He stopped Will Honeysack and said quietly, "Could you ask Bryce's campaign committee to stop politicking out on the church lawn, Will? I know it's election week, but today is the Sabbath."

Will laughed and agreed the campaign should stop at the front gates of the church. "Best message you ever preached, Jeb. I wish Gracie could have heard it. He'd be proud—and even prouder of the crowd you brought in this morning. The offering's three times higher than last week's. Good thing; I heard we're missing a bell."

Jeb voiced to Will a thought that had come to him this morning before he delivered the sermon. "I got us an idea on how we could help your nephew."

"Don't say? That boy needs help. A man ought to be horsewhipped for taking advantage of a young man's trust in these hard times."

"I got me a little cash, and I was thinking that if I bought up those chicks of his, I could raise them out in a barn on Ivey Long's place. I figure folks could use a good laying hen or a stewing hen every now and then. Ivey's got a barn with nothing in it at all, and if I pay him a little, he might let me keep chickens in it."

"That's generous of you. You sure you want the whole

lot of them, Reverend? He'd need at least twenty for the load."

Jeb liked the price. "Tell him I'll take them. He can find me at the church most days. I'll take him out to Long's barn." Jeb made a note to himself to remember to talk with Ivey. Then he dug out the cash and handed it to Will.

"You'll be like a savior to that boy, Reverend Jeb." Will shook his hand before he handed the offering plate off to Jeb.

Jeb watched Will as he headed out to corral Bryce's supporters and quell their enthusiasm for election week. He felt good about his poultry idea. A bunch of chicks at such a low price would soon turn a nice profit over the winter. With some lights and electricity, he could come up with a way to keep the barn warm. What few chicks he did lose would matter little, being bought at such a low price. But better than that, he'd be able to help out the nephew of a good friend. The idea was God sent, in his opinion.

Jeb felt the weight of the offering basket in his hands.

"I put a little extra in there, as promised," said Horace from beside him. He had Amy on his arm and several lumbermen waiting to speak with him about the coming work.

"Mr. Mills, I'd like to speak with you sometime," said Jeb. He still wanted to get it straight with Mills that he could no longer act as deliveryman for the bank. He would rather come up with his own means for making extra money, like the poultry deal.

"Sure thing, Reverend. Set it up with Mona. Better than that, let's break bread together." He looked at his wife, and she told Jeb she'd have him and the Welbys over that very week for supper one night. "How about Friday?" she asked.

Jeb acknowledged Amy's invitation. Behind them came Winona.

"Make it Tuesday, Momma. Best get our time in now before Reverend Nubey's dance card fills up for the week." Winona rested one hand on Jeb's arm. "I really took to heart your message this morning. It made me think and reflect on a few matters. See you Tuesday?" She sounded eager.

Amy smiled next to Winona. Their smiles mirrored their approval of him.

"Tuesday, then," Jeb answered.

Fern Coulter brought up the rear and handed Ida May off to Jeb in her usual fashion. "I could not get Angel to come to save my soul, Jeb. I don't know what's gotten into her, but you'd think she woke up this morning in a whole new world."

"Whatever it is, Fern, you can be sure I'm somehow the cause. That girl can stay mad at me longer than any woman I know."

He froze. Fern raked her fingers through her hair, pursed her lips, and then glanced away. She cleared her throat and, choosing to avoid discussing her own grudge with him, said, "She's a kid, Jeb. Give her a day or two, and she'll forget whatever it is she thinks you've done."

She lingered longer than usual, silent. When Ida May ran to join a group of girls, she let out a breath and said, "I think I need to make some things right myself, Jeb. I know it's hard to follow in Philemon Gracie's footsteps."

Her voice softened. "But you've exceeded everyone's expectations. I mean, just look at what's happened on one Sunday." She was more relaxed than she had been all year. "I've seen men here today who haven't shadowed a church door since they were boys." She swallowed and then continued. "What I'm trying to say is that it's time I had a little crow with my Sunday dinner. I'd like to ask you to forgive me, Jeb. I can't go on treating you like you're the worst man on earth when you're clearly one of the best."

Jeb withheld the urge to throw his arms around her. Instead, he touched her shoulder in as companionable a way as he could manage. He said, "You were right to call me the worst man on earth. I'll never measure up to Philemon Gracie. But I can grow too, Fern."

"Now I feel worse." She laughed, then returned his gesture by allowing her hand to pat his.

"I'm not meaning to make you feel bad, Fern." He delved further. "Do you finally forgive me?"

"I really do, Jeb." Fern shook her head as if to break the brief spell between them and took a step back. She snapped closed her handbag and then smiled. "Good things are going to come of all this. I'd best be going."

Jeb watched her leave. She gave him one last smile as she walked out chatting with three of her students. He did not know what to do now except let her go and feel satisfied with the acceptance of him she had offered. At least he could see her across the church and feel something besides hatred staring back at him. A grain of hopefulness was as good a start as any.

"They sure like you as the new preacher, Jeb." Willie ran up the steps, reveling in the attention showered on him by everyone, including some of the girls from school.

"Enjoy it while you can, Willie Boy. Jesus was popular too, just before they crucified him."

"You always got to spoil our fun, Jeb. I'm going to ask every girl in the church to go steady with me by the week's end. This is the life!"

20

Election Day brought every taxpaying citizen of Nazareth into town to vote at the library. The news had circulated about the Church in the Dell outlaw-turned-preacher. Young women waved at Jeb from the library steps. He tipped his hat to them as he walked around another "Bryce for Senate" sign on the library lawn. He tucked his voting stub into his pocket and headed for the jailhouse. Out front, Deputy George Maynard gabbed with some of the boys who had come into town to vote and gossip about the state police transport of Asa Hopper.

The Nazareth jail, built stone by stone by a group of town founders desperate for a place to keep offenders in the late 1800s, had seen at least two coats of paint the last fifty years. The painted brick in the alleyway had taken to peeling, revealing an old World War I advertisement that asked the locals to support the war.

Jeb could see Asa pacing back and forth inside the jail-house, one cell away from where he himself had been locked up a year ago. Someone had given Asa a pack of smokes. He lit one by another, awaiting his ride to

Cummins Prison Farm—the place known by lifetime offenders as The Jungle. Not many men had come through Cummins unmarked by stories of torture.

Maynard excused himself and disappeared inside the jailhouse office. Jeb heard the deputy call out Asa's name, followed by the familiar wham of the clanking jail doors. Jeb met Deputy Maynard at the front door. "Asa going down to the farm today?" he asked.

"Been a long time in the making. Shame to see a once-good family turn to ruin." Maynard stepped aside to clear the way as the state police prepared to escort Hopper out of town. Jeb heard the sound of chains scraping the jailhouse floor. He held out his Bible and said, "I'm the prisoner's minister. I'd like to have a word with him."

George Maynard nodded at the state boys. They allowed Jeb to pass. When Jeb made eye contact with Asa, the farmer lunged at him. The state police wrestled him to the floor while George said, "Maybe it's best you don't see Asa, Reverend. He's still testy about his wife signing away their land."

"Asa, I need to talk to you," Jeb pleaded.

Asa calmed himself and succumbed to the cops. "I'll let him talk, but only for a minute."

The policemen backed away but kept their weapons drawn.

"You've got some nerve, Preacher!" Asa shot back at Jeb.

Jeb breathed in and out and then said, "Telulah told me that the bank took your place for little to nothing."

"I had a deal in the works, a way to get government money to raise timber on my place. When I told Mills about it, he up and pulled together his henchmen to seal the deal for their own pockets. They stole from me and my kin. Why else would I go off and get drunk, half out of my mind?" He calmed and the cops released his arms. "What would you do, Reverend?"

"Not try and burn down half the town, Asa."

Asa slumped onto the bench inside the cell. He dropped his face in his hands and fell silent as stones.

"But I want you to know that I didn't know all the details of the deal. It was my fault I put my trust in the bank without reading all the fine print. That's why I came here today. To apologize."

Maynard cleared his throat and disappeared into the jailhouse office.

Asa shook his finger at Jeb. "You was paid off, and the whole town knows it!"

The cops lifted their gun barrels, cautious.

"I can't tell you that I wasn't paid for a delivery, but I thought it was a deal to help your wife out of her financial spot. I was trying to help," said Jeb. He thought his honesty might thread together a bridge of understanding. But it only seemed to make matters worse.

"I've you to thank for helping my family lose everything, then. Preachers is no different than bankers or lawyers. You all on the lam! Let's go, boys." Asa stood and moved gingerly through the jailhouse and toward the police car that would take him to Cummins.

Jeb watched Asa Hopper taken out of town in chains. For one full day he had taken the helm of the pastorate and led one man into ruin. In spite of Sunday's tide of jubilation, it seemed to him that tending a flock had so far brought nothing but sadness into the lives of others

When he had decided to follow in Gracie's legitimate footsteps, the life of a preacher had seemed noble. To Asa, he had been neither gallant nor helpful, and he was only just out of the gate.

Asa was gone and with him went Jeb's soul. He could not elicit a decent thought as to how he might get it back.

❋

Jeb could not find a good story in any of the books from his own small collection that might be usable fodder for his next Sunday sermon, let alone Sunday night and Wednesday evening. He decided to go back and pay a visit to the town library, the one building untouched by the riot fires on the block near the barbershop. He was cheered to find Fern's automobile parked out front amid all the others. By now school had let out, and the library had become the hangout for the high school students who were not slurping malteds at Fidel's, as well as the men and women still filing in and out to vote.

The library's musty aroma reminded Jeb of Fern's house, a cottage on Long's Pond that flowered inside with book collections and old college papers that lay in stacks on top of her bookcases. She was not like other women who kept their places like something to be shown off. Instead, Fern used every room for a place to study first one thing and then another. She had law books and science books, many from which she pulled tidbits to add to what the school textbooks meagerly fed her students.

He did not see her readily, and he needed to make short work of his research, so he meandered around the voters' tables and made his way to the quiet rear of the library, where he found a shelf labeled "Biographies." Several of the titles sounded familiar, so he pulled out a few and carried them in a stack to the only vacant table along the wall.

The first three biographies offered no charitable tales, but the fourth was the story of a man who had spent every cent he had to build a monument for the woman he loved. Jeb scrawled down the story's gist in his notebook and was about to leave when he heard Fern's voice. It warmed him to no end. She chattered away out of sight one aisle away and appeared to be deep in conversation with an old college friend who had come through town. Jeb heard the woman thank Fern for meeting her on short notice. He read a sentence twice and then gave his interest over to eavesdropping. Listening to her intelligent voice made him smile.

"I'm so sorry that you and I don't have more time together. Once I have these books checked out we can go to my place for a quick bite," said Fern to the woman. "How I wish you could stay the night."

The friend asked Fern about her classes this year and then said, "Whatever happened to that preacher fellow you once told me about. Jed or some such, right?"

"Jeb Nubey. He's finally made it into the pulpit. Our town minister has taken ill, and Jeb's assumed his duties. He's done remarkably well," said Fern.

Jeb pushed aside his books and decided to appear around the corner so that Fern could introduce her remarkable minister to her dearly loved friend. Before he could do so, the young woman commented, "Now is this the learned man you once were telling me about?"

"Learned? Dear me, no. I don't think I'd ever call him

learned." Fern hesitated and then said, "Or if I did, I was wrong. Maybe it was Reverend Gracie I was calling 'learned.'"

Her silly little laugh suddenly annoyed Jeb.

"He came out of Texarkana. A cotton picker, actually. Truth be told, a convict."

"And you almost married this man?"

"Lenora, keep your voice down. This library has too many wags wandering around in it today. Besides, you must be mixing him up with someone else. I never said we'd marry. Did I? If I did, I was speaking out of turn. Jeb Nubey's nothing more than an acquaintance. Here's what I was looking for. Let's take these books to the front and then we can go to my place."

Jeb did not move from his chair until he heard the women's voices fade away. The library had fallen silent except for a high school senior troubled with a head cold. Jeb picked up his notes and left the library, making certain Fern was nowhere in sight. It was a good thing he had not yet invited her to supper before the Wednesday prayer meeting. He would not want to bore her silly with his unlearned ways.

❈

Come Tuesday, Jeb woke up to a new resolve. He had been waiting for a woman who would never recognize him for anything but his sow's-ear past. Fern Coulter thought of him in the same light she regarded a stray pup—a nice feller to scratch around the ears, but not one allowed to linger around her doorstep too long for fear of fleas.

Tonight at the Millses' dinner party, he would acknowledge Winona's attentive signals and invite her to dinner Friday night. But first he'd find a way to discuss Asa's accusation with Horace. If Horace had used him to swindle the Hoppers out of their land, matters would have to be rectified. But the Millses were a reasonable lot, he decided. No one in town had sided with Asa except Jeb, and it had gotten him nothing but trouble.

Jeb dawdled around the house working on his sermon for most of the day. When the afternoon shadows crept up to the porch steps, he made certain Angel had started a meal of hot bread and soup for Willie and Ida May and then headed off to town. Angel had yet to come around in regard to the Hoppers. Jeb had decided to stay out of her arguments and keep her busy with other things. Eventually, she would see that he had nothing but the best of intentions where the Hoppers were concerned.

He swung by Honeysack's to pick up a bottle of men's aftershave and found that Freda was selling bouquets— the last flowers of the season, her sign said. She helped Jeb select the freshest bouquet for Amy Mills and sold him a small bottle of aftershave that smelled like something Oz Mills would wear. Jeb used the back room to slather up with the good-smelling stuff and then bid the Honeysacks a good evening.

"Must be an important date," said Will.

Jeb thanked them for the flowers and cologne and plowed through the doorway. In his haste to arrive promptly at the Mills house for dinner, he almost knocked down someone coming down the street. Fern Coulter's eyes widened in surprise.

"Pardon me," he apologized and then backed away,

more interested in being certain he had not crushed the flowers.

Fern found the matter more humorous than he did. She straightened her hat and sniffed the air. "What's that you're wearing?"

"Aftershave. Is my tie straight?" he asked, aloof. He made every effort to look as though his mind were elsewhere, not at all concerned that she had found him on his way to the Mills house.

She squared her shoulders as though she were framing Jeb in her sights. Then she reached up, gave the knot a slight jerk to the right, and said, "That's better. Where are you going?"

"The Mills home. Dinner party."

"Nice bouquet. I didn't know flowers were still available this time of year."

Jeb was about to tell her the flowers were simply a nice gesture for the hostess. But she had stopped smiling, and he enjoyed the way her small brows came together in the cen-ter. "If you'll excuse me, I don't want to keep the Millses waiting."

"Please give Winona my regards."

"Most assuredly, Fern."

"Jeb, is— Are—" Fern stumbled over her words.

Jeb kept moving toward his truck as she stammered around for the thing she was trying to utter. Finally she said, "I was wondering if you'd like to come to my place Friday night for dinner."

"With my new duties, you know my evenings have become so full, Fern. Sometime later, perhaps?" As he reached for the door handle, he suddenly felt his face flush. Regret sometimes turned him red as beets.

Fern nodded, and he left her on the sidewalk stunned as a rabbit. He had stopped short of telling her that he was not learned enough to keep company with a woman as academic as herself. But the sight of her staring after him in his rearview mirror was satisfaction enough.

❄

Amy Mills had invited any couple that had the slightest scent of prestige to her Tuesday-night dinner party. Jeb's bouquet was whisked away along with other hostess gifts, most of which cost much more than the fifty cents Jeb had squandered on Freda Honeysack's store flowers.

"Jeb, thank goodness you're here. The guest list is boring as all get out," said Winona.

"I'll make my presence known to your dear mother, Winona. Then, if you'd like, we can retire to the patio."

"No one's out there tonight. It's kind of cold."

But the way she said it, her eyes connecting with his, made Jeb believe that she warmed to his suggestion. "We can find something to help that, Winona," he said.

Winona took his arm and they found Amy greeting the wives of the men gathered in the study. The mood in the parlor was festive, celebratory.

Jeb saw Horace and the men grouped in the study— the same bunch he had introduced to Jeb as an investment group. Horace and the investors fired up cigars and patted one another on the back.

"If you'll excuse me for a moment, Winona, I'd like to have a word with your father."

"I'll have Henri light some torches out back. I'll bring two hot ciders," she said.

When Jeb entered the study, Horace announced him to the men, and they all gathered around him and slapped his back and shook his hand. "What's the occasion?" Jeb asked.

"Always the modest one," said Horace. The men laughed. One of them, a slight man with a thin mustache, said, "You've slain the giant, Reverend."

"With Ace Lumber money pumping through Nazareth, we'll put this place on the map. This will get all those laid-off men back on the payroll again, give them back their dignity."

Jeb silently mouthed, *I was only the delivery boy.* But then he realized he appreciated the accolades of the moneyed. He got a better buzz from it than from mountain hooch. It might take awhile to get used to the awkward feel of undying attention, but for now he let out a sigh and took to it.

"We'd tried everything to get those Hoppers to make a move. Asa was only being stubborn. It took a man of integrity to help those Hoppers see the light."

Jeb remembered his initial resolve and said, "I wonder, though, why the Hopper land was so important to the deal?" After a silent pause, he said, "There are other places suitable for timber, right? The drought has hit them as hard as anywhere else."

"But Roosevelt's New Deal is all about land conservation, as he calls it. Once we replant trees and flood part of the land from the lake next door, we'll have the perfect place to run lumber and grow a forest. We'll have the finest forest in the country and government money with which to run it." Mills tasted the end of his cigar.

"Whose idea was it to grow timber with government money, Mr. Mills?" asked Jeb.

The men all fell silent, each of them turning to gaze at Mills.

"It was Horace, of course." The man with the mustache spoke up. "He's the creative genius in the bunch."

The others laughed and shook the banker's hand.

"I'm relieved to know that," said Jeb. Now he had heard the other side of the matter. "Excuse me. I have a cup of cider waiting for me out on the patio." He needed time to clear his head and compare the stories of a convict with those of a group of respected investors.

❊

Jeb saw Winona's breath in the lantern light, a white mist floating veil-like around her head. She had draped a fur around her shoulders. Her face broke with gentle relief when she saw Jeb. "Glad you could come."

Jeb rubbed his hands together. "Maybe inside's a better idea."

"It's stuffy inside. Tell me what you and Daddy talked about."

"Men things."

"I'm not one of those women who has to be dismissed when matters turn to business. I worked in Daddy's bank for three years before going off to school."

"When did you decide to come home?"

Winona scooted aside and patted the bench next to her. "Join me. Unless you prefer we stand."

Jeb took a seat. "You've another year until you graduate?"

"That and the semester I've missed by coming home. I'm the only daughter in the Mills family. I came home to help out my mother. She needs me around sometimes for support."

"She seems to do well on her own," said Jeb. He cupped the cider and blew on it.

"It's a hard thing to be married to Horace Mills. Daddy's all business and meetings. My mother thinks she has to be the perfect hostess. She gets lonely. I can tell you all that privately, since you're the minister. You've learned how to keep private matters private, I gather, from Reverend Gracie."

"I plan to go and see him again this week. His daughter expects him to be released soon. But they're going to move to Cincinnati with his brother right away."

"How do you really feel about Church in the Dell being handed to you so suddenly? You're obviously learned and well studied. But to have it dropped in your lap so unexpectedly," she said, "has to be a jolt."

Her statement shocked him, considering Fern's assessment of him in the town library. He warmed to the girl right off. "Gracie trusts me to do the job. If Church in the Dell will be patient with me, we can learn together how best to manage the church duties."

"Aren't you lonely?" she asked.

Jeb nodded and gazed back at her, taking well to her interest in him. "I mean, I do have family. My family lives in Texas, mostly. But it's more than that. The pastorate is like having a window shoved down between yourself and the rest of the world. People look at you differently, especially men. I can't just go and play a game of pool at Snooker's. The men all see me as different.

Even the banjo I play is frowned on. I guess it will just collect dust up in my attic from now on."

"You played it here, for me," she said.

"I was Gracie's flunky. People can turn a deaf ear when they don't expect anything of you. But as the pastor, well, some people are still trying to get used to the organ. Banjo picking is straight from the devil—at least according to women like Florence Bernard."

Winona set aside her cup and said, "May I tell you something?"

Jeb read the candor in her face. He nodded.

"When I was going to State, I fell in love with a professor. I never told Momma or Daddy. They'd be so angry."

"Angry at you dating a professor? That doesn't make sense."

"I told him I loved him. That is when he told me he was married. He broke things off with me. I couldn't stand the thought of sitting in his class every day, watching another silly student be lured by his charm. So I came home. That's why I'm here."

"You have a brilliant mind, Winona. You can go to any campus in the nation."

She was enamored of his comment. "That professor . . . he called me stupid." She looked down, composing herself. "You're the first man to think I'm brilliant." Her smile could have lit up the patio. She moved closer to Jeb and allowed her coat to fall open.

Jeb reached up and clasped her neck. He pulled her face toward him and kissed her. Winona wrapped her arms around Jeb and kissed him back. "You know I've been hurt."

Jeb shushed her and they kissed again. Winona extinguished the lantern so that the only overseer of their patio party was the moon. Jeb felt the last traces of Fern slipping from him. It was not as painful as he had imagined.

21

Saturday brought a truck brimming with antique furniture and every earthly good owned by the Gracies to the front walk of the Catholic hospital. As Gracie was wheeled out of the hospital, some of the ladies wept, while most everyone else cheered for the departing minister. Gracie's face looked ripe for plucking, pink and more full of life than anyone had seen him in the last two weeks. Jeb walked beside Emily, who helped to push her daddy down the long walk to their waiting automobile. His brother, Geoffrey from Cincinnati, had arrived to help see the family all the way home. He ran to Gracie's car to open the door. His wife, Dolly, would drive the Gracie vehicle while he managed the large truck filled with his brother's belongings.

Jeb shook Gracie's hand and then grabbed him in a bear hug. "You'll be missed. You're already missed, Reverend," he told him.

"Don't worry over me, Jeb. I'm in good hands. You take care of this flock and those children the Lord's given to you."

Jeb pulled out the key the older man had given him. "You didn't tell me how heavy this is to wear."

"I was afraid you wouldn't take it." Gracie took the hands of the ladies as he passed them by. When he glanced back at Jeb, who did not know how to respond, he laughed out loud.

Jeb and Val Rodwyn helped Gracie into his car. As they backed away to allow the girls and Philip to clamber in behind their daddy, Val said, "Will Honeysack asked me to give you this. I almost forgot." He passed a folded note to Jeb.

Jeb tucked the note into his pocket. "I'm sorry Will and Freda couldn't come today."

"He had family in or some such," said Val. "Will and the missus dropped by earlier in the week to say their good-byes to Reverend Gracie. Can't say as I blame him. It's too sad this way." Val waved at Gracie and the girls and then headed back to his vehicle.

Jeb had helped Gracie's brother load his belongings from the parsonage. They all had decided it best to get the packing over and done with so they could take Philemon directly from the hospital on to Cincinnati.

Jeb felt a pang of sorrow as the Gracies motored away from St. Joseph's. He had kept his conversation with Gracie blithe that morning, not wanting to burden a sick man with problems he was leaving behind. He felt the weight of tomorrow's obligations weighing on him heavier than before.

Angel had come along with him to tell the Gracie children good-bye. She was waiting now for him in the truck. He was glad. On the way home they might have a decent conversation and ease the tension that had been building between them.

❊

"When will we move into the parsonage?" asked Angel. "Not that I've been in a hurry for the Gracies to go." She had as much sincerity in her tone as he had ever heard her use. "Emily is a decent girl. I don't think I really knew her that well until these last few weeks. She's not a fake at all, like I thought." She fell silent for a minute or two and then said, "It's sad to see them go."

"How about Monday? The old Long house is too cold to stay in much past that."

Angel let out a sigh, relieved more than she'd been willing to admit. "A real kitchen again and a good bed."

"Best I load up on some coal."

Her eyes followed a diner they passed along the way and a sign that said, "This way to Bathhouse Row." Then she said, "I got a letter from Aunt Kate. I figured Willie probably told you."

"Good news about your momma, I hope."

"Same as always. Good day and then a bad day."

"I think one of these days your momma's going to sit up in that bed and climb out ready to be her old self again. Next thing you know, she'll be bossing everybody around, same as you."

She seemed cheered up by his words. "I can say one thing—I'm glad not to be living in an attic with Effie and her screaming kid."

"Me too. I'd not have anyone to fight with."

"Oh, you and me will fight again. You're dating that lunatic from the bank's daughter."

Jeb had taken Winona to Beulah's the night before and come home smelling like perfume. Angel had noticed it right off. "How nice is that?"

"Something's not right about her. I don't know. Can't put my finger on it. You know she ain't got Fern Coulter's brains."

"Winona's a smart girl. College educated and better at math than anyone I know."

"She's got you figured out, that I know. When she saw you coming, she took one look and knew all it would take was a wiggle of that figure of hers and you'd be slobberin' like a hound."

"Let's change the subject."

The sun took one last breath and gentled behind the silvering hills.

"It's getting dark," said Angel. She shivered.

"Good thing. I can't wait for a little peace and quiet. This preacher business takes the wind out of you." He hadn't had a full night's sleep in the last two weeks.

"It'll be quiet. Sundays is good for quiet."

❉

At dawn, Jeb pulled out his best white shirt, laid it across his bed, and picked up his sermon notes to study. The last hour before Sunday breakfast had become sacred, a time of shedding off what remained of the week so that he could stand clean as bleached cotton before the congregation.

As he returned to his bed, he lifted yesterday's shirt from the chair where he had undressed the night before. Beneath it on the floor laid the folded note from Val. He had forgotten to read it. He carried it with him back to the bed and read it as he leaned back against the feather pillow. Then he sat up. He reread the note, but found it just as mysterious as the first reading. It was not signed by Will Honeysack. Truth be told, he did not recognize the scratched signature at the bottom of the note that looked like "Red," or perhaps "Fred." The note read:

Dropped by address on delivery. No one about. Left delivery inside.

Red

Jeb pulled on his socks and padded into the parlor. After looking around the room, he saw no package or parcel. He could not remember ordering anything from Honeysack's store. He shrugged and decided he would ask Will about the note before the morning's message.

He dressed early, drank coffee, and then pulled on his coat. As of next week, when they moved back into the parsonage, he would be only a rock's throw from the church. Like Angel, he had to admit that the move back to the comfortable house behind the church would be a relief.

He woke her up. "I'm driving early to the church. You all ride in with Miss Coulter and don't give her any lip."

Angel moaned and then lifted her head. "I'm going, Jeb. Don't be so bossy. I hope you made coffee. I feel like the dickens."

"Don't fall back to sleep," he told her. He left and went outside to warm up the truck.

❋

The water flowed green and cold under Marvelous Crossing Bridge. He drove behind the chapel and parked in front of the parsonage to leave more room for the new parishioners. The parsonage was dark and had a lonely look about it with the Gracies gone.

A sound caught his ear. He looked up, expecting to see perhaps a flock of geese winging overhead. But this was a murmuring sound, a rising and falling commotion that couldn't be caused by geese. He waited and heard it again. The sound was coming from inside the church.

He stamped his boots on the rear porch steps before turning the knob and opening the door to the sanctuary. A sudden flapping and clucking caused him to freeze. He couldn't believe his eyes. Perched along and under the pews of Church in the Dell were two hundred white pullets. The smell from an evening of that many chickens roosting indoors had Jeb covering his nose with his coatsleeve. He coughed, ran out for fresh air, and then staggered back to the doorway to survey the mess.

"What idiot would do this?" He was completely at a loss. It had to be a joke gone awry. Not knowing what else to do, he began chasing the chickens away from the lectern and the altar. But as he herded them down the aisle, more of the feathered creatures flapped around him, hopped, and skidded onto the platform. The noise was deafening.

Every pew was ornamented with feathers and overnight roostings. Jeb checked his watch. Only an hour until the service started.

That is when he remembered the note from Will Honeysack and his nephew Herschel's delivery of chicks.

He yanked it out and read it again. Somebody had messed up the delivery instructions. And over the last month, Herschel's postponed shipment of chicks had grown into pullets.

Jeb slumped down onto a pew. Soon half the town would be filing in under the tolling church bell. The church bell? He groaned. He had completely forgotten about the bell. He had not had time to think about finding and purchasing a new one. Of course, it was a slight matter compared to the mess he had walked into this morning.

"Tarnation!" he yelled.

The pullets scattered.

Think! Think! He could open the doors and send the pullets out into the freezing cold of morning. But after chasing the young hens out of doors, he'd still have to clean up the parting love gifts left him overnight—in less than an hour. And the birds would surely flock under the trees. Some of them might actually survive. He imagined the birds collecting around the church grounds as people arrived. Somehow he had to get them all gathered into one place and out of sight.

He remembered three slumbering Welbys cozied under a blanket. If he rallied a few men along with the Welbys, they might salvage some of the flock and get them into coops. Maybe Will Honeysack would help. This was, after all, his nephew's deal.

He tried to imagine explaining that to the head deacon before his first cup of coffee. He shooed a pecking hen away from his feet and bolted for the door.

❄

Angel and Willie ran down the aisle waving and yelping like they were herding cattle. Ida May kept trying to gather pullets into her skirt so she could name each one. Will Honeysack and his visiting nephew Herschel held cages open while the women and the Welbys ran the pullets through the church.

"I'm sick as I can be about this whole delivery business," Herschel apologized. He had expressed his deepest regrets to Jeb for the botched delivery at least a dozen times, if not more. He had paid two teens, one named Red, to deliver the pullets to Jeb, he said. The boys, down on their luck and in need of some fast money, had mixed up the orders—*Meet Jeb Nubey at said address and ask him where he wants them delivered.* Wanting to be free of the delivery, they had found the back door unlocked, dropped off the pullets, and, just as Herschel had instructed, delivered the cages back to him so they could pick up their money.

"It's as much my fault as anyone else's," said Jeb, trying to ease Herschel's guilt. "I plumb forgot to ask Ivey about his barn. Then I forgot to look at the note Val handed to me yesterday."

"Law, they smell like the devil!" said Freda. She and Herschel's young wife had chased hens and held their noses until they were out of breath.

"So you bought all these chickens, and for what? What'd you think we would do with two hundred of them?" demanded Angel.

"Jeb, the women will finish cleaning up for you. Herschel and I are going to take these out to Long's barn. We'll stop him on the way to church and make sure he knows why they're on his place."

The sound of car doors slamming outside brought everyone into the aisle.

Willie came running up the pew rows, herding three more pullets ahead of him. "Folks is pulling in to church!" he hollered.

"It smells like a barn in here!" Angel fell back against a pew. "I'm going to become a Methodist. They're quieter."

Ida May piped up. "Maybe they'll think angels has been here." She blew a handful of feathers into the air.

"I don't smell anything," said Jeb. "Act calm, Angel. No one will notice."

Freda looked worried. Will and Herschel disappeared out the back door.

Angel sat up, picking feathers from her dress. She let out a sigh, grabbed the bucket of soapy water the women had brought over from the parsonage, and shoved it under a pew.

Jeb held out his hand to the first group of women who came through the door. "Morning, ladies! Beautiful day, ain't it?"

❋

The morning's sermon went better than Jeb had imagined it might. More than once he witnessed white tufts floating through the air like celestial droppings. Josie Hipps had swatted curiously at them and then gone back to her nodding. Florence Bernard kept sniffing the air but was too polite to comment. Doris Jolly sneezed throughout the entire morning and finally sneaked out the front door altogether until time for the benedictory song.

As Jeb led the congregation in the closing prayer, he heard a clucking sound from the rear of the church. Angel's and Willie's heads lifted in unison. A white pullet crossed the aisle between the two last pews and disappeared. Angel said something to Willie.

Jeb raised his voice and tried to drown out the commotion as a wave of muttering shot through the congregation. Eyes peeped open to glance around nervously. As he spoke the final amen, he noticed a few of the women whispering back and forth before politely resuming their forward and genteel postures.

Willie slid out of the pew, the first to hit the aisle. In a flutter of squawking and feathers, he swung the remaining pullet into the air by the feet and then disappeared through the front door.

Jeb quickly descended to the center aisle to draw startled gazes back to the front. "Sister Jolly, lead us as we go, if you will, in a departing chorus. 'I'll fly away, oh glory, I'll fly away . . .' "

Angel hid her face in her hands.

22

The chimneys puffed with hazy gray and black smoke, mixing with the late October air. The hollow was cold, and few families had the good fortune to smoke a wild turkey or a goose for a Thanksgiving that was only several weeks away. The Bluetooths had stopped selling their soap and leather along the roadways due to the cold, and most of the merchants had more to sell than the locals were willing to buy. But the pinch of the last two winters was easing, and more families than not were chatting up the need for a Christmas social in the hollow come December.

Jeb could hear Florence Bernard and Freda Honeysack above the din of women who had gathered in the church to plan the festivities. He closed the door to the study and returned to finish the church books. When Gracie had pulled away with his children the church had scarcely had two nickels to rub together. But the past several Sundays' offerings had brought in some hefty donations from Ace Timber. Jeb studied the signature on the most recent check but did not know the benefactor—a man whose surname was Farnsworth. The first name he could not decipher.

He recorded the check along with the usual dollars, dimes, and pennies given by the Church in the Dell flock. In spite of the increase in attendance, the fact that so many were still out of work while waiting for Ace Timber's full operation to move in had not increased the giving. Without the Ace Timber donation, Jeb might not have had enough to pay himself or keep the lights on.

He breathed a prayer of thanks and tallied the bank deposit. He still had not made mention to Mills of no longer acting as the deliveryman for the bank, but the banker had not brought up the matter, either. Bringing it up over dinner with Mills as he courted his daughter would have been nothing short of ill-mannered. Besides, the pastorate had begun to fill every minute of the day with house visits.

The raucous laughter out in the sanctuary indicated the committee women were in good spirits. During his two and a half months in the pulpit, Jeb's approval among the Church in the Dell elect had risen incrementally day by day. He stuck his head out the door and said, "I think that in keeping with the Christmas observance, ladies, we should plan on enjoying a smoked ham from Smithfield's farm." A few ladies voiced approval.

"True, Reverend. Best hams in the state," said Freda.

Florence said, "He's not a member of the church. I doubt he'll take much off his price."

Jeb pulled a couple of bills out of the bank bag and said, "We had a good week. Here's two dollars to put down on it. Order the ham."

The ladies cheered.

As Jeb walked the deposit out to his truck, he heard two women conversing in the sunlight near the church drive. One planted pansies near the churchhouse sign while the other complimented her work. She turned in time to see Jeb.

"Morning, Reverend," said Winona.

Winona had found numerous reasons to visit the church over the last few weeks. She had shown up at the parsonage and enticed Jeb out onto the porch in spite of the cold on many a night after the Welbys had fallen asleep. This morning she held out a bag to him that smelled of things fresh baked. "Momma baked biscuits this morning. I thought you'd like some." She wore a yellow dress with cherries dancing along the collar. The color made her face sallow. She had always looked fresh from the department store, but today crescents of blue under her eyes made her look as though she nursed a cold.

Jeb thanked her. He accepted her gift and was excusing himself to leave when she said, "We're still on for Friday night, aren't we?"

Jeb said, "Of course, just like every Friday night. Willie's been sick with something, but I figure he'll be on the mend by Friday."

"His sister sees to him."

"Influenza's going around. Can't be too careful these days, especially with youngens." From the looks of her, he half-expected Winona to say that she had been fighting the flu as well, but she changed the subject.

"Looks like you're going to the bank," she said.

"Appears I am." Jeb smiled.

"If you don't mind my suggesting that I give you a ride, we can ride together. I've been wanting to share something with you. But with all the goings-on at the church, we've had little privacy lately."

"Long's I can drive. Don't look right for you to be driving me around."

❊

They had driven within a mile of Marvelous Crossing Bridge when Winona leaned toward Jeb and kissed the side of his face. Then she said, "I saw Fern Coulter at Honeysack's at the crack of dawn. She scarcely said two words to me. Have you noticed she's been acting kind of funny lately? Not to gossip, but she's never been the most friendly person in Nazareth."

Jeb had noticed Fern leaving church earlier than usual the last couple of weeks. "Fern's got her own ways. I quit trying to figure her out long ago."

"She's not from around here and that may have something to do with it. Oklahoma people have their own ways. We have ours."

"I don't suppose you drove all the way over from your place to talk about Fern Coulter." For some reason, Winona's questions about Fern irritated him.

"You're starting to know me better than myself, Jeb. I have a letter here with some news about that family in Pine Bluff."

Jeb could not recall what family in Pine Bluff, but his irritation kept him from commenting.

"Now all of this came about after I had scarcely mentioned to my friend from out of town that you might be looking for a home for the Welby children. I hadn't even thought of it at all myself because that's your business, and you clearly said you weren't interested. And that's final as far as I'm concerned. But yesterday this letter came, and this family is looking for a little girl Ida May's age. They are willing to take all three children just so they can have a little girl like Ida May." She waited a moment as if for Jeb to comment and then added, "I think that speaks well of them."

"Winona, I know Angel's had her problems, but with the Hopper boy out of the picture, she's settled down a tolerable amount. Packing her and Willie and Ida May off with strangers might upset the applecart for these kids, so to speak."

"I knew you'd say that. But you've not exactly been yourself, what with taking over the minister's role here at Church in the Dell. Who can blame you for not being able to think straight? You look worn out all the time, up at dawn visiting sick people. Up at all hours with farmers and sick cows and women in labor. Then to have to take care of someone else's children on top of all that. I mean, if they were your own, then certainly I could see you doting on them. But that oldest girl shows little respect for you, and don't think these loose-tongued women don't notice it. She doesn't understand your role like Emily Gracie understood her daddy's place in the community. You'd never hear her up at the town Woolworth's spouting off about her daddy."

Winona covered her mouth with her hand. The longer she spoke, the more the momentum of her subject carried her further into a kind of unwitting anxiety.

"Angel's been spouting off at the Woolworth's about me?"

Winona fell as silent as snow.

"You already told me, Winona, so you may as well spill it out."

"To hear her tell it, you conspired against the Hoppers."

"Angel said that in front of everybody?"

"If everybody is the town mayor, the school headmaster, the man that sweeps up the streets, and the apple hawker on the corner near Woolworth's."

Angel had been so polite of late that Jeb thought she had finally let go of the Hoppers.

"It wasn't my intent to tell you all that, just the part about the Pine Bluff family. She'll hate me now more than ever. You can't tell her, Jeb."

"Angel doesn't hate you."

"Last Sunday she sidled past me down the church aisle and the look she gave me would melt nails."

Jeb had believed that things between them were on the mend. He also thought of how he could have left her behind in Little Rock to be pecked on by the hungry buzzards devouring her Aunt Kate and her wretched brood. Angel had yet to appreciate the life he had given her. "Let me see that letter from Pine Bluff, Winona."

Winona pulled the letter from her handbag, but then hesitated. "I feel awful about all of this."

Jeb slid the letter out of her hand. "What time is dinner again?"

"Friday night at seven. Unless sooner is better." She slid out a stick of gum and snapped her bag closed.

"The sooner the better," said Jeb. It seemed easier to embrace the new life in front of him than to try to keep piecing together the mess from the past. "We're driving to Hope, if that's all right with you. There's a new place that's open for dinner. I'll pick you up Friday night at six."

A logging truck hugged the side of the road. The driver caught sight of Jeb and Winona approaching in the

rearview mirror and then, letting out a gaseous stream
from the growling engine, rolled forward. Jeb saw the
three newly employed men sitting on top of the freshly
cut timber like monkeys with their cups full of pennies.
He laughed. "There's a sight for sore eyes."

He'd deal with Angel tonight.

❄

Angel had settled back into the parsonage as though
she'd never left it. She had pinned up magazine pictures
of movie stars in a frame around the window. She leaned
against a picture of Claudette Colbert. She closed her
eyes and held her breath.

Jeb pounded against the door. It was only a matter of
minutes until he dismantled the lock from the outside and
threw open the door. "Angel, you may as well unlock the
door! Hiding yourself won't help matters!"

Angel huffed and finally marched to the door and
turned the lock. She kept her back to Jeb as he marched
in behind her. "You aren't listening, so what's the point?"

"In front of the mayor, the whole town, you trashed
my name. I'm the preacher of these people, and you go
off half cocked because of some silly boy crush. This is
serious, Angel. I shouldn't have to explain about reputation to you. You're old enough to know better!"

"I barely said anything at all and to one person. If it
was carried further, is it my fault?"

"So you mouthed off down at the Woolworth's?"

"I know you think things is going right for you, Jeb.
But you're just blind to matters. The Hoppers are gone,
and now you don't have to see the hurt in Mrs. Hopper's
eyes or think about the way she feels when she can't feed

herself or her kids at suppertime. You don't see because you made it all go away! I remember a day when you saw people like the Hoppers as humans instead of trash."

"I don't know if you've noticed, but things have gotten better for Church in the Dell, not worse, and not just for us. This town's lumbermill is up and working. They's a whole new timber operation settling down right here in Nazareth and I for one am proud to be part of it. The Hoppers were in a fix, yes, but Asa had too much pride to let anyone help. Now he's in prison, and his family's been put out, but I didn't put them there. You're taking on confusion like a leaky boat takes on water, Angel."

"Beck told me he'd write when they settled, and it's been a whole month. If they've broken down along the road somewhere with no one to help them, we'd never know."

"What do you expect me to do? Go driving up and down the road hollering out Hopper's name and hope to find them?"

"You shouldn't have let them leave, Jeb."

"None of this matters a hill of beans anymore, Angel. Some people are beyond help. I have a church to run, bills to pay, and a flock that needs tending. This church was dying when we came. Remember? Now it's a fine little place with a congregation and respectability."

"Maybe I don't know much about preachering, but this kind of respectability don't sound like something God would take to." Angel fell back onto her bed and brought her hands up over her face.

"Angel, I need to tell you something. I know we've had our differences, but I've always loved you, Willie, and Ida May." He hesitated, not knowing if he should deal the next hand.

Angel sat up and at once read his expression. He saw anxiety suddenly wash over her face. She pulled her knees against her chest and swallowed hard. "If it's an apology you're wanting, I'm sorry for what I said at the Woolworth's, Jeb."

"They's a family in Pine Bluff that's been looking for a little girl to call their own. A girl Ida May's age——"

"You're not sending Ida May off, Jeb, without me! She'd be scared to death."

"They're willing to take all three of you." Jeb pulled the letter from his trouser pocket.

She stared at him for the length of time it would take for a trapped bug to measure the marvel of a web and then said, "You can't throw us out!" She wiped the tears from her cheeks, angry. "If this is the way it is, Jeb, then why didn't you leave me in Little Rock?"

"This will give you the momma and daddy you been needing. I can't do for you in the manner you need anymore, Angel. You're bullheaded and I just keep giving in. I don't want you to end up like your cousin Effie."

"I hate you!"

"Why you want to make me feel like a louse? I'm trying to do right by you. Thousands of youngens are out wandering the roads, and you got a family that wants you, Angel. They can care for you and make sure you stay out of trouble. With a good family you can make something of yourself."

"If I won't go, neither will Willie or Ida May. They do as I say."

"Ida May needs a momma, not a dictator."

"You was mean when I met you, and you're mean still! Nothing's changed about you, Jeb Nubey. You might wear better things now or part your hair different, but you is still the same mean man that crawled into Nazareth rain soaked and looking for a free meal ticket. All you've done is trade people like the Hoppers like you're trading a mule. You get respectability and anyone in your way gets the boot!" She hid her face in her pillow and sobbed.

Jeb took a deep breath but didn't answer her. The whole matter of Angel left his heart stranded on a bad stretch of road.

23

Jeb took a shovel to the thin sheet of ice that had formed overnight on the rear porch steps. When he put away the shovel, he found the crawl-space door ajar. A raccoon had most likely found its way beneath the church for warmth and to forage for a midnight meal. Jeb stuck his head into the musty space. A three-foot spread of potatoes had frozen. He raked out the damaged tubers and piled them into a burlap bag.

When he stomped into the church, his muttering brought a loud laugh from the front. He looked up, surprised to find he wasn't alone. "Fern."

"I'm glad it's me standing back here and not Florence Bernard. She might mistake your muttering for swearing."

Jeb tried to apologize.

"I like that about you. You always make me laugh."

Jeb took off his hat and grabbed the broom. The new floor required a good sweeping every other morning, and it gave him a reason not to look Fern square in the eyes. When he'd first seen her standing in the light from the windows, he'd had to jolt his memory so that he could even remember why he was supposed to be angry with her. "Could I help you this morning, Fern?" Or did you drop by casually to poke fun? he thought.

"If you'd give me the chance, I'd like to call a truce."

Jeb recalled the scene in the library, remembering the manner in which she had described him to her uppity friend from school that afternoon. He stiffened. "You probably think someone of my caliber has time for chitchat. That's understandable. I know my reputation with you." He swallowed and continued. "My eyes have been opened to a lot of things this past year, including how you feel about me." He swiped a cobweb off the wall with the broom, but kept looking at her, ready for one of her snappy comebacks.

"Since I've taken to teaching only the lower school and tutoring an hour after school, I have an hour now between my two morning classes. I noticed Angel was not her usual self. Downright surly, if you ask me. I thought now would be a good time to ask you about her." She was refusing his argument, elevating herself above him again.

"That's another thing. You think because you and me once had—that we were once, *nearly,* anyway—that you can put your hands in things that don't concern you."

Fern turned ashen. "I should leave."

"I realize that I'm not the best substitute daddy in the world for the Welbys, but I've made do the best I can."

"No one can argue the fact."

"What I'm trying to say is that you don't have to be so involved in the Welbys' lives anymore. Like coming over every Sunday to button Ida May's dress and making biscuits for the kids." The more he talked, the more sickened he felt. While his intent had been to defend himself, the result had hurt the woman he could never quite shake from his thoughts.

"No one makes me do that. I do it because I like it."

"Angel's big enough to do that. You might see things turn better between the two of you if you'd back off." His voice quivered.

Fern stiffened. She opened her handbag and pulled out a handkerchief. Then her eyes lifted to Jeb. "I can see," she said, "that I've only made things worse."

Jeb felt the broom handle fall from his hands. He saw her tears and the way the corners of her eyes turned down as she saw something in him that pricked down deep into her soul and left her without words. Fern was never at a loss for words until he had gone too deep with the blade. Come to think of it, he had never known the plumbing depths of any woman's threshold for hurt, let alone Fern's. That was kind of a nuisance with which he had learned to live.

She gave in to him by saying nothing at all. Jeb wanted to swear at himself for hurting her. He tried to find the words to say how sorry he was for being the backside of a mule. But all he could do was watch her turn from him, like the last leaf falling from the last branch in November. As hard as he tried to mine Fern from his heart, the farther she became embedded.

"I'm sorry I interrupted your work, Reverend."

"Could you tell me your reason for coming?" he choked out.

"To invite you to dinner Friday night."

Jeb remembered his date with Winona, but nothing would make him tell her. "I wouldn't be good company, Fern." He felt as if he were choking.

She turned at the last second and held the church door open. "I guess you want to tell me why not."

"I'm not a learned man," he whispered just above the sound of an icicle falling outside onto the porch. He was a complete fool now.

Fern took two quick breaths. She waited at the door, confusion causing her brows to furrow. Then her eyes widened and she shook her head as if arguing with someone. She left and the door slammed behind her.

Jeb pondered the minutes that had just passed. It seemed to him that over the last few weeks, every choice that had seemed right had curdled like turned milk. Right and wrong, up and down, yes and no all seemed to carry the same weight until he tossed one or the other at the feet of the person whose life he was affecting. It seemed to him that God kept handing him the white ball or the black ball to cast into the box of fate. Every choice he dropped had fallen through space, black and menacing, fatefully hateful. Systematically, he was squashing every life that had loved him, and every time he did, his own got a little smaller. While elevating himself in the eyes of so many, he was left more miserable than the day before.

He heard Fern's engine turn over. Then he looked at his feet to see if any bullet holes riveted his boots. After all, his habit of shooting himself in the foot had become his new sideline.

❄

Jeb found the longer he rubbed down the pews the madder he got, so he took a drive into town to have coffee and find a place to soothe the ocean that stormed his thoughts. To his good pleasure, he found Hayes Jernigan sipping coffee at Beulah's when he took a stool at the bar. The lumbermill owner asked Jeb to join him. "I need some good company, Hayes," said Jeb.

"You sound troubled, Parson." Hayes held out his cup to allow Beulah to fill it and give him a smile.

"Just when I think I've learned all there is to learn about women, I find out I'm still in grammar school."

Hayes let out a laugh that drew the attention of some of the other lumbermen parked against the far wall. When they returned to their mumbling, Hayes said, "Women are like a good herd of cattle. You inspect them for good proportion and healthy eyes and teeth. But somehow, as the years pass, you start to find out just how little some of the heifers pass muster."

"Molly know you're comparing her to a cow, Hayes?" Beulah asked, miffed.

"All I know is that women want you to know all the rules about them, but they don't want to tell you. You have to play this guessing game. Then you get all those womanly rules figured out in your mind and blam!" Jeb slammed his fist against the counter and made Beulah flinch. "They up and change the rules on you."

A few of the lumbermen clapped and then held up their empty coffee cups to Beulah. She threw down her wiping towel and disappeared into the back.

"Looks like you up and gave the whole morning crew a coffee break, Hayes," said Jeb.

"We're having a meeting. When they saw you come in, Tuck Haw said I'd better give you the lowdown on what's going on at the bank."

Beulah brought Jeb his coffee and a biscuit but wouldn't look at either of them.

"I knew that to take on this bigger job with Ace Timber, I'd need some new equipment and some working capital to pay my boys until we knock out this first job. The Hoppers had the best timber woods, thick and pretty, but hardwoods need better blades than we've been using making barrels."

Jeb tried not to flinch when Hayes said "Hopper."

"So I knew the bank would have no problem making me the loan for the expansion of the mill's business. But Mills, he put me off for several days. I was beginning to worry when he sent for me. When I come in, he danced around prettier than a burley-cue girl, using all kinds of words, like he thought I would be too stupid to understand."

Jeb pushed aside the biscuit.

"But bottom line is this: Ace Timber wants a piece of the Jernigan Mills pie. A big piece, if you catch my drift. They're willing to front us the money directly—for a share of the company."

"Stockholders are not a bad idea," said Jeb.

"Fifty-one percent is the piece of the pie they're asking. Don't they call that 'controlling innerst' or some such?"

Jeb did not know how to answer.

"Tuck Haw, he says his brother's wife's cousin—they got a place in Texas—says that Ace Timber took over an operation not far from Texarkana. All the men that had been laid off were put back on the line, but at half pay. You do that to our men and they won't be able to pay the landlord, let alone put grub on the table."

"Half pay is slave wages, Hayes. You and I know that. Did you say that to Mills?" asked Jeb.

"Mills says he is only passing along the offer, that he don't know nothing about the hiring practices of Ace Timber. He told me not to jump to conclusions."

"Mills has the town's best interests at heart, Hayes. Don't you worry none. I'll go down to the bank this afternoon and meet with him. We'll get this straightened out." Jeb patted Hayes's shoulder.

"I told the boys you'd be on our side. They have this idea that you're in Mills's back pocket. But you're not crooked like some say. I know that about you."

"Who says that, Hayes? I want those rumors to stop!" Jeb slammed his hand against the counter. This time all the lumbermen fell quiet, like stilled spindles. Jeb spun around and came onto the floor. He wanted to tell the lumbermen that he was a man of honor, that he had not aided a pack of rich scoundrels in offing with a poor family's inheritance. But it seemed his words lately had the wrong effect on matters. He decided it was best to allow his actions to speak for him. "You boys don't worry yourselves over this Ace Timber matter."

Tuck Haw's gaze lifted above the others. Jeb could not tell if Tuck was glowering or giving him the thumbs-up. He left Beulah's and headed for the bank.

❄

Afternoon light bled slowly onto the floor of Horace Mills's office. The clock on the wall had a tinny sound, ticking off the seconds like the timer on a detonator. Mona had led Jeb directly into Horace's private office and left him sitting for a quarter hour, waiting to meet with the banker, who had been tied up all morning in an unnamed meeting. Just as Jeb had twisted a second window tassel into a braided tangle, Horace burst into the study, blustery, apologetic, and muttering under his breath.

Jeb lifted from his seat by the window and sat in the chair that faced Mills head on. "I should apologize to you, Mr. Mills. You weren't expecting me. I should know in times like this that bankers keep a tight calendar."

"Reverend, as always, I'm glad to see you. It's good for a banker's soul to stop and break bread with those who don't spend their living spinning deals." He held out a dish. "Have a candy?"

"Mr. Mills, I'll cut to the chase. I just came from Beulah's where the lumbermen from Jernigan's operation were holding a meeting."

"And you think I'm involved in some scandal to skim profits from the town lumber industry."

"I'd never say something like that," said Jeb.

"But you thought as much. Jeb, you should know that lumbermen are a different breed of men. They're tough—love to live by the sweat of the brow—and they look out for one another. A kind of brotherhood, if you will. I expect them to ask questions about the winds of change that have blown into Nazareth of late. It's their right and privilege. They have to look out for kith and kin, so to speak, and protect their own interests. But their clannish ways might cause them to sniff down the wrong trunk or peep into a hole that has nothing more in it than harmless rainwater. You catch my meaning, I'm sure."

Jeb reached into the candy dish.

"Not too many years ago, I met up with the man who started Ace Timber. He was a fine man, a man of means. But he sat me down, lit me up a really fine, fine stogie, and shared his story with me. He was an orphan boy, brought up in a foundlings' home. Never heard tell of such harsh surroundings as was told to me by him. But that boy had enough pluck about him to go off and learn the lumber trade. He saved every dime until he could buy into a little sawmill operation up in Houston. From there, he kept reinvesting his profits and buying up more and more operations until he had his own company. While other mills floundered when the Depression hit—and it hit the lumber industry like a stack of dynamite—his operation survived. That boy was the fellow you met that night at Amy's party. Fellow by the name of Jefferson Watts."

Jeb nodded. "So he's the owner of Ace Timber? Land partners with those two railroad men?"

"I swear, Reverend, you do pay attention."

"What interest does the railroad have in Nazareth? The railroads passed up Nazareth for another town back in the turn of the century, I hear," said Jeb.

"Men like Watts, Lepinski, and Steele are entrepreneurs. They deal in deals; they're the kingpins of deals. So they find men of like minds and invest together. It's over your head, I'm sure. Preachers don't have to worry about such things."

"Money deals, no, Mr. Mills, I don't get involved. But human folk, they're my business. Those lumbermen, also my business."

"I understand. I ask your cooperation in the matter in helping to quell any insurgencies from the Jernigan camp. You are a peacemaker, Reverend, and this town knows it. Heaven's bestowed upon you a fine way of massaging troubled hearts into harmony. Harmony is essential to the makings of a successful town."

"I don't know what to make of your use of the word 'massage,' Mr. Mills."

"Now that you're here on business, though, I think it's time to help you with the church's fund-raising efforts." Mills reached into his desk and pulled out a long envelope.

Jeb rubbed his eyes and temple and then said, "Mr. Mills, I think it's in the church's best interest that I no longer make deliveries for the bank. I know I should have told you before now. These hard times make for surly parishioners. The one thing Philemon Gracie tried to teach me is to stay out of town politics and mind those interests that might bring conflict."

"Conflict, Reverend? I assure you there is no conflict involved. Consider yourself the bearer of good tidings to the hurting families of Nazareth. They need suffer no longer through this whiplash of a Depression."

"I want to know the name of the family." Jeb stated it as quietly as he could manage.

"Bluetooth. Injun family. Leastways, the husband's Injun. Old man ran off and left her. Same old story, same as what's happened to so many good families in Nazareth and every other town in the county."

"Is that a bank foreclosure, Mr. Mills?"

"Offer, Reverend, to prevent foreclosure."

Jeb came to his feet. "I will not do it, Mr. Mills." He backed out of Horace Mills's office. "The last time I did this, I didn't sleep for weeks. Maybe you have a right to foreclose on those that aren't making their payments, but I can't let you use the office of the clergy to *massage* your way into deals. Not for any amount of money."

Jeb did not stop walking until he came to a stop in the

middle of Main. A Ford drove around him, came down on the horn, and left him in a cloud of road silt.

By now Angel would be walking Willie and Ida May home from school. Jeb imagined how Angel would be worrying over how she would tell her brother and sister of this new family from Pine Bluff that would take them in. She would paint Jeb in dark colors, hateful terms that made him out to be a louse.

He thought of what had just transpired in the bank president's office. At least this time Angel would be only half right. He had shed the louse title, if only for a night.

24

A deep cold had seeped into Nazareth by Friday night, coating every stick and tree in a hoary rime. The hollow blued like the veils of some ice queen, and nothing remained of November except the meager meals planned by the local families for Thanksgiving.

When Jeb arrived at the Mills estate to pick up Winona, he could smell potatoes and peas simmering in pots generous with butter.

Winona appeared at the door, dressed in blue and some feathered headgear that made her face look soft and round. "I'm not ashamed to say I've changed outfits three times waiting for tonight to come," she said.

Jeb remembered how he had left matters with Horace, but only said, "Is your momma or daddy about?"

"Sitting down to dinner, but let's go. The walls start to close in on me when I've been here too long." When Jeb lingered, she gave him a pleading look until he turned and escorted her to her automobile.

"My friends have been to this restaurant in Hope. They tell me good things about it." He opened the door for her on the passenger side.

The drive from Nazareth to Hope was so quiet that Jeb finally decided to query her. "I stopped by the bank this week to pay your daddy a visit."

Winona shuddered and pulled her fur around her shoulders, saying how she wondered if she would ever be warm again.

"Business, of course. Your daddy didn't mention it?"

"Bank business, Jeb? You want to talk about bank business on a night when we can shoot for the moon and get away from everything that corrals us day after day?"

"I suppose you're right."

"When we leave behind this shabby old town tonight, Jeb, let's make a vow, you know, like a pact between us. You'll be you tonight—not Reverend Nubey, but Jeb. And I'm not the daughter of the town banker. Just Winona."

Jeb sighed. "We are who we are, Winona."

"Not tonight." The tension in her tone made her stop and gather her thoughts. "I want to tell you that I've been jealous of Fern Coulter for a long time. But not in the way you imagine. I envy her knowing you as a scoundrel. I want to know that side of you."

"I've left him behind, for good."

"Then bring him back. For me, tonight, Jeb." She leaned across the seat and brought her face close to his. "I can be bad too."

Jeb smelled her perfume and considered what he wanted to say. Instead, he said, "I tried the bad-guy life. I don't recommend it."

He drove them across Marvelous Crossing Bridge. When they left behind the lake, he could see the slightest glimmer of moon on a distant pond. Long's Pond. A light, faintly yellow, shone beyond the pond, and he realized Fern was home. He imagined her sitting alone at her kitchen table eating a bowl of warmed-over soup, and it saddened him.

"Oh, look there, yonder. Oz is in town. You always know when you see that Packard of his parked out in front of Fern's place on a Friday night."

Jeb held tightly to the steering wheel to keep Winona's car from sliding into a ditch. The tires swerved, and he jerked the wheel to bring them right again.

"I'm sorry. Does that upset you?"

"Icy patch. You were saying—something about being bad?"

"You pay attention to me, Jeb, to what I'm saying. Not many fellas are good at that kind of thing."

"Tell me about this professor friend. He broke your heart. I can tell that about you."

"I never heard history told like he could tell it. That's what first drew me to him. It was a stupid sophomore crush, and I look back on the way I behaved and I hate myself for allowing him to use me."

"You never told your momma. Maybe you should. Amy seems like a sensible person."

"Who tells Daddy everything. I can't take the disappointment in his eyes. Daddy has this way of looking at me and making me feel like I'm twelve years old again. When I was twelve, he made me feel six. I can't measure up to that person he imagines me to be." She kissed Jeb on the side of the face and then sat back against her seat. "Jeb, can we talk about something else?"

"Tell me about this restaurant in Hope. You mentioned your friends have gone to it before?"

"It's not a big restaurant. But they have beer. How long's it been since you had a beer?"

"I just got my first pulpit and don't plan to lose it."

"I like that about you too. You got this religious conviction and this bad-boy image all rolled into one delicious package. One dance with me, Jeb, and one beer. You do that, and I'm all yours."

"Winona, it's not an easy thing you ask of me." He remembered how he had sat by and watched Oz twirl Fern on the dance floor. "One dance, as long as none of our church members are around?"

"And a beer."

"No beer. I'd never stop with only one."

"One dance, then." She allowed the fur to drop behind her and came up on one knee. She kissed Jeb on the corner of his mouth, twice, softly. Her hand came down his chest and rested on his thigh.

Jeb knew he should do the sensible thing: turn around and take Winona back home to join the folks for a plate of potatoes and peas. But he kept driving toward Hope and giving in to this girl's imaginative sense of discovery. His hand dropped and rested on top of hers. Her skin was soft, and he decided that she smelled of something costly, like the kind of perfume a girl would pick up in Little Rock.

She lifted her hand from time to time to brush Jeb's hair away from his forehead or make a soft circle around his earlobe with her finger. "You better know right now you're in trouble with me, Jeb Nubey."

She whispered most everything she said between

Nazareth and Hope. Her words seeped into Jeb's head like sweet icing melting on fresh-baked cake.

❄

Automobiles filled the parking lot around the Candlelight Café and Bar, every chrome fender and headlight red and blue with neon from the flashing bar sign. Couples drifted in and out of barroom doors framed by tobacco halos.

Jeb helped Winona back into her wrap. The freezing air sent them both running inside and laughing at how the cold dictated their pace. Winona passed a couple of bills to a maître d', who led them to a red booth in the restaurant's farthest corner. She made a turn like a cat does before lying down and said, "No religious types around here."

"Except for us," said Jeb.

"You mean it, don't you? I mean, this preacher act's not an act." She scooted next to Jeb in the booth and turned down the offer to check her coat.

"I could tell you anything, Winona. How would you know the difference?"

"By the way you treat me. We made it all the way to the restaurant, didn't we?" She said to the waitress, "Two beers for starters."

"I'll order, if you don't mind. Coffee for me. Beer for the lady, please."

"May as well give me coffee too." When the waitress left to turn in the order, Winona said, "You think one beer's going to corrupt you?"

"How about if I don't talk about your daddy's business and you don't talk about mine?" Jeb wearied of how

Winona kept pointing out his constraint, like he was some provincial spinster. He remembered a time when he made the same judgment on others. He watched men around the bar using coy talk with the ladies and knew by heart all the best lines. The smell of tobacco and gin brought back memories of girls he had sweet talked and ditched just like this college teacher had done to Winona.

"You just take yourself seriously. I think it's sweet."

"You think that religion's about being good, Winona."

"Let's decide what's good to eat here." She opened a menu.

Jeb pulled down her menu and made her look at him. "Have you ever read anything by Pascal?"

Winona lifted the menu back up. "Friday-night special looks good. Pascal. He's that guy down in Florida that writes on playing the horses and such. I know a lot more than you think, Jeb."

Jeb sighed. Fern would roll her eyes at Winona right about now while Blaise Pascal rolled over in his grave. He picked up his menu, then laid it down and said, "Winona, I don't think I can send the Welbys away. Not to Pine Bluff or Timbuktu or anyplace."

"No one is forcing you to do it, Jeb. It was nothing more than an option. You know about options, don't you? You got two choices, so you pick one and see how things turn out. In your case, you got this string of kids to think about while you're taking on this church and all its churchy business. So you weigh your options. My daddy does that when he makes a decision." She closed her menu and smiled. The blue feathers in the flashing light made her look like a peacock.

"You're like your daddy. You have a way of looking

disappointed when things don't go like you planned. Are the Welbys so bad for me?"

"They aren't your kids, Jeb. One day you're going to meet the girl of your dreams and she'll want a family with you. Not someone else's family." Winona heard the small band on the other side of the bar strike up the first note. "Someone promised me a dance."

Jeb followed Winona out onto the floor. But while she had played the aggressor all night, now he pulled her back next to him and took the lead. Winona laid her head against Jeb's shoulder. She all but crumpled against him, demonstrating the same vulnerability he had sensed the first time they kissed out on the patio. He smelled her hair and felt the soft way her hand slipped into his.

"I'm sorry about how I've acted with you, Jeb. I really don't throw myself at men." She drew up and looked at him. "And I understand why I need God. It's because he wants me to follow a better way than my own."

Jeb nodded, half surprised at her sudden conversion.

"You ever lost your head and then wished you hadn't?" she asked.

"It's been a problem for me."

"Nazareth's not a place that offers a lot of options. Tonight, when I saw you standing in the doorway looking the way you look in that dark coat, I lost my head. I want to start over and act like we just met."

"How many starts you need out of the gate before you're satisfied?"

"Until I get it right with you."

Jeb spun her around, and they wound up in front of a window that gave them a view of the crisp night. The sky was black, with stars frozen in place in a celestial lake.

Winona laughed and that caused Jeb to ask her what was funny.

"I'm the only girl in church that's danced with the minister," she said and then laughed again.

Jeb wondered how long a girl like her could keep secrets.

❋

Jeb and Winona talked all the way back to Nazareth. She talked of owning a horse once and training for an equestrian show. Her vocabulary improved as she spoke of topics that interested her. When Jeb finally pulled into the Millses' long drive, Winona let out a sigh and said, "You've given me the best gift I've had in a long time, Jeb. A memory I intend to keep."

"Let me walk you in," said Jeb. He helped her put on her fur again and escorted her all the way into the parlor. The only light in the room was the dim electric glow of a fake candlestick sconce. Horace and Amy Mills and all the household servants had retired for the night.

"Come up to my room."

Jeb's eyes gazed up the staircase. He wanted to oblige. "I'd better get back to the kids."

Winona pulled off her feathered cap and fluffed out her curls. She looked impish in the dim glow. "You wanted to tell me something when you first picked me up tonight. I should have let you speak. Sometimes I'm bad about avoiding confrontation."

"I'm sorry if I seemed confrontational."

"I know about your meeting with my father. Word gets around fast when Horace Mills doesn't get his way."

"And you think I'm crazy for telling him no."

"Don't put words in my mouth, Jeb."

"I didn't take on this pulpit to be a delivery boy, Winona."

"You're the first man I've ever met that would stand up to Horace Mills." She snugged up close to him again. "But I want you to know my daddy's quite the persuasive man. He doesn't take to 'no' often. I mean, he's a gentleman and all, but he knows what he wants."

"I can't be used like that. I'll never forget the look that Angel gave me when she found out I had delivered the Ace Timber offer to the Hoppers. At first I thought she didn't understand adult things. But now I think she probably understood more than I give her credit for."

"My daddy hasn't done anything wrong, Jeb, if that's what you're saying. He's an honest banker, and that's hard to come by in these hard times. The Hoppers lost out because they didn't think ahead."

Winona sounded like a recording of her daddy. He pulled away from her. He made with an apology that sounded lame to him, but the hour was late and he was tired. "Time for me to go, Winona."

"I don't want you to leave, Jeb. You're the best thing to come into my life in a long time."

Jeb kissed her until she gently pulled away. "Dinner again next week?" he asked.

"Why wait?" Winona followed him to the door. Her face grew taut and the girlish waif disappeared. "Remember what I said about Daddy, Jeb. He has his job to do. He'll see that it's done right. You might consider honoring what he's trying to do for this town and for Church in the Dell."

"You're a loyal daughter, Winona. But my loyalty has

to be with people that need my help. Who will help them if I don't?"

"The church must be doing well now, then, if you can help out the people that need it, as you say."

"All thanks to your father. But everything ultimately belongs to the good Lord."

"Pick your battles, is all I'm saying." Her brows lifted in the center of her face. Anxiety never looked so pretty.

He kissed her once more good night and then braced for the freezing cold. As he climbed back into the old truck and pulled away, he could still smell Winona's perfume on the cuffs of his sleeves. He saw her slender silhouette as she watched him from her window. Her windowpanes looked like bars from a distance, with Winona the comfortable captive. Jeb did not care how pretty she looked in feathers. He would not become a slave to Mills's growing machine.

25

*F*lorence Bernard dropped by with a list of things she needed to collect from those who could contribute to the Christmas social. She tapped outside the small room in the church where Jeb sat paying the bills. "Morning, Reverend. I'm here to pick up the money for the Christmas ham."

Jeb stared, blank as a summer chalkboard.

"You remember the Christmas social, don't you? I'm elected to pick up the Smithfield ham that you told us to order. Smithfield will want the rest of his money."

Jeb stared at the figures in front of him. The offering had brought in exactly two dollars and twenty-one cents. No special gift from Horace Mills or Ace Timber. At the dismissal of the Sunday morning service, Horace had lingered politely at the back of the church until his gaze passed over Jeb like a cloud. He had offered a sympathetic smile. Without saying a word, he had sent a clear message to Jeb. Winona had smiled at him with a similar sympathy before being escorted from the church between her mother and father.

Jeb had risen at dawn to pore over the stack of bills,

which included the light bill, the lumber that Jeb and Will had used to repair the front porch, and the monthly mortgage. Now the old radiator was about to sing its last song. After doling out a generous donation to the starving Wolvertons, the church bank account was sputtering to draw air. The remaining payment had come due on the floor, which was only half installed since Mills had paid just enough down on it to have the work started. The floor extended only across the front altar area, stopping two feet from the front pews. Children had been taking turns tossing marbles under the unfinished framing. Jeb had assumed the floor job would be paid off by Horace, since the project had been his brainchild. But his contribution was plainly withheld.

Angel had outgrown her shoes, and all three children needed new stockings. With the potatoes half gone and the pantry stock dwindling, Jeb did not know how he would pay the mortgage. If he asked the bank for an extension, he would have to go through Horace Mills. His pay had been nothing this week, and he wondered how many more weeks he could go without an income from the church. "Morning, Florence. What's that you're asking?"

"I've come to collect from the church for the Christmas ham. You told me to order it. For a large group, I ordered an extra large one. But Smithfield wanted half down now and half when we pick it up in two weeks. You only gave the committee two dollars. He says it's from a prize sow, so I can't wait to carve it up and serve it. Everyone's had it so bad this year; it's going to lift spirits."

"How much you need now, Florence?"

"It's ten dollars and twenty cents, so half that, Reverend, or three dollars and ten, plus the two we already have."

Jeb knew that would take more than this week's entire offering. "Can Smithfield take half of half, or a couple of dollars down?"

"I'll ask him." Florence paused at the doorway. "Everything all right, Reverend? You look like someone died."

Jeb's fingers drummed the chair arms. He stared at the floor and then said, "Let me know if Smithfield can take the smaller down payment." Before she could get out of the building, he stepped out of the office and said, "Florence, maybe we should settle for the smaller ham."

She pressed her lips into a frozen smile and said, "Whatever you say, Reverend."

After she left, Jeb knew that his pride was the only thing keeping him from telling Florence the social should be cancelled. At least to tell Smithfield that the church would need to order a smaller ham might have removed some of the weight of the money woes. But the levity of the party preparations had lifted the spirits of so many of the women that it seemed a sin to change plans midstream.

He prepared the bank deposit but instead of heading for the bank, he left it in the small safe beneath his desk. It seemed best not to let Mills know how little the church had to deposit.

The sound of slamming automobile doors brought him to his feet. When he stepped out into the sanctuary, he found Deputy Maynard hauling Edward Bluetooth inside. "I caught him, Reverend!"

Edward's contorted face softened when he saw Jeb. "Preacher, you'll vouch for me. He won't listen to me."

Maynard threatened to backhand the boy, but Jeb stepped in. "Deputy, I do know this boy. What's the problem?"

"Guess what I found him melting down out in his momma's barn. Nothing but the stolen church bell."

"I'd never do that!" Edward yelled.

"Edward, you took the bell?" Jeb asked.

"He won't listen to me. He wouldn't listen to my momma, neither, so what's the use?"

"Maynard, let him go. I'd like to hear what he has to say." Jeb patted the pew and invited Edward to take a seat.

Edward jerked away from the deputy and joined Jeb on the pew. "Reverend Gracie bought some of my leather one day. We got to talking, and he asked me what else I could do. I told him I could do lots of things. So he asked me about the church bell, if I could come take a look at it. I came one day and no one was around. So I climbed up all the way into the steeple and saw the bell needed fixing bad. So I decided to surprise Reverend Gracie and take it home in my wagon. I left him a note. Didn't he tell you?"

"Reverend Gracie grew sick, Edward. He's gone home to Cincinnati. He was in the hospital awhile. I'm sure he forgot to mention your repair of the bell."

"I fixed it real good. It's ready to hang, only before I could get it back into my wagon, this deputy arrested me."

"You don't believe him, do you, Reverend?"

"I'd stake my life on it," said Jeb. He stood. "On behalf of the Church in the Dell, Deputy Maynard, please release Edward. He's a good boy. I'll vouch for him."

"I hope you're not sorry, Reverend."

Jeb waited for the deputy to leave. "I'll give you a ride back home, Edward." He invited Edward into the parsonage. "I need to make a list of things I need from the store. I'll only be a minute."

Jeb quickly inspected their pantry and found last week's canned goods running low and a sack of dried beans only half full. The coal scuttle was close to empty; he would have to get up several times in the night to stoke the potbellied stove with more wood. He counted his folding money. After paying for a new truck part, giving money to the Wolvertons to buy coal oil, and taking Winona Mills to the Candelight Café for an expensive evening, Jeb had two dollars left.

The thought of the Bluetooths' land offer lying atop Mills' desk waiting for him to buckle under the weight of the Ace Timber land scheme left Jeb feeling sick at heart. He would ask Edward about their situation.

Edward sat smiling out in his truck. On the way out to the Bluetooth land, Jeb said, "Tell me how your momma's doing, Edward."

"Not so good. I think Reverend Gracie thought that if he gave me work, it would help our family."

It had escaped Jeb that Edward would need payment for the bell. He reached into his pocket and found he had a small amount of cash.

"I know we Bluetooths don't show up at the whites' church, but even so, my momma prays every night. I fixed the bell for her. So no charge to you, Preacher."

"I'm paying you anyway, Edward."

"I can't take it. I did it to bring a blessing on my momma. She needs one right about now."

Jeb drove him home. The two of them together loaded the repaired church bell onto the truck. "Looks like a new bell, Edward."

"Just in time. Momma needs a miracle."

Jeb pulled away from the Bluetooths'. He was headed for the Bank of Nazareth.

❉

Horace Mills found Jeb's request humorous. "A loan, Reverend? Why? Is the church in trouble?"

"I'll use my truck as collateral, if need be. I want to see Church in the Dell make it through the winter. It's best I don't take a salary for a while."

"No offense, Reverend, but your truck could be hauled away for scrap metal."

"Gracie tried to warn me, but I wanted to trust you. Ace Timber is nothing but a front to take land from people in Nazareth—"

"That haven't planned for the future."

Winona had said that, Jeb remembered.

"But it's no front, Reverend. You're wrong about that. Ace Timber's a legitimate partnership and a company that has blown into our town like a breath of fresh air. Reverend, you have to remember that you are a charity and I'm a lending institution. My business *is* business. When a man like Asa Hopper or those Indian Bluetooths squander what they own frivolously, get behind on their payments, it's my place on behalf of my shareholders to make the hard decisions. When you stepped in to bring a healing balm to these tough decisions, I felt it was good for the bank and for the town— a way to show people that we aren't coldhearted. Most banks are foreclosing. We're finding buyers for those that are in trouble."

"Ace Timber is taking advantage of the poor, Mr. Mills. The office of the clergy can't be used to help land sharks. Now I'm asking you to front the church a loan. My truck is surely worth something."

"You going to walk from house to house to visit the sick and dying when you lose that truck? Church in the Dell would not be here if it weren't for men like Jefferson Watts, and yes, even me—men willing to step in and see that this town gets to keep a spiritual token in spite of hard times. Church in the Dell is that spiritual token, and you have the privilege of passing out that token every Sunday and Wednesday. Everybody needs hope, and somebody has to pay the bill for that kind of hope. You try and make it more than that and you're elevating your station higher than any of us intended."

"I'm wasting your time," Jeb said.

"Take this blasted offer to the Bluetooths and tell them that signing on the dotted line is for their own good!" Mills pulled out his wallet. He counted out several twenty dollar bills. "This is your pay for you and those ruffian children you insist on keeping around." He counted out another stack. "You give this to Ethel Bluetooth just for signing. She's down to her last can of soup, I hear. Hurry now, and get this money to them before they starve, Reverend. When you look back on this later, you'll remember this day as one where you were savior to a hungry family. Give yourself back your dignity. Begging's for railroad tramps, not men of the cloth." He scooped up the cash and walked around the desk to meet Jeb face-to-face.

Jeb felt the cash and the Ace Timber offer slide into his hands. He felt weak, as though he had taken a punch in the stomach. Mona opened the door and let him out. She slipped into the banker's office with more papers for Mills to sign. Jeb heard her ask Mills why he insisted on being so generous with the ones who would never appreciate his efforts. Mills replied, "If it weren't for my daughter's insistence, and a promise to Philemon Gracie, I'd not give this charlatan preacher the time of day."

❄

Ethel Bluetooth stirred a boiling pot of lye soap out by their front porch. Edward sat on the front steps with the afternoon sun warming his head. He formed a scrap of leather around cardboard in the shape of a shoe sole.

"Preacher!" Edward yelled. "Momma, it's the preacher I've been telling you about. You know he picked up the bell."

"Your boy has a talent, Mrs. Bluetooth."

"I'm sorry you haven't seen me around your church. Some people don't like it when I bring my boys around. I think the old people still have funny ideas about Indians. Edward, go inside and bring out two cakes of soap for the preacher." She looked at Jeb. "On the house."

Jeb tried to turn her down, but she said, "We're not selling much right now anyway."

"The banker told me that you might be needing some money for food," said Jeb.

She spat on the ground. "Horace Mills ain't nothing but a robber, a big bandit out taking people's houses from them. Like he did the Hoppers'." She drew out the paddle and propped it against the porch railing. Then she grew stiff, blinked once, and said to Jeb, "It isn't true you're helping Mills and that timber company take people's land from them, is it? I never believed none of that about you."

Jeb turned the envelope over twice in his hand without looking up.

Ethel saw the envelope. She took two steps toward him and said, "I've defended you, Reverend, every single time."

Jeb saw Edward standing in the doorway listening to his momma question Jeb. "You'd never work for Mills, would you, Preacher?"

The wad of cash in Jeb's pocket felt like an anchor weight. He drew it out, hoping the cash would soften the blow. "Mills asked me to give this to you, to help with your groceries for a while."

"You think I ought to sign those papers, Reverend?" Ethel began to cry.

Jeb moved toward the porch. He laid the cash on Ethel's porch and then backed away. "No, ma'am, I truly don't. As a matter of fact, I'm taking these papers back to Mills and telling him that I wouldn't let you sign them. I don't know how far behind you are on payments, but surely if enough people know about this, they'll help."

"Help the wife of a Cherokee? You tryin' to be funny, Reverend?"

"If we don't sign the papers, we can't keep the money," said Edward. He scooped up the cash and tried to give it back to Jeb.

"Consider it a loan, one backed up by Church in the Dell. Mrs. Bluetooth, you go and buy your family some necessaries. I'll take these papers back to the bank and tell them you need more time, that you plan to keep your land."

Ethel ran up to Jeb and threw herself against him. "Reverend, I never saw no one do nothin' like this. You're not like any preacher I ever saw." She cried.

Jeb excused himself. He tucked the money that Mills had paid him in advance for making the delivery back into the bank envelope with the unsigned documents.

He didn't know how the rest of the day would turn out. But at least for the Bluetooths, it would be a better one.

❄

An old rowboat had been left tied up for the winter beneath Marvelous Crossing Bridge. Jeb pulled one end of the rope and brought the boat to shore. He rubbed the splintered wood and studied the inside of the craft. It had not taken on any water. He picked up a cane pole from inside the boat as he stepped into it and, using the thick end of the pole, pushed away from shore. He buttoned his coat, the woolen one that Winona had found so handsome. The last two mornings had not given way to a warm afternoon. The sky had clouded after he left the Bluetooths. By Christmas, if the cold weather persisted, the land would be a hard shell of frozen crust. Jeb shivered.

The boat passed a cottage that had once been overgrown with lilies and a cloud of butterflies. The winter had turned the leftover flowers of last spring into a thick patch of tough brown reeds. Jeb had taken Fern on a boat ride past this cottage once. He remembered how taken in she had been by the gardens and cottage—and taken in by him.

He allowed the craft to drift, driven by a northern wind. The boat passed by shacks and shorelines littered with old rusted bicycles and other abandoned items.

It seemed to him everything that had bloomed in his life had died and been left to rot. The children he had taken in were growing up wild and as near starvation and need as when he had first found them hidden like refugees in the back of his truck. His role model had been taken from him, sick and possibly destined to live out the last of his years on medication and sedatives. His dream of leading Church in the Dell as a respected leader had taken him back to his point of beginning, a man who lived among suspicion and mistrust by those who had extended their faith in him. The harder he worked to succeed, the more pain he felt he brought to those around him. The worst part was not that he had somehow gotten entangled with the wrong woman, but that he had let the best one slip away. For the life of him, he could not remember why he had elected to serve in the office of clergy. Somehow the mission had lost its meaning.

Jeb pushed the cane deep into the water to keep the boat near shore. But he had drifted too far, and the pole could find no bottom from which to push off of. He laid it inside the hull of the boat and rubbed his arms vigorously. He would have to wait for the boat to drift closer to shore.

Jeb questioned God. Gracie had taught him to do that in times of crisis—to ask God the hard questions, to look in the Bible for answers. But the more he thought about his role in Nazareth, the more he hated what he had become. He thought of the Hoppers wandering the roadways like nomads with no place to call home. Then he imagined Angel coming home from school, expectant of a long-awaited trip to the Woolworth's to buy stockings for her brother and sister but being told that things had changed. The lack of money seemed to echo across the water with no one to hear.

Jeb could not understand how a body could get in so much trouble just by following the so-called leading of the Spirit. Philemon Gracie had a gracious manner about him, even when life took him through troubled waters. Jeb realized what a far cry his life was from Gracie's. Men like him were cut from finer cloth, hand tailored by unseen hands for the pulpit. Jeb had fooled himself into thinking that he could rise to the occasion with any sense of purpose and mission.

He pulled his coat tighter, turning up the collar around his throat. That is when he felt a cold prick against his chest. With one hand he drew out the chain that held the trinket given to him by Philemon Gracie. With the other he clasped ahold of the key, turned it over, and whispered, "Do Not Lay Down Your Plow."

Jeb's head dropped forward and he hid his face, in case anyone from shore might think it strange to see a man in a drifting boat crying.

26

Jeb found the letter from the Pine Bluff family. He had looked for it for two days. He found it under his own bed. It had been shredded into a thousand pieces.

"Angel, you come here!" he yelled.

"It's time to leave for school. Bye!"

Jeb heard the front door slam and the ensuing voices of Ida May and Willie as they ran in the cold to catch up with their sister. Jeb watched them disappear around the church with holes in their stockings. He took the handful of shredded letter and threw it into the kitchen waste can. Thanksgiving was two days away.

A movement from out front brought him onto the porch. He saw two men placing ladders against the side of the church. Next to them, Winona chattered.

Jeb slipped on his shoes and met them out in the churchyard. "Morning."

Winona smiled, but Jeb knew it was only because he had not taken the bad news to her daddy yet about the Bluetooths. After his first cup of coffee, he would march into the bank and ruin what remained of their relationship.

"Morning, honey," said Winona. She had not called him by any endearing names until now.

"Ladders and measuring tapes. Something I should know about?" Jeb asked her.

"It's impossible to surprise you, Jeb, what with you being around so much. But up in Hot Springs a man—an artist, really—designs stained-glass windows for churches. And—here comes the surprise—we're buying stained-glass windows for Church in the Dell." Her cheeks reddened as her joy at having shared such good tidings bubbled over.

"We're buying? Who is we?"

"Daddy, me. Momma's helping me pick them out, but I want you to come along too."

"We have a floor that's half finished that we haven't paid for yet. Church in the Dell can't afford a Christmas ham, let alone stained-glass windows, Winona."

"Church in the Dell won't get a bill for these windows. I asked Daddy to have his investors pitch in, what with the work you're doing for them." She said quietly, "With the mood he's in right now, you can imagine how hard this was for me to coax out of him."

Jeb regretted that he had not already told Horace Mills he was turning down the delivery boy job once and for all. If he had to sell off household furniture to pay for the Bluetooths' cash gift, he'd do that too. But the thought of Winona measuring for stained glass made him even more angry. "While stained glass is beautiful—" he began.

"Church in the Dell will be the envy of the county."

"But I don't want stained glass."

"You need it. It's tradition."

"I can't see through it, Winona. What's the point of a window you can't see through?"

"It's not that you want to see through it. You just want to look at it, appreciate it for what it represents."

"It represents money that could be used elsewhere."

"The windows are a donation, silly. You don't understand."

"Like the church floor?"

"You'll get your floor. You and Daddy are working things out."

"You don't understand, Winona. I don't want stained glass."

"He knows what he wants, Winona. He's the pastor of Church in the Dell."

Jeb spun around, shocked to see Fern eavesdropping while the two of them argued. She'd come from inside the church.

"Nobody asked your opinion, Fern," said Winona.

"I want something I can see through. That's all," said Jeb.

"Perfectly understandable." Fern smiled at the two men who stood holding the ladder.

"Fern, you are the worst person to discuss this with. You and your plain-Jane ways." Winona turned her back to Fern. "Jeb, I'm sorry for surprising you. We can discuss this later."

"Plain-Jane, as in I decorate my walls with bookcases? Winona, my decorating habits have nothing to do with the minister's decisions. Reverend Nubey wants windows he can see through. It's simple enough for me to understand."

"Fern, you understand, don't you?" asked Jeb.

"I finally do," she said.

"I'm glad to hear that." Jeb turned to Winona. "No stained glass for me. I'm done with all that."

"It's taken you long enough," said Fern.

"I wish someone would explain it to me," said the man at the bottom of the ladder.

"Jeb, that's not the only reason I came by," said Winona. "Since you're turning things around for the church, I thought you'd like to know that family from Pine Bluff wants to meet the Welby children this weekend. Sunday, they said."

Jeb could see several samples of stained glass leaning against Winona's car. She had been the impetus all along, her daddy had said, for hooking Jeb into the Ace Timber deal. Now she was bullying her way into church decisions and decisions on his whole life. He looked at the workmen. "You fellers look worn out. Go inside for some coffee, and then kindly help Miss Mills gather up all of her belongings and take them away."

"Angel told me you were shipping them off to Pine Bluff," Fern said matter-of-factly.

"I'm not. That is, I was going to, but I've changed my mind."

"She told me about Edward Bluetooth too," said Fern. "I'm glad you didn't have him thrown in the jailhouse."

"Angel doesn't know anything."

"If you don't want the stained glass, then I guess I'll give back the money I worked so hard to raise," said Winona.

"Or give it to the Hoppers," said Fern. "If you can find them. I hear they're in dire need."

"You two come back here and take this ladder,"

Winona said to the two hired hands. "Forget coffee. Jeb, I don't know why you're acting like this, but I don't deserve any of it." She turned away. Then her hand came to her forehead. She teetered right and, without warning, slumped against the church wall. Her forehead slammed against the side of the building and then she wilted right onto the cold brown grass.

"Is she kidding?" asked Fern.

"We'd better get her up," said Jeb. "Looks like a genuine faint."

❖

Jeb and Fern waited outside on the porch of the doctor's house. Horace and Amy Mills came driving up.

Fern sat next to Jeb on the porch swing. "Here comes Papa and Mama."

The couple marched past Jeb and Fern without a word and bolted into the doctor's house. After a few minutes, both of them could hear Horace ranting like he had lost all sense of reality. The front door slammed open. Horace ran out and lunged for Jeb. Amy followed, grabbed his arm, and begged him not to beat up the minister.

Jeb started to come off the swing, but Fern grabbed his arm. "Remember who you are," she whispered.

"Horace, calm yourself!" Amy shouted.

"Mrs. Mills, what's going on?" asked Jeb.

"It's Winona." Amy crumpled into a rocking chair. She sobbed into a handkerchief and then composed herself enough to say, "The doctor's examined her. He says she's pregnant."

Fern looked at Jeb. She got up out of the swing and went to Amy to comfort her with a hug.

"I told Winona to stay away from you. You're not a real preacher. I don't know what you are, but now you've ruined our daughter's life. You better tell me next you love her," said Horace.

Jeb had never heard Horace Mills sound so vulnerable. He shook his head. "I don't."

"Jeb, maybe you should wait and discuss this with Winona," said Fern. All the color had left her face. She could not look at him.

"He doesn't love me, Daddy." Winona listened to them from behind the screen door. She held a cold compress to her forehead. "It's not his baby."

Jeb looked at Fern. All of the life that had just washed out of her seemed to come flooding back as she breathed a sigh of relief. He said, "Winona, I think you need to have that talk with your momma and daddy now. It's something you can all work out together."

"Jeb, I'm sorry I've dragged you into all of this mess. When I saw you, you just seemed the best daddy for my baby. I thought if you worked for my daddy and his investors that he would be more accepting of you for my sake. We'd all be the happy minister's family." Her words sounded like they'd been mixed into a salad of sarcasm.

"So all that talk about you wanting me to help Jeb, Winona, was your way of finding a solution to your little problem?" asked Horace.

"You always taught me to be a problem solver, Daddy."

"You aren't my daughter," said Horace. "This isn't how I raised you."

"Sure it is," said Winona. "I learned from the best." She turned and disappeared from everyone's sight.

Jeb took a breath. "Mr. Mills, I'm sorry to give you another piece of bad news, but I wouldn't let Ethel Bluetooth sign away her land. But I did give her the money. If you want my truck to cover it, it's yours. I told her that I'd ask the bank to give her more time. If you ask me, the Bluetooths are good for it."

"You keep your truck, Reverend," said Amy. "We'll keep this all between us, if you know what I mean. Horace, we'll send Winona away for a while so no one has to know."

"She'd be better off with you, Mrs. Mills, her own momma." Fern rubbed Amy's shoulders and then returned to the swing to sit next to Jeb.

"This is Nazareth, Amy. You can't keep anything a secret here. Winona will stay with us. We'll see her through this. Reverend, thank you for bringing my daughter to the doctor. We'll take over from here." Horace collected his wife from the chair and without another word took her back in to face their daughter.

Jeb and Fern drove back to the parsonage together. Fern said little. Jeb said nothing at all. But somehow the quiet was good between them.

❈

Jeb delivered the Ace Timber offer back to the bank. He handed it to Mona, glad to be rid of it. "Please count the money, Mona. I want to be sure we're in agreement that it's all there. All except what I gave to Mrs. Bluetooth."

"You ought to take your payment out of it, Reverend. I think he's expecting you to anyway," she said.

"Best I don't." He waited while she counted out the crisp twenty-dollar bills.

"In case you're looking for him, Mr. Mills won't be coming in today." Mona pushed away from her desk to take the envelope of cash behind closed doors.

"I gathered as much."

Jeb left the bank. A weight had been lifted from his shoulders. And just this morning he had agreed to string a banjo for a man who had driven all the way from Hope to ask for Jeb's services. Word was spreading and he, for once, was glad. He couldn't let women like Florence Bernard guilt him into starvation, at least where the Welbys were concerned.

Before he could climb back into the truck, of all people, Florence Bernard came running up to him, red in the face and out of breath. "Reverend, it's all over town what you did for the Bluetooths. That Angel of yours has quite a good little public-address way about her. I'm glad you're letting the Welbys stay. They're good kids, really."

"I'm picking up my banjo again, Florence."

"So I've heard."

"Is there anything I do that the whole town doesn't know about?"

"Not really."

"Pardon me, Sister Bernard, but I've got a man to meet about a banjo stringing." Before Jeb could make his way around the front of the truck, Florence said with a smidgen of timidity, "I've been wanting to ask you about the whole banjo business, Reverend. Is it proper for you, a man of the cloth, to be playing the devil's instrument?"

"Only when I want to chase away the devil," said Jeb.

She watched him drive away. Thanksgiving was two days from now. It was time for the families to gather and give thanks again for how God had seen them through another year. Maybe "Depression" was a bad name for something that brought folks so close together.

27

Christmas in Millwood Hollow brought the smells of pine and smoking chimneys, bells chiming on the doorposts of every family, and finally the Church in the Dell Christmas social.

The ladies' Christmas social committee had draped holly and garland over every window and windowsill. The schoolchildren had spent days pasting and gluing paper chains for the tree. Jeb and Fern had found the perfect pine one evening on a walk by the stream. The two of them went back together and cut it down the night before the social and nearly killed one another dragging it through the woods toward the church.

"You're pretty strong, I guess, for a woman."

"It's a good thing you brought me along or you'd never get this thing back," she groaned, yanking hard.

"This scrawny tree? I'm only letting you help so you'll feel useful."

"Letting me? Maybe I'll let you take it back all by yourself."

Before Fern could walk away, Jeb grabbed her around the waist and pulled her next to him. "Forget the tree. I'm not letting you get away with murder anymore, Fern. You have to answer for what you say to me." He smiled down at her. "Tell me I'm the strongest man you know."

"You're not." She laughed, biting her bottom lip.

" 'Jeb Nubey is the strongest man, the most intelligent, and good-looking to boot.' Say it."

She shook her head, no.

Jeb kissed her, at first just a soft brush against her lips to test the waters. Fern lifted her face to kiss him back.

He drew back his mouth. "Say it," he whispered.

She let out a sigh with mock exasperation. "Jeb Nubey is the strongest man, the most intelligent, and most persistent—"

Jeb squeezed her close to him.

"All right, good-looking."

Jeb kissed Fern while pine and the distant scent of snow perfumed the woods.

"Can you believe we're here together?" she asked. She reached inside his coat and wrapped her arms around him.

"I'm dumb enough to believe it," he said. They kissed until Ivey Long's sleigh bells could be heard ringing down the road. "You owe me a wagon ride, Fern Coulter."

"You're on, Reverend!" They raced to the road, all the while dragging the tree behind them.

✼

Willie climbed a ladder and stuck Ida May's home-crafted star atop the tall evergreen. Jeb and Fern had situated it at the front of the church on the half-finished floor.

Angel carried a platter of fig cookies across the room

and offered the first hot batch to Fern. "Miss Coulter, I heard you liked these. You take all you want."

Fern was stunned. She took a couple of cookies from the platter and thanked Angel.

"It was Jeb who told me you liked figs."

"I'll remember to thank him, Angel." She smiled at him across the room.

"Maybe I don't say it enough, but I think he's all right, at least for a feller from the sticks." She waited a moment and then added, "In case you were needing my opinion about him."

"I think he's pretty all right too." Fern helped Angel pass around the cookies.

"I can't tell you, Reverend, how excited the whole town is about this party," said Florence. "I don't know if Church in the Dell is big enough to hold everyone."

"It always works out," said Jeb. "Don't do any good to worry." He greeted Will and Freda Honeysack as they came through the door. Freda handed Jeb a fruit basket. "Happy Christmas, Reverend Jeb."

Fern and Angel came around with the cookie platter. "The Bluetooths are here," said Fern to Jeb. "I was hoping they would come."

Ethel carried in a basket full of soaps and candles wrapped in straw ribbon. "For the children," she said to Jeb. She meandered through the party guests and laid her basket beneath the tree.

Several more families arrived, each one bearing a food offering for the Christmas shindig and a sack of home-made gifts to be distributed to all the children.

Edward Bluetooth entered with a heavy wooden craft of some sort.

Jeb met him at the door and offered to help carry the wooden object. "Edward, you been building something, I see."

"A manger. For the Christ child. I'll put it near the tree. Then can I ring the new bell?"

"Not until midnight," said Jeb. "It's tradition."

"I wish I would have known. I could have brought a doll for the manger." Fern watched the boy lay the manger between the basket of soaps and a sack of candy from Woolworth's.

Soon the church filled to overflowing. Jeb helped Florence carve the smaller Smithfield ham. She said to him, "After you donated those smoked chickens, looks like we'll have plenty."

"Here come some fellers to pick with me," said Jeb. Several men entered bearing guitars and a fiddle.

"Those are the boys that play pool down at that pool hall. They don't play worldly music, do they, Reverend?" asked Florence.

"*Decent*'s the better word, Sister Bernard. *Decent* music." Jeb excused himself to greet the last few guests who entered the church. Some of the women placed crudely wrapped gifts beneath the tree, completely encircling the base with presents.

Jeb peered outside into the frosty night.

"You look good in that shirt, Reverend," said Fern as she came up behind him.

"Christmas isn't as bad as everyone said it would be, is it, Fern?"

"If it were perfect, it wouldn't be Christmas."

"Fern, if I had my wish, I'd want to make everybody's pain go away. I wonder if I'll ever get over feeling like that."

"Gracie would call you a good student just for wishing such a thing. But when things are imperfect is when we see the truth about God's love."

He felt her arms go around him. "Want to do a little necking in the woods with the minister, Miss Coulter?"

"Preacher, look what I got!" Edward Bluetooth ran toward Jeb and Fern holding a doll. "I prayed for God to give us the Christ child for the manger. It was in the first bag handed to me." He ran back to the circle of children to place his gift back into the crude manger.

Fern dabbed her eyes. "Jeb, you'll have to tell Edward that God gave him the Christ child long before tonight."

"I think he is starting to understand that on his own."

"He's told you so?" asked Fern.

"Edward and I have been praying for the Hoppers to find a home. His momma made a contact in Hot Springs after writing to a relative of the Hoppers. Ethel Bluetooth has invited the Hoppers to come and stay with them. I think it's going to work out."

"Edward's had two prayers answered, then. Jeb, look, the kids have gathered around the manger. They're wrapping the doll in cloths just like the Christmas story."

Angel pulled out her harmonica. She played to her friends around the tree, wheezing out what sounded as near a Christmas carol as anything else she tried to play.

Jeb picked up his banjo and carried it to the platform with Fern on his arm. Fern joined the Welbys and Edward at the manger. Jeb gave Florence Bernard an assuring smile. The three musicians, also lumbermen, pulled out their guitars and fiddle and joined the preacher in a night of music. It filtered out into the night, rising above the pines, a prayer of song.

Nazareth's Song
Reading Group Guide

1. We find Jeb Nubey all at once thrust into the ministry. His deepest need is to find legitimacy and respect in Nazareth. How important is respect to the pulpit and do you believe the pastorate has maintained a degree of respect in modern society?

2. Jeb derives his education primarily from Philemon Gracie and self-study. Education by apprenticeship has gone out of vogue. Would students today find benefit through an apprenticeship?

3. Fern Coulter is uneasy with Philemon Gracie's departure. Is her mistrust of Jeb based upon knowing his past or because she was stung as a romantic interest?

4. Angel is sensing a conflict in Jeb's ideals. She believes the Hoppers are being treated unfairly, like outcasts. Is it popular in the church to bring aid to outcasts? Does the church do a thorough job of mending the wounded?

5. Jeb rushes to bring peace to the town riot. Gracie would not have gotten involved, although he most certainly would have made himself available to the wounded and jailed. Jeb's involvement eventually caused a conflict of interest as the pendulum of popular opinion swung away from Horace Mills. When

is the role of a peacemaker acceptable and should we ever refrain from political involvement?

6. Horace and Winona Mills both offer monetary gifts to Jeb and Church in the Dell during a time of great need. But eventually the money is found to be tied to Mills and his special-interest group, Ace Timber. Should the modern church accept funds from groups not otherwise affiliated with churches or ministry? From government funds?

7. Jeb's involvement in the lumber mill's woes draws men to church that had never shadowed its doors. Jeb is pleased to see his decision has caused the church to grow. But eventually these same men's livelihoods are threatened as Ace Timber gains control of the town lumber industry. Is church growth at any cost a viable solution for reaching those who don't know God?

8. Angel and Jeb are at odds as Jeb struggles with his role as a stand-in father. What authority issues are raised when a non-birth parent tries to counsel a child?

9. Winona lures Jeb into her web of deceit so that she can use their relationship as a handy explanation for her pregnancy. Jeb has moments where he senses her eagerness, but then he allows Winona to continue in her seduction. Is it that easy to lay aside common sense and spiritual restraints in order to settle for a false love?

10. Jeb finally sees the danger of trading lust for real love. He finds in Fern not only a romantic interest, but friendship and the seeds of trust. He had to earn all of those things and it took time. Is it popular to

take time for a relationship to grow before seeking intimacy? Is it practical or even possible considering our modern mores?

11. Jeb comes to realize that community respect is less important than choosing to do what is good, right, and honest. Jesus knew popularity for only a short season. With Jesus as our model, is popularity the most important quality we can gain as an individual or as a church?

And there's more from Patricia Hickman . . .

WHISPER TOWN

Book Three in the Millwood Hollow Series

❋ ❋ ❋

Life is getting more complicated for Reverend Jeb Nubey. Angel, the oldest of his "adopted" orphan waifs, is now a teenager and is making his life miserable. Jeb is still keen on pursuing the charming schoolteacher, Fern Coulter, but his old adversary, Oz Mills, is crowding the way. A mysterious crime in the apple orchards has the whole town speculating, and to top it off, an infant girl has been left abandoned on the preacher's doorstep. The fact that the child is black adds tension to the situation, and Jeb is forced to look at some of his neighbors in a new light. As Jeb gets caught in the vortex of Depression-era southern racism, his leadership of Church in the Dell is tested, as is his ability to keep his growing family safe.

Available June 2005